LOVE, MOM

LOVE, MOM

Editing: Tracy Liebchen

Proofreading: On Pointe Digital Services

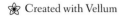 Created with Vellum

LOVE, MOM

MOM

A psychological thriller

ILIANA XANDER

PROLOGUE

I've never hurt a single person. But right now, I want to punch the face staring at me from the national newspaper's front page. A picture of *her*, with that signature red lipstick and long raven hair. The pretty face of a monster.

BEST-SELLING AUTHOR FOUND DEAD

Elizabeth Casper, 43, better known around the world as E. V. Renge, the author of gritty thrillers, was found dead in what appears to be a "freak accident."

She is survived by her beloved husband, Ben Casper, and their twenty-one-year-old daughter, Mackenzie Casper.

The world is in shock at the tragic loss of the talented soul gone too early. Fans all around the world gather for a massive tribute to the literary genius.

Oh, the lies...

The cold smile taunts me from the newspaper in my trembling hands, and I have the urge to carve it out and wipe it from my memory.

She had it coming.
She deserved to die.
I just wish it had happened sooner.

PART 1

ONE

MACKENZIE

You'll probably never see another memorial service like this one—without a single tear shed.

My mom's memorial service is the grandest performance of the year or, perhaps, her entire life.

The mob of fans outside St John's Memorial Center doesn't know that. They think that their mass gathering is organic. They don't know about the money being poured into publicity, influencers, gossip columns, and book bloggers.

Since Mom's passing, her novels have topped the book charts again.

Look, Mom! You are dead, and everyone is still cashing in.

The newspaper headlines have been going crazy in the last week, proposing all sorts of wild theories.

*E. V. RENGE DIES TRAGICALLY
AT THE PEAK OF HER CAREER.
ACCIDENT OR...*

That's why that guy standing at the back of the room is here. Middle-aged, with a funny mustache, dressed in a suit and tie.

"This is a private event. Please, leave," Grandma says to him curtly in a hushed whisper.

As soon as she walks off, her smile disappears.

You don't need to be super observant to spot a gun holster under his suit jacket—he is a detective. He came to our house two days ago. I opened the door, and he started asking me about Mom until Grandma flew up toward us like a furious hen.

"Mackenzie, leave us, please," she ordered, blocking me from him. Then, when I walked around the corner, she told the detective in a clipped tone, "You should be ashamed of yourself—talking to a child who just lost her mother."

Now, the man is forced to leave again.

The newspapers and bloggers have been suggesting all sorts of crazy theories about my mom's death for days. The truth, as per investigators, was more banal—Mom slipped, fell, and cracked her head on a rock while taking her usual morning walk in the woods adjacent to our house.

"Misadventure" is what they called it. Coincidentally, Mom's bestsellers are full of misadventures.

Don't get me wrong, some people might be sad.

That bitch, Laima Roth, who is talking to the publisher right now like this is a regular business meeting? For sure. She has been my mother's agent for over twenty years. She can now forget about the future book releases they were planning. Though, I'm sure she'll capitalize on special editions, sprayed edges, book boxes, and whatnot. This enterprise will never dry out.

We cremated Mom several days ago in a private arrangement attended only by a dozen or so people. Still, there were no tears.

This memorial service is for publicity. For "friends," they say. To pay their respects. Respect was pretty high on Mom's list, but friends? Not sure she had any true ones, though the eloquent speeches they've been giving in her honor for the last two hours made it sound like she was Shakespeare, no less.

The streets outside the building are mobbed, but the crowded memorial hall is eerily quiet, whispers ricocheting between the walls.

On one side of the room is a giant author portrait of Mom in a lacy high-collar blouse and red roses in the background. It says *E. V. Renge* under it. The middle-aged quirky photographer hired by the publishing house is snapping pictures of it from every angle. With the publisher, the agents, and Dad. He asked me to pose, too, but I refused.

Screw them.

On the other side of the hall is a picture of Mom in her office. She has full makeup and her hair done, but she looks somewhat dreamy sitting in front of a bookshelf. Her real name, Elizabeth Casper, is under her informal picture. This version is for other sources, like the local newspaper, the church Grandma goes to, and the charities Mom used to donate to.

I prefer to stand at the back of the room, away from this spectacle, next to my grandpa who doesn't give a crap—and never did—about my mom. Or my looks, for that matter.

Grandma does. Earlier at the house, she asked me not to put on my usual black lipstick and heavy eyeliner.

"And wear something appropriate."

I almost always wear black. Coincidentally, that's very appropriate for a memorial service. Just like my black eyeliner and the lipstick I put on anyway.

Grandma, of course, is dressed in Dior and expensive jewelry. She makes sure she talks to every attendee.

Dad is dressed in a slick black suit, and he looks dashing. He is somewhat sulking, but that might be because of the withdrawal. His parents live only four hours away, but they have been staying at our house since Mom's passing. Grandma controls Dad's too-early-in-the-day intake of booze. With Mom gone, she proudly took over the household.

Me? I want to cry, I really do, but the reality hasn't hit me yet. I want to be sad, but I always felt like Mom never cared enough about me. That made me very bitter in recent years, and we grew apart.

My best friend, EJ, says I have delayed grief. Maybe I'm just heartless. I asked EJ not to come, because I didn't want my best friend to see how screwed up my life has been, well, pretty much as far back as I remember.

I'll see him at the house where we are having a catered party tonight for the "close circle." I'm sure it will be a party though they call it a celebration of life.

I look around the room and cringe when I see the familiar figure approach Dad and shake his hand. That's the dean of the university I go to. I look away and roll my eyes. Mom used to rub shoulders with him. "For your future's sake," she said once. She even did a lecture at my university and donated money, in fact. I won't be surprised if they set up a monument in her honor.

Mom's therapist is here too. Two of her editors. Her three assistants. Our family lawyer. Most of her "friends" are simply people she worked closely with.

I want to cry, I really do, but I can't. For the last week, since the accident and while I was staying home instead of at my studio apartment in town, I constantly thought about her, what we had, our little screwed-up family. I felt sad, just not overwhelmingly sad like I am supposed to be, I guess.

Dad checks his phone and hurriedly walks away from everyone and toward the door. There, I notice another man in a baseball hat who turns around and walks away. Dad follows.

This would be a good time to tell Dad that I have a headache and am about to have a mental breakdown—lies, of course—and I need to leave. Emotions bubble up inside me, but I can't figure them out. Mostly, I want to be away from these people.

I walk out into the empty hall connecting to another small hallway and see Dad talking to the stranger at the very end.

I start walking toward them and slow down when I hear a hushed whisper, "You scumbag."

The hell?

I step to the side, behind the doorway, where I can't see them but can clearly hear them.

"Not here," he hisses. "How *dare* you?"

"How dare I? I have the right to be here."

"Get out. Now."

The man chuckles quietly. "Does she suspect anything?"

"Who?"

"Mackenzie."

My heart gives an uneasy beat at the sound of my name.

"Don't you dare mention my daughter."

"Oh, she doesn't? Well-played, Benny-boy."

Benny-boy? My father? Who the hell calls him that?

"I said, leave," Dad adds more desperately. "Just... go. We'll talk later."

I step closer to the doorway to peek around, and the hardwood flooring under the carpet squeaks, it freaking squeaks.

Dammit.

I stand still like a deer caught in the headlights. I hear muffled footsteps, and Dad appears in the doorway. As soon as he sees me, a panicky look crosses his face.

"What was that about?" I ask and peek around the doorway, but the mysterious man is gone.

Dad wipes his face with both hands. "Nothing."

"Were you arguing with someone?"

"No, kiddo, just talking." He reaches inside his jacket and pulls out a flask.

"Do you know that man?"

Dad takes a nervous gulp and exhales slowly. "I've never seen him before."

That's a clear lie.

He hides the flask back in his jacket, then winks at me. "You okay?"

"I can't be here. These people—" I don't finish and, rolling my eyes, motion toward the main hall.

"I know. I know." Dad closes his eyes and pinches the bridge of his nose.

"*You* okay?"

Dad and Mom weren't exactly a perfect couple. Especially lately. They fought more than ever before, and that's only what I saw during the weekends with them, because for the last two years, I've been renting a small studio in town, close to the university.

Dad inhales loudly and exhales through puffed lips, then manages a fake smile. "Yeah, kiddo." He gently pats my shoulder. "It'll all be fine. You can get out of here if you want."

"See you at the house," I say and turn into the hallway that leads to the back entrance.

The biggest performance will be outside as soon as everyone exits the building. The fans from all corners of the country are the ones actually grieving. The publishing house already brought an in-house PR team to navigate the event. Yes, they call it an event. A hired group of actors will cause havoc and scream obscenities and desecrate one of Mom's portraits, proclaiming E. V. Renge a devil. Because, you know, there is no bad publicity. I know that because I was informed beforehand. Right after I signed an NDA, a non-disclosure agreement. This stunt secretly conjured by the PR firm is supposed to rake up insane sales for the books.

I definitely don't want to exit through the main entrance and right into a pack of paparazzi and crazy fans.

I exhale in relief when I step outside the back door of the building and, making sure there's no one in the parking lot, walk to my car.

My phone rings.

"Thank God," I blurt when I answer. "I'm out of there."

"Hey, Snarky, it's almost over." EJ's reassuring voice is like a balm for my soul.

"You are coming over, right?"

"Already on my way. Might be there before you."

"Watch out for the paparazzi in front of the main gate, okay?" I unlock my car door to get in. "I'm sure there will... Hold up."

There's an envelope on the driver's seat, and I frown in confusion, picking it up.

"EJ, hold on." I put him on speaker, get in the car, then study the envelope. "What the hell..."

"You okay?" he asks.

"Not sure," I say, my heartbeat spiking as I read the words on the envelope.

From #1 fan. XOXO

TWO

Fame, even in the literary world, comes with praise, fan mail, stalkers, and occasionally, a random vial of urine or bloodied underwear. Yes, there are crazies out there. I won't talk about the more morbid stuff. There's plenty of that too.

Nervously, I peer out through my car's windows. The parking lot is packed with cars but not a single person in sight.

"Kenz, what's up?" EJ asks worriedly on speaker.

"Fan mail," I reply, turning my attention back to the envelope.

"Something crazy?"

"What's crazy is that it was inside my car."

"Did you forget to lock it?"

"Tsk, dude, I know better. I hope it's not ricin or something. I should just toss it."

"Open it! It might be entertaining."

EJ is always excited about Mom's fan stories.

"Okay, okay!" I rip the envelope open.

Carefully, I spread it open with the tips of my black-polished nails and peek inside. You can never be too careful with fans. Stranger things have happened. People send all sorts of stuff to my mom. Love letters, threats, their own manuscripts, toys, cookies, locks of their hair. A bottle of urine—that was nasty. Some guy sent her a photoshopped picture of him and her, covered in his semen.

"Come on, spill. What is it?" EJ asks impatiently.

"There are papers inside. Someone's teary letters, probably."

"Read them."

EJ loves that kind of creepy stuff. He graduated from my university a year ago and does various freelance IT jobs. He might be a brilliant programmer now, making more money from coding jobs online at twenty-three than an average adult. But when I met him several years ago, he was a nerd. He told me he had stayed for a second year in junior high because he had skipped classes and spent all his time on the computer at home. He is still a nerd, but he just found a gang of like-minded people. Sometimes, that makes all the difference in life.

I pull out the papers from the envelope and unfold them.

The letter is handwritten and consists of three papers, one side of them fringed, like they've been ripped out of a notebook.

"Come on!" EJ urges me impatiently.

"Hold on! Jeez. Patience is a virtue, you know."

The first page only has several lines that I slowly read out loud:

Want to know a secret?
Love, Mom.

THREE

"What the hell," I say, then angrily look at the second page and feel my hair stand on end.

I can see the familiar names on the paper, a date from twenty-two years ago in the top left corner. Location: *Old Bow, Nebraska*.

If that's someone's sick joke, it's an elaborate one, because I know that place. My parents went to college there, more than twenty years ago.

"Snarky, you there?" EJ asks.

"Listen, I'll call you back."

"Everything okay?"

"Yeah. I'll call you."

"You'd better."

For the next five minutes, I don't move. I read the three pages from the envelope and feel my insides twist. I reread them and turn the pages to make sure there is nothing else I missed.

I don't know much about my parents' past, but I know where they come from. The story on the pages seems personal, intimate. Mom never cared to tell me much about her past. Why would she now?

"Complicated," she used to say.

Knowing her novels, I would say it was screwed up. The critics called her imagination "brilliant." I personally think it's batshit crazy with its roots obviously in the past. And what parent tells their kid about their screwed-up past?

My first reflex is to shove the pages into a giant chest full of the similar stuff written to my mom over the twenty years of her publishing career. She keeps a chest in her office at home. It's an old gothic thing, the size of a tomb, dedicated to her fan mail.

But I'm curious. What if these letters are really from Mom?

There is one thing I can do to check the authenticity.

I start my car and drive to my parents' home.

Our house is an hour outside town. I insisted I didn't want to stay home while getting my BA, considering Mom didn't let me move anywhere out of state for college. So, at least I got some freedom by moving into town.

I visit my parents often, every other weekend. After Mom's passing, I've stayed at home. Of course, it was Grandma's idea so that "we could bond through grief." That's her wording. Though I'm pretty sure none of us is grieving.

An hour later, I pull into the private road that leads to my parents' estate. It's a seven-thousand-square-foot house on five acres, with an additional guest house, a pool, and a natural pond next to a lake surrounded by forests.

A security guy, hired by the PR firm, nods to me. But I should've expected that one wasn't enough, because two hundred feet up the road, here they are—several men darting out of the thick woods with cameras, flashing pictures of me as I approach the main gate.

"Mackenzie, do you think your mother's death was an accident?"

"Mackenzie, will you be finishing her current novel?"

"Miss Casper!"

"This is private property!" I yell at them through the glass. But they know that. They don't care. At least, when the metal gates slowly open and I drive in, they don't dare follow.

A minute later, I'm walking into the house.

An overwhelming sweet scent wafts into my face—hundreds of flowers sent from friends, colleagues, and fans. The house is crowded with catering staff preparing for the evening reception.

I make a beeline straight to Mom's office, the envelope in my hand.

The office is locked. Mom was the only one with the key, or so she thought. We could only go in when she was there. But I know where Dad keeps the spare. I caught him sneaking in months ago. Mom never knew about it, and the fact that this was even happening shows how screwed-up my parents' relationship was.

Right now, I really need to get inside that office.

I walk to the small indigenous mask by the guest bathroom and sink my hand into the mane of its thick fake hair. In the soft rubbery base of the skull is the office key.

"Bingo," I murmur. Dad still keeps it there, which is a relief.

I hurry to the end of hall and unlock Mom's office, then lock the door behind me.

I've never been here on my own, only with her. The only reason I was ever curious is because she always locked this room. That was her writing haven, she said. Not anymore.

I'm waiting for the grief to strike me suddenly, sneak up on me, here, of all places, but it's not happening. Not a tear. Not even sadness really, just bitterness.

Mom and I were never close. I was told that a small trust fund she set up for me would cover my entire education, but that's about it. Nothing extra. No inheritance. Everything goes to my dad. I would like to be a hypocrite and say that we don't love our parents for their money, but Mom made millions and didn't leave me a penny besides the college fund. I'd be lying if I said that this fact doesn't piss me off or at least rubs me the wrong way. So, yeah, I wasn't Mom's fan. Her trying to teach me a lesson? Fuck whatever. I'll be fine on my own.

Right now, I'd like to learn what the purpose of this anonymous letter is. Maybe, the lesson is still coming. If this little prank turns out not to be a prank but a farewell letter from Mom, I could do better research later.

The only thing I need to check its authenticity is the small frame on the giant mahogany desk. That frame was—wait, drum roll, please—Mom's reminder of how much she'd achieved. Right. Typical pat on her shoulder. Inside the glass frame is the first page of the original manuscript of *Lies, Lies, and Revenge*, Mom's first novel and the internationally acclaimed bestseller that sold millions of copies and put E. V. Renge on the map.

This first page could probably sell for thousands of dollars right now. It's handwritten on some old page from a journal Mom wrote as a teenager. Yes, that page is that old, almost thirty years or so. My mom started writing her bestseller at the age of sixteen. Talk about genius, right?

But I need this little piece of memorabilia to compare with the pages I got from an anonymous fan.

I sit down right on top of the desk—Mom would've killed me—set the framed page down flat on its surface, then flatten the pages from the envelope and study them.

Obviously, I'm not a graphologist or a forensic examiner, but I lean close to both samples and inspect every letter. The way the Is are wavy on top. The way the B in Ben, my father's name, curls at the bottom. The commas, the quotation marks, the way one word is underlined twice in the letter and identical in the framed first page, right under the *Prologue*.

Five minutes later, my neck hurts from leaning down, my eyes sting from squinting, and an uneasy feeling is gathering in the pit of my stomach. The handwriting on both the framed page and the letters is identical.

"Huh," I muse to myself.

Still, that doesn't prove that the letter came from Mom.
But that's not what makes me curious.
It's what she has written at the end of it:

This secret will now be yours.

LETTER #1

When you are young, you don't fall for the sweet guys. You fall for the wrong ones.

First love can be toxic. Occasionally, you choose to stick with it. Ben Casper was exactly that.

Why did I even fall for him? Ah, that's the question. Our present is often a collage of our past deeds. I wouldn't call my past a mistake. A despicable chain of events, more likely. But I'll get to that in time.

What's more important is that everyone in my past was a taker. Ben? Ben had the gift of making those around him feel special. He was the first guy who paid attention to me in a way that made a girl swoon.

So, I swooned.

I was in my senior year of creative writing. I lived in a small college town, Old Bow, Nebraska. The town stretched for two miles along Main Street and was surrounded by lush forests. It felt secluded. It suited me. My past would not catch up with me in a place like this, or so I thought.

I first saw Ben at the campus cafe. I stood by the vending machine, and he locked eyes with me.

"Cool lipstick," he said with a nod. "Red, like a strawberry."

Not blood, like everyone else remarked, but strawberry. Can a guy get more romantic than that?

He grinned with that boyish smile that felt like a fresh breeze wafted into a stuffy room. It promised easy laughter and walking hand-in-hand and a possible heartbreak. But you don't think about heartbreaks or the fact that the boy is way out of your league or that his friends at the far-end table snicker about you and give you condescending once-overs. You don't care, because when that boy walks over to that table, he looks over his shoulder and grins at you again and winks, and there is no stopping the hard beating of your heart and the flutter in your stomach and the thoughts spinning a mile a second with the images of what would've happened if he only took time to get to know you.

But then he did.

A week later, I saw Ben at the Seminar Hall. This time, he was alone, no friends around to steal his attention.

"Oh, hey, Strawberry!" he called out to me.

My legs felt weak, and that treacherous flutter in my stomach was back when he approached.

"You took the first prize in the Short Story Competition, huh?"

I couldn't stop myself from blushing. "Yes."

"Congrats!"

"Thank you."

"You gonna be the next Sylvia Plath."

My heart gave out an excited thud—he liked literature. Never mind the fact that it was Sylvia Plath tribute week; it said so right on the award board next to us.

"Rock on, Miss Elizabeth Dunn."

My name! My name never sounded so cool coming out of anyone else's mouth! My heart wanted to leap out of my chest and plant itself at his feet—he knew my name! Never mind that it was on the award board with my picture right next to us.

"It's Lizzy," I murmured.

"Lizzy?"

"Lizzy," I echoed.

"Lizzy." He grinned. "I'm Ben."

I know. "Hi, Ben."

"Hi, Lizzy. Have you written any other cool stories?"

"You like to read?"

"Of course! I love a good story."

Ben didn't care about reading and almost failed English II in the first year. But I would only learn about it later. As well as other things. That he barely passed most classes. That his uppity parents paid his way into graduation. That he already had a drinking problem. That he didn't get accepted into any internships. That his friends, a popular crew, made fun of me. That I was his little secret for months, until everything in our lives started spinning out of control and became a train wreck.

No, that would come later.

But that day, as I stood before him, my starving heart begged for him to talk to me for one more minute.

There was something about Ben that made people want to gaze at him. His laughter was the most wonderful sound in the world. His dimpled grin made my knees weak. And when he casually asked for my pager number, "Would love to hear more of your stories," I fumbled and blushed in embarrassment. I didn't have one, only the house phone.

I would write about it later, about our first time, and the second, and the third, about the happy days and sleepless nights, coy smiles and bitter tears, cheerful dates and a nasty betrayal.

But later that very day, he picked me up from the house, took me for dinner at his favorite place, then out to a movie. Then we got a bottle of wine and minis of booze and went to my place, a shabby studio above the convenience store in town. He didn't seem a bit baffled by the miserable size of it. I wanted him to see it, knew this might be a one-time thing and was all right with it. This would be the night I would write about for months, I thought.

We drank and laughed, and he pulled me against him.

"Do they taste like strawberries, too?" he murmured against my strawberry-colored lips and kissed me and whispered, "We are not going to do anything you don't want to."

An hour later, we were naked, and he was doing *everything* I wanted him to do.

Late into the night, he was sprawled on my bed as I sat next to him and read him excerpts of the novel I had been writing for years. He gazed at me with those luminous blue eyes full of awe that made me feel on top of the world.

I grew up in a group home, a loner, and was thrown out into the big world with nothing but the clothes on my back and social housing. But I was a smart girl. I worked three jobs. I got a college grant and full scholarship. I was determined to make my way out of my crappy life.

I wanted to impress Ben so badly that night that I told him the one thing that made me dream. "A literary agent is interested in my novel."

He instantly lit up. "Really? Cool! Will it actually get published?"

I shrugged shyly. "I hope so. The agent is talking to several publishing houses. She says my novel is brilliant."

He pulled me closer, kissing, kissing, kissing me everywhere, making me giggle and swoon and feel like finally, *finally*, after the horrible events at the group home, life was working out.

"You are"—he pulled back and looked at me like I was the biggest treasure he'd ever seen— "amazing, Lizzy Dunn."

He gazed at me for the longest time, that intense gaze I couldn't quite figure out then, though I did later.

To my surprise, Ben returned the next week, and every week since then. Usually, late into the night. Slightly tipsy, always happy, with that dreamy smile and soft, "Hey, Lizzy, baby," and we would have sex and he would make me read to him and praise me. Praise is the greatest trick with women.

He loved my long black hair with straight bangs. And my strawberry lipstick. "So Kat Von D." He loved my stories and dark twists I always tried to impress him with.

Ben and I were from opposite sides of the track. I didn't have friends besides John, the guy who worked at the local coffee shop.

Ben, on the other hand, was happy-go-lucky, a party head. I knew I would never click with his crew. I hung out with them a couple of times until one of the girls got drunk and said to me, "The only reason Ben keeps you is for your talent. Otherwise, he'd never look twice at someone like you."

But I knew that, you see. Some have attractive looks. Others have talents. I didn't want Ben's friends. I wanted Ben, someone who could be only mine. And I didn't want to be out there, attracting attention. I knew what it could do. Like it did once. I was comfortable living in the shadows.

I never told anyone about the three boys at the group home back at Brimmville, what they did to me. No one needed to know my past. Definitely not Ben.

But *you* should.

As always, I'm getting ahead of myself, my beautiful girl.

You see, the thing with Ben is, he came from money but had zero merits. His only talent was his smile—dazzling, charming, cute, or apologetic if needed. Whichever way it shined, it made people's heads turn. It was his gift. That was about the only gift he had. So, he surrounded himself with popular people, and on occasion, the talented ones, making up for his own lack of personality.

I only realized that later. But by then, I was already in love and found out what he was doing behind my back. Then came the first heartbreak, but I was determined to work things out.

It all was great until *she* came into our lives, twisting her sharp claws into his heart and into my mind, dragging my past into the daylight.

She made me do things I'd never done. She brought out the worst in me. She dug up my old sins.

But then, she made me write the best stories.

So, here we are.

This secret will now be yours.

Someone might tell you lies. Someone might spread awful gossip about my past. But this—this diary—is the truth.

FOUR

"You think this is legit?" EJ asks, passing the pages back to me. He takes the joint out of his pocket and lights it.

We sit in the gazebo by the pond that's tucked away into the woods only a short walk from my parents' house. We stayed at the party at the house for exactly one hour. That was one hour too long, and no one cared when we snuck out.

"The handwriting matches, I told you."

EJ takes a drag and passes me the joint.

"Plus, it sounds just like them," I add. "My parents."

It's nighttime. The dim solar lanterns in the gazebo corners light EJ's chiseled cheekbones and puckered lips as he exhales a cloud of smoke. He leans back on the bench, his hands locked behind his head. He has a handsome profile. Somehow, he's a far cry from the awkward nerd I met only several years ago. He's wearing Converse sneakers, jeans, and a black hoodie, the same type of hoodie that used to look like a potato sack on him and now looks sexy. Though I should probably not use that word in reference to my best friend.

"You got some strange mail, sure," he says thoughtfully. "Leave it. It might be nothing."

"What if it's some sort of clue?"

EJ turns to look at me. "To what? Your parents' love story started with a one-night stand, Snarky. It's not the story of the century."

"Oh, my god." I cringe. "That's all you got from it? I'm talking about the woman."

"What woman?" EJ shrugs. "There is no name. What are you supposed to get out of it? Ask your dad."

True, I could try to coax some stories out of Dad, now that Mom is gone. It always felt like Mom watched him like a hawk, curated every word he said, even when he drank too much.

"Ask him what, though?" I wonder out loud.

"Exactly my point. This letter is vague. It's just some preamble to—"

"What?"

"I don't know what."

I have so many questions. When did she write this to me? Months ago? Right before she died?

"Why do I only get this? This!" I shake the papers in the air. "Where's the rest of it?"

"Maybe there's nothing else."

"She was talking about some boys who did something to her."

"Maybe she started writing this story and then... you know..."

He doesn't say it, but I know he means the accident. People are so sensitive about words. She died, and that's that.

Yet, my chest tightens, and I try to focus on the suspicious letter to make the grim thought go away.

I feel EJ staring at me. I turn to meet his thoughtful stare. "What?"

His gaze softens. "Kenz, I think you are substituting grief with some mystery you are trying to milk out of this random fan letter. Maybe someone is just messing with you."

Disheartened, I don't answer. Instead, I pull the hood over my head, lie down on the bench, and take a hit off the joint.

I like these moments with EJ. I like when he calls me Kenzie or Kenz. That's when I know he is serious or concerned. Snarky was what he called me when we first became friends. The nickname stuck. I don't blame him. I'm not the easiest person to get along with. Dad says I got it from Mom.

"What does it feel like?" EJ asks after some time.

"What does *what* feel like?"

"This new reality, with her gone."

I shrug. He knows Mom and I were never close. Our family wasn't a happy one, and that's because of Mom.

My mom was 1) "A bitch," as per Dad's side of the family. 2) "Complicated," as per my father. 3) "Brilliant genius," as per the literary world. 4) "Queen," as per her fans. She spent hours a day in her social media groups. She donated signed copies to charities all over the world. She was nicer to her fans than she was ever to me. And definitely way more generous with moral support for them.

I'm not yet a great writer, but I try. I love writing. When I decided to submit a piece for the college writing competition, Mom was the first to read it.

She shrugged. "You have a long way to go, sweetie." Always that "sweetie." I hated it. No help from her, no pointers. She just handed my story back to me like it was beneath her to help me work on it.

I won first place, thank you very much, and celebrated by getting shitfaced with EJ. Professor Salma of creative writing said I had a future.

Mom only gave me a condescending smile, a cold "congrats," then wrote in her social media post that she was proud of me and hoped that one day, I would follow in her footsteps. Emphasis on "follow." Like I will always be in second place.

Whatever.

So, Mom? Yeah, she is a complicated bitch with a brilliant talent and a sweet personality in public. *Was.* I should've written a beautiful eulogy to impress the literary world, but I was speechless for days after they found her body. Still am. I don't know how to process the fact that I miss her, or how to deal with the sudden void in my life. Yet I am not grieving, I don't think. And there is no one besides EJ I can tell that I miss her presence yet I don't grieve her. It's bad. You shouldn't say that about your mom.

"My dad had a fight with some dude at the memorial service today," I tell EJ as I pass the joint back to him.

"Like a fist fight?"

"No. Like a conversation gone wrong. Dad called him a scumbag. The guy called him Benny-boy."

EJ chuckles. "Called *your* dad that?"

"I know, right? There was something off about that convo."

"There's something off about your whole family, Snarky. No offense."

He's not wrong.

The worst part is that there's this nasty feeling inside me that there are a lot worse things to come. And they have something to do with the letter I received.

FIVE

A loud laugh and a curse from behind the gazebo make me sit up.

"Hi, sorry! Sorry! Hey!" A drunk couple stumbles toward us.

The dude puts his palms up as if in surrender. Next to him is a hot brunette in a mini dress and a man's suit jacket over her shoulders.

He sniffs the air. "Looks like you have all the right stuff."

The brunette giggles, wobbling on high heels that sink into the soft ground.

The joint is gone, and I motion with my eyes to EJ to get up.

"The place is all yours," I say as I walk off the gazebo steps, EJ following.

"Sharing is caring!" the guy shouts at our backs, then laughs in unison with his date. "Come on, guys. You have the good stuff."

"I'm pretty sure they've snorted plenty of good stuff already," EJ says under his breath with a soft chuckle.

"All these people make tons of money," I say bitterly as we walk toward the house, "and they still want to score something for free whenever they can."

"Yeah. Listen, your folks' house is killer, but not when that whole circus is here," EJ says apologetically. "I'm gonna bounce."

"Yeah."

"Yeah," he mimics me. "Hey, Snarky."

I don't look at him but feel his fingers approach my face about to pinch my nose.

It irritates me when he does that. I react in time and slap his hand away before it reaches me, tripping as I walk.

He grins at me. "You'll be all right?"

"I don't need a babysitter, EJ, if that's what you're asking."

"Okay. Come back to town, yeah? We'll hang out, get takeout, play some video games, talk."

"I will."

He is leaving, and I already feel sad. EJ is my best friend. I really don't care for anyone else. He says I'm like my mom—a recluse, a loner, sometimes strange.

He is just being cocky, of course.

EJ is only a few years older than me. We met at some lame party when I was a freshman in my first year at university. That was when I was still trying to fit in. He was a nerd. I was a rebel. Neither of us was popular by any definition. We clicked. He helped me set up my online writing platform, and in no time, we became best friends.

He already had a place of his own, much bigger than mine, where we started hanging out until I got my own little studio.

EJ's parents are scientists who relocated to the West Coast several years ago. EJ visits them often, but since we met, EJ ended up at many of my family's holiday dinners. Calling those gatherings "family dinners" is an overstatement, considering they are big affairs with dozens of guests. They usually include Mom's latest protégé, some industry professionals, and of course, her agent, Laima Roth, who I can't stand.

Anyway, while EJ and I both appreciate personal space, he's become part of an online community for programmers who do all sorts of jobs in cybersecurity and coding. While I still nerd out by writing on online platforms and making pennies, he attends all sorts of conferences and conventions across the country and makes good money.

I'm surprised he didn't drop me as a friend. But then, he wouldn't. Trends come and go, but friends stay. EJ is a sweet person.

His Dodge Charger speeds away from the house, and as I watch the tail lights disappear in the dark, I feel bummed out. I like being by myself. Unless it's with EJ. But lately, we spend less and less time together. He dates now and then, whereas my dating life leaves much to be desired.

I walk back into the house that's now quiet. *Quieter*, to be exact. Most guests have moved outside to the pool deck. I can hear a small group of Dad's friends down in the billiard room.

Laima is in the living room, pretty wasted, talking to some rising star in literature who apparently was Mom's protégé, like many others before him. And he might be talented, sure, but that's not why Laima's hand is on his thigh, the wine in her glass about to spill onto his pants because she's distracted and leaning into him with her double Ds, or triple, I'm not an expert. He's not too enthusiastic about it by the looks of it. Considering that he is barely over my age and Laima is old enough to be his grandma.

I walk to the kitchen and look around at the neatly stacked bottles of booze left after the caterers cleaned up. If EJ stayed longer, we could've had shots. But I don't drink much, and definitely not by myself—that would be going down Dad's path. If what I read in the letter is true, Dad's indulgences into booze started around my age. *No, thank you.*

I spy a small tray with Italian pastries and decide that would be a smarter choice. Grandma always taunts me about how skinny I am. I've told her many times that the almost exclusively black clothes I wear make me look skinnier. I'm five foot four and a hundred pounds. That's called small. But she's convinced in her head that I am bulimic.

"Just like your mom used to be," she often says.

Fingers crossed, the references to my mom will now decrease to avoid potential triggers.

With a tray of pastries in my hand, I walk toward the staircase.

Suddenly, a rustle in the hallway catches my attention. I walk over to check, but it turns out it's not a rustle. Voices are coming from Mom's office.

Well, isn't that a surprise? As soon as Mom is gone, her office becomes public domain.

I press my ear to the closed door and hear Dad's voice.

"What did you want me to do, Mom? She was the one who had it under control. He was *her* problem."

"He was everyone's problem, Ben. She just figured out how to benefit from it. Right in front of your nose."

"Oh, cut it out!"

"I'm sure she justified it by calling it stress relief."

The sound that follows is Grandma's chuckle. Grandma knows how to push buttons. Especially my dad's.

This conversation is odd, just like the one Dad had with the mystery man at the service.

"We need to figure this out," she says.

"Figure what out? I thought it was all figured out a long time ago."

"Does it look that way? Elizabeth wouldn't agree, would she?"

"She is dead."

"Exactly my point, Ben. Are you really that stupid?"

"Oh, what are you talking about?" Dad asks almost shouting.

"Shh. No need to drag the whole party in here," Grandma says in a hushed whisper. "Do you know who came talking to me again today? Right after the service? That detective."

"About?"

"Saying that they still have a reason to believe that it wasn't an accident."

My jaw drops. That's the first time I'm hearing about this from my family members.

"I'm not surprised," says Dad, and there comes a sound I can't discern.

"Keep it together, Ben," Grandma hisses.

A chill runs down my spine because I realize what that sound is—it's Dad's drunk chuckle, a nasty little sound that grows louder and turns sinister in the span of several seconds. It's cut off abruptly with his sharp words:

"She had it coming. For years."

SIX

VIRAL is written and underlined on the whiteboard of the lecture hall. Professor Robertson's voice drones on as I sit at the back of the lecture hall and scroll through social media.

For days, E. V. Renge's fans have been organizing all sorts of gatherings around the world. Tarot card readings, cosplay parties, streaming them online, with the trending hashtag #ForeverRVNG, because, you know, her pen name is an anagram for "revenge."

I can't stop thinking about the letter I received.

Last night, I opened Mom's first bestseller, *Lies, Lies, and Revenge*, and reread parts of it. The crazy plot acquired a new meaning, though I might be exaggerating. I still can't quite stomach the gruesome details of what was done to the main heroine in the book and then what she did to the culprits.

The professor's loud voice pulls me out of my thoughts.

"I'll upload the latest assignment onto the digital board. See you all next week," he says.

The lecture hall of over fifty students starts frantically packing their books and laptops. Only then do I realize that I snoozed through almost the entire lecture.

"Are you following what's happening online?" Sarah asks me. "With your mom and everything, you know."

Sarah has been sucking up to me ever since that lecture assignment about E. V. Renge's books.

"I don't care," I snap.

I grab my shoulder bag and go down the steps of the auditorium, past the professor's desk, when he calls out to me.

"Miss Casper? May I have a word?"

Ugh.

I don't think that professors realize how awkward it is when they single you out among others and request to "have a word."

I walk over to his desk and meet his sympathetic eyes—I know what this is about.

Professor Robertson teaches my social studies lecture. Kind eyes, cashmere sweaters, and frameless glasses. He is soft-spoken but entertaining and probably everyone's favorite professor.

He says that since we are taking social studies, we are part of a social experiment too. Hence, "giving us a choice" as much as possible—his words.

That was how he found out I was the daughter of the famous E. V. Renge. Well, he and everyone else who didn't know yet. That lecture started a shitstorm.

It happened during his lecture about the power of small things that change history.

"You've all read *The Tipping Point* by Malcolm Gladwell," he said that day, his arms crossed at his chest as he leaned back against the lecturer's desk and studied the audience. "At least, that was the assignment, and you will get tested on it. Not the book. I know you can download the detailed synopsis online." He scanned the audience with a knowing smile. "Our next topic will be artificial intelligence, so you will have an opportunity to tell me how it's integrated into your daily life. Now. Back to the current one. I want your understanding of the concept of trends. What makes things go viral. The power of chance. A momentum."

The thing everyone likes about Professor Robertson is that he doesn't lecture. His way of teaching is by having a conversation. Engagement, he calls it.

"Today, *you,* yes, *you* are going to tell me what we are studying next," he said during that lecture, smiling mysteriously. "I'm passing around small pieces of paper. You are going to take a minute to think about one single phenomenon, something that is trending right now, or has been recently, that has had a considerable impact on our society. Be creative. Whether it's Taylor Swift or HeyDudes or character AI or 'aura points.'" Someone in the audience laughed. "Don't be vague. Be specific. Write it down. One thing only."

In five minutes, all the papers were collected into a cardboard box that Professor Robertson had his hand in, stirring them up. He pulled one piece of paper out and set the box aside.

"Let's hope it's a good one," he said. "Because whatever this is" —he lifted and shook the chosen piece of paper above him—"you will write a two-thousand-word essay about it."

"Ouch!"

"Oh, man!"

All sorts of reactions came from the lecture hall as the professor grinned and unfolded the paper.

"Let's hope no one put anything stupid," Sarah murmured next to me.

"Oh. That's interesting." Professor Robertson scanned the audience after he read the piece of paper. "Apparently you are writing an essay on"—he paused for emphasis—"the book phenomenon." He cocked a brow. *"Lies, Lies, and Revenge* by author E. V. Renge."

He smiled at the audience who exchanged glances.

Claps and excited cheers erupted from everyone, while I wanted to sink through my seat.

It sucks living in the shadow of your talented parent. I lied as a junior when people looked at my last name and asked if I was related to Elizabeth Casper. Until Mom did a signing at my university library—a huge deal. Of course, she mentioned me, with a proud smile on her face that rarely appeared in real life.

Naturally, I was screwed. Not as much as the senator's son in my class whenever the politically woke discussed any major political events. On second thought, probably worse. Yes, definitely worse.

"Okay, okay!" Professor Robertson raised his hand to calm everyone. "I have to agree. The books by E. V. Renge gained a huge following in the last few years thanks to the social media boost. Here's the tricky part." He studied the audience, summoning complete silence. "You are going to *read* the book *Lies, Lies, and Revenge*, if you haven't done so yet." Disappointed grunts went around the lecture hall. "Yes. Calm down. I'm going to read it too, since"—he pressed his palm to his chest—"guilty, I haven't read any of her books yet. Many of you will cheat, I know. So, here's a heads-up. You will write your essay in class the next time. Yes, right here, so I can make sure you don't use AI. It will be exciting to see your handwriting."

The frustrated boos went around the audience again as Professor Robertson chuckled.

"Yes, Mr. Stepanchuk!" he called out to Alex, several rows below me, who was glancing at me from behind his shoulder, his hand raised.

I glared at him, mouthing for him to be quiet, but he only grinned like a fool.

And then it was too late.

He got up and said in that pompous voice, "Just so you know. We have the author's daughter among us."

"Is that so?" Professor Robertson raised his eyebrows in genuine surprise.

Alex turned to point at me. "Mackenzie Casper. Her mom,

Elizabeth Casper, writes under the pen name E. V. Renge. It's not a secret, FYI. Just so we have transparency here."

Transparency, my ass. I swear, I wanted to cut Alex's vocal cords. I still might.

"Her mom is hot," another smart-ass commented.

I'm pretty sure I heard the words "milf" and "ew."

Sneers went through the auditorium.

If I could have a superpower, I'd wish I could disappear.

Professor Robertson called me over after the lecture.

"I didn't know E. V. Renge was your mother."

"Yeah, well. You are in the minority."

As well as Sarah, who became like a piece of chewing gum stuck to my shoe sole, because she was a longtime E. V. Renge's fan.

Professor Robertson smiled. "It's all right. Let's do one thing. Skip the essay, considering your connection. But if you can instead talk about what inspired your mother's books, that would be great. Maybe you can give us a little personal insight."

The next week, when I told him that I wrote an essay instead, because of NDAs and whatnot, he nodded in understanding. When he read my essay, he said, "No wonder. You've always had a great sense of words. It must be from your mother."

Here we go. Everyone thinks the best part of me is inherited from her. I hate that. As a kid, I desperately tried to find her approval. She was a book goddess, but I spent less time with her than her fans did. I mean, she was obsessed with herself, with her books. I don't know what I did wrong. Maybe she hated me for the failure my father was. She called him that during one of their arguments.

Me? I don't know what changed when I started growing up. I've always enjoyed reading and writing, but when I started university, I really got into writing and have been taking a creative writing course.

Here's another unsettling thought.

I have a feeling that my mom distanced herself from me as soon as she found out about my hobby.

It felt like Mom never wanted me to write.

SEVEN

Now, two months after that excruciating study of the trending phenomenon that was my mother, Professor Robertson looks at me with pity as he summons me.

"Mackenzie, how are you coping?"

I don't need to cope, I want to tell him, but then he'll think I'm heartless.

"I'm all right."

"I know it's tough, Mackenzie. Especially when she had so much attention, and you were part of it."

"You didn't know her, Professor. She was..."

Mom was too big for the room. She was too cool for school. She cut sharper than a knife. She could really make you feel important. Make you feel like shit, too. She could. She had a way with people. She walked into the room, and everyone's eyes were on her.

I sigh, remembering Mom with an indifferent stare that she perfected at home.

"We weren't close," I say instead.

"I see." The professor studies me with pity.

"With her gone, it's... it feels kinda empty, you know?"

"Are you seeing a counselor?"

I roll my eyes. "What, like I'm the only person in the world who lost someone?"

"No, of course not. Your family is helping you cope?"

My family, right. Wouldn't he want to know about my family?

I pick at the corner of my shoulder bag, trying to excuse myself, but strangely, he is the only professor who seems to be genuinely concerned, unlike most others who ask just to kiss ass.

"How is your health? Are you doing more tests?"

I knew that was coming.

If the whole ordeal about my mom's books wasn't enough, I also had a seizure during his lecture three weeks ago and had to go to the campus emergency room. They sent me to see a specialist. Not surprisingly, my parents, who never really gave two shits about me, didn't even look through the medical bills or wonder why I was at the specialist.

I should've kept my mouth shut, but when Professor Robertson inquired about my health the week after that, I told him what the doctors said. He stared at me with pity like I was already half-dead. Now, every time he asks me about my health, he looks at me with sadness like it's only a matter of months until I croak.

I told Sarah, too. In contrast, she looks at me like I'm an exotic creature because I have some inherited condition that I need to take pills for. I didn't get a chance to tell Mom or Dad. Now, there's never a good time.

Some might think it's weird that strangers know more about my health issues than my parents. In psychology, there's a not-so-remarkable common term for it—dysfunctional family.

That's double pity from my professor.

I can see it on his face. He looks at me attentively as if my expected grief is supposed to manifest itself on my skin or something. Teary eyes, maybe? Saggy mouth? Shaking chin?

"I'm fine, Professor," I say, trying to contain my irritation. "Honestly, you know what's better? When people don't constantly remind me of what I just lost."

He nods apologetically. "I understand and apologize."

I feel bad right away and give him a weak smile.

"If you ever want to talk, I'm here," he says and pushes himself off the desk, signaling that the conversation is over.

Thank God.

He is not the only one "concerned." There are other professors, of course. Some are exaggeratedly nice to me. Some feel like I'm entitled, so they despise me for the sheer fact that my mother was a celebrity.

Right now, I want a burger with a fizzy drink and to get back to my writing, which I haven't done much since Mom's accident.

I stop at the local burger joint for takeout, then walk fifteen minutes to the two-story apartment building that hosts twelve apartments rented out to students.

I have a car but mostly only use it to get home on weekends or to drive to EJ's, who lives about a ten-minute ride from me. Dad asked me if I was coming home tonight, but I had one more class in two hours, so I told him I'd be home very late.

I open the front door of my building and walk up the stairs to the second floor. Struggling with the take-out bag in one hand and my shoulder bag in the other, I rummage for the keys and finally manage to shove myself into the apartment. Right in the hallway, my foot slips on something on the floor, and I slide like a clumsy skater on ice until I catch myself.

"What the hell," I murmur and look down.

There's an envelope on the floor with my fresh boot print on it.

I curse at the asshole who still puts envelopes under the door. Must be the super of the building or someone from the student association.

But when I pick up the envelope and turn it around to see the name of the sender, there's none. Only the familiar phrase that sends my heart racing:

From #1 fan. XOXO

LETTER #2

I could pinpoint the exact beginning and end of the happy days. The day Ben took me out for dinner was the first. The first time I saw *her* in town was the latter.

For several days before *her*—I always think of events as *before her* and *after her*, as if she was a marker of some twisted turn in my own story—I was finishing my first novel.

Ben showed up late that night, smelling of booze and pizza. A wide smile on his face, his tipsy eyes gleaming as he wrapped his arms around my waist and pulled me toward him right in the doorway, kissing me, walking us in, and kicking the door closed.

"Missed you, Lizzy," he whispered, his kisses sloppy and urgent.

And though that had become an already well-practiced routine of us tumbling into my Murphy bed and having quick sex, something about that night felt different. Much later, I realized that was the night *she* showed up in his life.

Fifteen minutes later, we were done, and Ben was already falling asleep.

"I'm just going to chill for a minute," he murmured.

That meant he would stay the night and leave early the next morning. So, I sat for some time by the window, in the dark, by candlelight, and wrote.

I loved writing by candlelight. It felt romantic, somehow old-school. Writing with a pen instead of a computer felt like a talent in itself. It required patience. Not that I could afford a computer anyway. Occasionally, I used a quill, an old thing I got from an antique shop on Main Street. It came with a half-empty bottle of ink.

It was one of many such nights when I would study Ben's naked body on my bed, and flashes of what those three boys did to me years ago would start creeping back.

"Wanna play, Lizzy?"

I was fifteen. They were a year older. I was a loner. They were a popular trio. But mostly, they were cruel—the quality that often goes hand-in-hand with good looks in teenagers.

"Hold her, Brandon. Shh, pretty girl, no need to scream. You scream, and it will hurt. We don't want you to hurt, right? No, we don't."

Writing those words was like getting paper cuts.

"Good girl. So pretty. Aw, don't cry."

It was bitter—seeing their smiles the next day, like *it* had never happened. Brandon's arm around my shoulders in class. "How are you, Lizzy?" Smiling while I wanted to stab his eyes out with a pen.

But as I wrote down that story from memory, another feeling began taking root inside me, soothing me—vindictive satisfaction. They were gone, long-gone. And I was here, turning the awful past into a twisted tale of revenge that one day would find its readers.

They say writing about the past is reliving it. What I found out was that writing the past down and changing the outcome was therapy.

That's how my first story was born.

Lies, Lies, and Revenge.

I wrote down exactly what they did to me. But the barn fire they died in a month later was too easy of an outcome.

You see, in real life, they received their punishment, simple and way overdue. But on paper? Oh, on paper, they received revenge. Twisted, dark, bloody, with screams of pain and pleas for mercy.

Punishment is white. Revenge is red. Mine was bloody-black.

That night when I sat by candlelight and edited yet another chapter, I smiled. My main heroine, ten years after what she'd suffered, had become strong, confident, and successful. She took the law in her own hands. "The Tailor," the authorities called her, or, supposedly, the maniac male, who tortured, killed, and sewed live mice into the three men who all graduated from the same group home. Three men who, years after the group home, had become powerful and successful, but one day, their lives started falling apart. Within a span of several years, they were broke, publicly humiliated, and ostracized. That's when they met their tormenter and—very soon—their killer.

I wrote about thick gut-wrenching revenge. Their slow descent into madness as my heroine ruined their lives. Their screams of pain when she tortured them. And I wrote it with a smile, changing my own story into what would be the proper revenge.

Still, then, I thought I was the only one who knew what really happened the night of the barn fire.

But that was about to change.

Several days later, I was at a cafe where John worked. I'd met John in that very cafe the day I moved to Old Bow, and we had become close friends.

I stopped for our usual chat that often came with a bagel and coffee on the house. What are friends for, right?

He was my only friend, besides Ben. I entertained the thought that he liked me. He had even asked me out once, right before I met Ben. But then, Ben happened, and there was no room for anyone after that.

I was leaving the coffee shop when a blast from the past stopped me in my tracks. That past had messy brown hair, intense dark eyes, and a haughty smile that I had hated all through the years at the group home. The past was dressed in a swanky shirt hanging off one shoulder and ripped jeans. And it had a name —Tonya.

That should've been the first red flag—she wasn't surprised to see me as she walked in, right into me. But *I* was.

"Hi, Lizzy," she said, studying me up and down.

I don't think I answered right away, my first instinct being to run, to run from my past, but sensing it was too late.

"H-hi," I finally managed. "I didn't know you lived here."

"I do now." She smiled that cold smile that didn't reach her eyes.

I didn't want to talk to her for longer than necessary. My orphan past had somehow caught up with me, and I hoped I'd never see her again. I said goodbye and started walking away.

"Hey, John! How is it going today?" I heard her voice behind me and halted at the door, looking back.

John beamed at her. "Hey, Tonya, great now that I see you."

My insides churned—they somehow knew each other. I had a feeling she would get a free bagel and coffee just like I did.

Just then, she turned and locked eyes with me. That's when I knew, I felt it in my bones, that she wasn't in Old Bow by accident.

I scrambled out of the shop, my heart beating wildly in my chest.

I asked John later, "How do you know her? That girl from earlier?"

He shrugged. "She just moved in, I think. She's friendly. Cute, too."

Nothing could've prepared me for what waited for me at home that night.

A note, a simple note, inside my studio, right on the kitchen counter. A scrap of paper with words that sent chills down my spine:

I know what you did to those three boys in the barn.

EIGHT

"I think my mom hurt people," I say to EJ on the phone. "I need to find out more. Want me to bring the letter over?"

"Get your ass here!"

Yes, sir.

Besides being a good programmer, EJ now has a wide network of connections who are very good at finding hard-to-find information online, and not always legally. Maybe, that's what I need right now.

Half an hour later, adrenaline rushing through my veins, I take two steps at a time as I hurry up the stairs to the third floor where EJ's apartment is.

I almost slam into a blonde dressed in fashion sports sweatpants, a hoodie, and Prada sneakers.

She gives me a condescending once-over, her gaze lingering on my black lipstick.

"Spooky," she says and walks past me down the stairs.

That's Monica, EJ's ex.

I listen to her steps echoing downstairs then turn to look at the window and see the lights of the red BMW outside flashing as she unlocks the car and gets inside.

I could be one of those cool rich girls if my parents ever spoiled me. But as it stands, I'm lucky to have a used car at their expense. I'm making a little cash writing stories online, but that's pocket money, nothing fancy.

I feel a prickle of envy. Monica paid for that luxury car herself. I know that for a fact. I also know that Monica is a successful online influencer, and not just a pretty face but a tech girl. Also, she is thirty years old. Also, she should find someone her own damn age to shag instead of EJ, who is almost a decade younger. She is supposed to be his ex. At least, that's what he told me. Maybe, he lied.

"You are a beautiful girl, Mackenzie," Mom used to say. "Don't let the boys ruin that. They always want to get their sticky hands on pretty things like you. Boys will be boys."

I hate that phrase, the lame excuse for predator behavior. Mom stopped saying that I was beautiful when I started wearing dark makeup and black lipstick. But I always kept her words in mind. Only now, as I learn about her past, do they start making sense.

My mood drops significantly within several seconds as I ring EJ's doorbell. I'm sure that Monica and whatever she and EJ do together is more exciting than my silly fan letters.

"You miss me already?" EJ says with his million-dollar grin as he opens the door. As soon as he sees me, his grin is replaced by the slightly embarrassed cute smile.

"It's just me," I say, walking past him. "Are you back together with her?"

Right away, I cringe at having asked. Not that I care. I shouldn't. I might have sounded a bit judgmental.

"Nah. She was picking up a game prototype I helped her with."

"Whatever." I plop down into the armchair. "None of my business."

EJ's cute smile grows into a grin again. "Jealous, Snarky?"

"As if."

49

I feel stupid having asked about Monica.

EJ grabs a couple of Fizzys from the fridge and passes one to me.

"Where is it?" he asks, eyeing my bag as he drops into his computer chair.

So, he's still intrigued by the letters. *Good.*

I take the envelope out of my bag and pass it to him, then sip on the fizzy drink as I study him out of the corner of my eye.

What a difference several years can make! EJ is not a scrawny skinny dude with glasses anymore. He started working out. He wears contacts. He travels to conferences for programming and software development. He's had several girlfriends, though he won't tell me much about them, like it's a cool secret I'm not worthy of. Except Monica, that brainy Barbie. I've met her before. I didn't like her, hated her, actually.

He only laughed. "You need to get laid, Snarky."

"Shut up."

"I'm serious."

"Because, what? You just lost your virginity, so you are all hot stuff?"

He laughed loudly at the joke.

I lost my virginity at a party during my first university year. I told him it sucked. He said sex was cool. We left it at that. We never discussed that kind of stuff afterward. Like I said, awkward. I didn't want to imagine him naked. I mean, he has a nice body, but the last thing I want is to think about what my best friend does to girls in bed.

EJ reads the pages hungrily, leaning with his elbows on his knees. He tilts it a little toward the giant multiple lit-up desktop computers. It's always dim in his apartment during the day and dark by night. The decorative neon signs are always on, painting the walls in cheerful colors. So are the multiple computers that make his place look like a hacker's den.

"Okay." He straightens up in his chair and turns the pages,

making sure he didn't miss anything. "You have the previous ones on you?"

I do. I carry them with me, because every time I think about them, I have the urge to reread them.

I pass him the first envelope, and he takes out the papers and examines them.

"They are written on the same paper, same notebook by the looks of it. They are all ripped out carefully."

"Right."

"Your parents... Yeah. That was some first date," he says with a little smirk and meets my eyes. "Clearly, you are following in your mom's footsteps."

I roll my eyes.

"Okay, but the mention of the three guys..." He traces a line on one of the pages with his forefinger. "Now it's pretty clear that something happened. They did something to your mom. And I'm not imagining when I say that the incident, whatever that is, is a bit too similar to what happened in *Lies, Lies, and Revenge*."

"Yeah," I say uneasily.

"Shit," EJ curses under his breath. "I mean, she grew up in foster care. So did her heroine. She mentions the three guys. Her heroine has exactly the same story. You think she was..." He clears his throat, not wanting to say what we both think.

"Raped?" I prompt.

"Yeah," he says.

"Yeah," I echo.

He exhales loudly. "And then that note, *I know what you did to those three boys in the barn*."

"Listen, she wrote fiction, okay? You don't think that she actually did something that... You know, what she wrote about in her books... At least not as gory, right?"

I stare at EJ, hoping for him to contradict me. I can see his Adam's apple bob as he swallows and licks his lips.

"Okay, here's what we gonna do." EJ turns to the computer in the center of his desk and pulls up the search engine page. "What was the name of the group home she grew up in?"

"Like I'm supposed to know that?"

"Jesus, Kenz," he murmurs disappointedly.

Mom didn't like to talk about her teenage years. I never insisted. Journalists, on the other hand, were fascinated with her, to say the least. They researched her extensively. Mom rarely gave interviews, so they looked for the information elsewhere.

"Here." EJ clicks on an online article with a picture of the group home. "This guy wrote about her group home, Keller Foster Care Facility in Brimmville, Nebraska. Let's see."

I rise from the couch and lean over EJ's shoulder to take a closer look at the article.

"Okay, don't breathe down my neck, yeah?" he says, turning to look at me.

"Well, jeez, sorry." I step back.

"No, it's just I want to see you when I talk to you, you know?" He gets up and drags the armchair toward his desk, leaving it right next to his chair. "There." He pats the seat and gets back into his own.

EJ has this weird thing where he insists on locking eyes with people when he speaks. He says he doesn't trust those who can't look him in the eyes. If I didn't know EJ well, I'd say he had some childhood trauma where he's afraid to be stabbed in the back. When I told him that the first time, he laughed and called me an idiot. But that's EJ, he's just... different.

He starts typing, sifting through more search results online. "If something happened, a crime, we will find it, okay?"

I bite my lip as I watch him type a mile a second in a search bar. The words "rape," "assault," "group home," town, state, and other keywords flicker on the screen, and I can't believe these are the words we use to research my mom.

Nothing comes up.

"Okay," EJ says, not even slightly discouraged. "Maybe that wasn't a public case. Or not a case at all."

"She never mentioned it, never said anything in her blog. This is the first time I heard about it. So, yeah, maybe it was a secret."

"Okay. But if there was a fire, then it should be in the local newspapers, right?"

"I mean, it was in the nineties."

"So?"

"It's old. How are you going to find it?"

"Snarky, the nineties weren't that long ago."

"Yeah, our lifetime ago."

He snorts out a laugh. "It wasn't the Middle Ages, you know."

His fingers swiftly run over the keyboard, typing, as he argues with me.

He has long fingers, sort of delicate, whereas his body is muscled. Not in a meat-head kind of way, but taut, a far cry from his stick-figure several years ago. Even in his sweatpants and a T-shirt, like he's wearing right now, he's attractive. I can see why Monica would go for a guy six years her junior. EJ is smart, too.

Me? It's not the first time I've seen people give me bizarre looks. My dark hair with the matching black lipstick and heavy eyeliner are not exactly the norm.

"Unapproachable, rebellious, wanting to push people away," Mom used to say.

That's the way I like it.

I'm still staring at EJ when he suddenly claps his hands and shoots them in the air with a loud, "Bingo!" almost making me jump.

My eyes snap to the computer screen.

"No freaking way," I murmur as we both gape at the article from almost thirty years ago with a grim headline that makes the goosebumps break out on my skin:

BARN FIRE AT GROUP HOME PROPERTY KILLS THREE.

NINE

I didn't want to go back in time and think that Mom was a killer.

But here we are.

I brush that thought away, but it keeps coming back as EJ and I finish reading the article and lean back in our chairs, sinking into silence.

In the mid-nineties, a barn fire claimed the life of three teenage boys who lived at the Keller Foster Care Facility. Authorities suspected foul play, but the investigation was deemed inconclusive and soon closed due to the lack of evidence.

"Or," EJ finally says, "most probably, it was closed due to the lack of state funding."

"It would be helpful if we knew what made them suspect it was foul play."

"It says in the article that as per the toxicology report, the teenagers who died were highly intoxicated."

"So much so that they passed out?"

"Probably."

"All three of them?"

EJ shrugs.

"Sounds fishy."

EJ turns to meet my eyes. "You think your mom had something to do with that?"

"Oh, my god, EJ! That's not what I meant."

We sit in silence and reread the article.

"Okay, listen," EJ says, rubbing his lower lip with his thumb in contemplation. "This case has to be an old file. It might be public domain. We can request the files."

"You can do that?"

"Doesn't hurt to try. If we can't do it legally, then I'll get my buddies to get it elsewhere and fast." EJ wiggles his eyebrows at me.

"They can do that?"

"Sure."

"For free?" I probe carefully, because I don't have extra cash to spare, though funny enough, after the accident, Dad asked me if I had enough money for expenses and offered more. Mom always controlled the finances of our family. Now, I suppose, it's all in Dad's hands, and Dad is a lot more generous.

EJ leans over and gently pinches my cheek. "Maybe you'll have to pay with your body, Snarky," he whispers mockingly.

"Ew." I bat his hand away.

He laughs and elbows me gently. "Of course, for free. Anything for a friend."

EJ once explained to me briefly what sort of jobs he does. He swore that they were all legal. Though he told me stories about some of his online buddies who do hacking jobs and all sorts of stuff that can get them in a lot of trouble.

It's already close to midnight when I get back to my parents'. I contemplated staying at my apartment in town, but then thought maybe Dad would feel lonely in the giant house. My grandparents left this morning. To be honest, that's a relief.

There's still a security guy at the gate but no more journalists snooping around. Just like everything, celebrities' deaths are hot news but transient, taking backstage when something more exciting pops up.

The only lights on in the house are on the first floor. I park my car and pray that there are no guests or annoying PR people inside. It's been a while since our house has been peaceful.

The area on both sides of the front door is crowded with flower arrangements. That's just the spill-over. The entire hallway and living room are stuffed with bouquets from friends, colleagues, and fans. Despite it being late October, our house smells like a flower garden. I want to tell Dad that it looks like a funeral home. Of course, I won't. It might hurt his feelings.

The house is eerily quiet when I walk in, and I sigh with relief.

I drop my bag by the coat closet—Mom would've reproached me for that, of course. *Not anymore.*

The house phones ring. We have two: one in the living room and one in the kitchen. I glance at my watch—it's midnight, yet someone is calling the landline. That phone has been a nightmare in the last week since what happened to Mom, yet no one bothered to unplug it. I actually think Grandma secretly loves all the attention lately. It's not a nice thing to say, but that's the truth.

To my surprise, the door to Mom's office is wide open. I step to the doorway and see all the lights on, including the desk lamp.

Dad is rummaging in the desk's drawers. A half-empty whiskey glass and an open bottle sit on top of it, next to the desktop computer—looks like Dad has been there a while. I wouldn't be surprised if he is celebrating his parents finally vacating the house.

Right away, I notice a flat-blade screwdriver sitting on top of the desk, as well as stacks of documents and all sorts of envelopes.

Holy crap.

I stifle an amused chuckle.

I know Mom kept most of her drawers locked. She valued her privacy. *Well-well.* It looks like Dad got impatient and, not finding the keys, broke into the drawers. He has held out for over a week since Mom's passing and until Grandma and Grandpa left.

There's only one reason for it—he is looking for something that no one besides Mom was supposed to know about.

TEN

"What are you doing?" I ask, crossing my arms at my chest and leaning on the doorframe.

Dad jumps, startled.

"Jesus, Mackenzie!" He presses his hand to his chest then takes a gulp from his whiskey glass and wildly looks around the desk. "Looking for some papers."

"Mom would've killed you if she saw this," I say with a sad smile.

"Yeah, well..."

No one has touched her things yet. Not her clothes upstairs. Not her collection of cars. Not her favorite coffee cup in the kitchen.

I push off the doorframe, walk toward the desk, and sit on the edge of it.

Dad knows that Mom would be furious at me for doing this, too. She hated nonchalance and loose manners. Now, Dad and I are on our own, and it almost feels like the security guard we've had monitoring us for years is gone.

"What papers are you looking for?" I ask. "Need help?"

"Um... Just stuff."

I chuckle. "Just stuff?"

He waves vaguely around the room. "Life insurances and whatnot."

"Insurances? Like multiple?"

"Yeah, we have those."

"For you and Mom?"

"Mom, me, you."

"Me?" That's the first time I've heard of this. "Why do I have life insurance?"

"Mom insisted we get it."

Are you kidding me?

Two things bother me about this scenario.

One, there was no reason for Mom to get life insurance for me. I mean, I'm twenty-one. Why would she insure my life unless she thought something might happen? I never told her about the emergency room or the visit to the doctor's weeks ago. I cried that day, I tried to talk to her. But she had some online conference scheduled, so I didn't tell her out of spite, imagining how one day, I would just drop dead, and she and Dad would regret that they never paid me more attention.

I'm exaggerating, of course. The doctor said my condition is not severe if properly monitored. The prescription he gave me would keep it in check. Considering that it's a genetic condition, maybe Mom even knew about it all along and never told me not to scare me.

That's what suddenly dawns on me. If she knew it could get out of hand untreated, maybe that was the reason she got a life insurance policy for me.

I shake that awful thought away.

The second thing that bothers me is Dad. I feel he is not just looking for insurance paperwork. Stuff like that is always available online. Many of the legal papers are at our family's lawyer and in safety deposit boxes. There's a safe in the basement, too.

Instead, it looks like Dad is trying to find something he doesn't want anyone else to find. Something Mom kept locked away even from him. And that makes me curious.

ELEVEN

Nothing in this family is what it seemed only days ago.

"Dad, did Mom have friends in college?" I ask just to keep up the conversation so I can observe him.

His eyes dart toward me a little too fast as he leans back in Mom's chair and takes a sip of his whiskey.

It's a giant gothic chair with claws for legs, black wood, and intricately decorated animal horns. Something out of the Viking age. When Mom sat in it, she looked majestic, like a queen of the underworld. Dad looks like a peasant. It seems it's swallowing him whole.

"Not really," he says without looking at me.

"I mean, you guys partied in college, right?"

"Not your mom. She was a loner. She liked to"—he waves his glass in the direction of the bookshelves—"stay home and write. She was a recluse. And... Yeah." He looks around the table with sadness.

"I mean, like maybe one person?" I prompt, remembering the mention of some guy named John.

Dad gives me a smile that's far from genuine. "Listen, what's this about?"

I want to tell him about the letters but then change my mind. They are supposed to be a secret. Mom and Dad hadn't been getting along lately. Not at all. In fact, Dad doesn't seem to be grieving much.

"Just wondering. I want to know more about her."

Dad takes a deep breath, as if I'm twisting his arm, and scans the room. His exhale is heavy, his gaze somewhat nostalgic.

"Your mom... She was a fun person. Until she wasn't." He goes quiet.

Great. So insightful.

But then Dad continues. "She was kind and full of life. Until... Some things happened. She... We moved to the East Coast right after you were born, and then, a year later, when her first book came out, things just started changing so fast. So fast," he repeats in a whisper, still not looking at me.

Again, he didn't tell me anything I didn't know.

I only now notice that Dad is quite loaded, which is not unusual these days at this time of night. Dad has drinking down to a science, the perfect formula being not to pass out.

He does look sad, somehow lost. He's only forty-four, but he has plenty of grays in his brown hair. He is still slender, but his posture is stooping.

He reaches into his pocket, pulls out a cigarette holder, and plucks out a cigarillo.

On reflex, I hold my breath, wondering if he'll actually dare to light it. Mom didn't let him smoke in the house, let alone inside her shrine.

But he does. The lighter in his hand clicks and lights the tip of the cigarillo. He inhales tastefully and exhales a cloud of smoke as I watch in disbelief. He takes another drag, then another, chugs the rest of the whiskey in his glass, then flicks the ash into the glass and sets it on the desk.

That's it. I'm sure Mom's ashes just caught on fire in the urn. Her ghost will come to haunt him.

Dad sits in silence, and for a moment, I think he forgets I'm here. Or maybe he's completely wasted—his eyes are clouded, his gaze vague.

"We used to be happy," he finally says, staring at the desk. "When the book was released, it was an instant sensation, on the New York Times Best Seller List for months. We traveled. We bought our first house. Not this one." He motions aimlessly with a cigarette, his nose slightly scrunched up in what I realize is aversion. "Our first place, simpler. I invested into a business, then another. They both failed. I lost that money. That's when she said, 'You can't even keep the money that I give you.'"

Dad chuckles bitterly. "E-li-za-beth... I once rhymed it with Macbeth. She didn't like it. Well..."

He scratches his brow with his thumb, then wipes his mouth with the back of his hand.

"She was... She was always the talented one. The genius," he says with a tiny snarl. "I was *the husband* of E. V. Renge."

Dad flicks the ash of his cigarette on the floor as I stare in shock, afraid to interrupt him. He's never talked like this about her. He'd never dare.

"That wasn't even the problem. It would still be fine. Me and her—it was always supposed to be me and her. And you, when you came around." He finally looks at me and flashes a boyish grin with dimples. "Of course, you, kiddo."

I love Dad's grin. That's one thing that hasn't changed about him in years. No matter the mood or appearance, that grin always melts people's hearts.

"But then..." Dad's grin vanishes in a second. He snatches the whiskey bottle off the desk and takes a big gulp.

Whoa. This would be a good time to stop him, but I want him to keep talking.

"Then?" I prompt in a whisper.

"Then *he* showed up in our lives. And it all went to fucking hell," Dad says angrily.

"Who?"

Dad chuckles nastily, takes another gulp from the bottle, and sets it down with a loud bang. His head bobs a little.

"The guy she's been shagging behind my back."

My jaw drops.

Dad shrugs drunkenly. "Sorry, kiddo. You are old enough to know the truth about your talented mother," he says with a poisonous snap.

I want to know more, but Dad's eyes are drooping. I think he is tapping out. In a moment, he tilts his head back against the chair and closes his eyes.

Quietly, I leave.

At least now I know one thing for sure—my parents have enough secrets for another bestseller.

TWELVE

For over six years now, the closest person to me in our household has always been our maid, Minna. Sad, isn't it?

It's around nine in the morning when I come downstairs to the smell of breakfast.

Minna greets me with a sympathetic smile. "How are you, Miss Mackenzie?"

"I'm all right."

She awkwardly looks in the direction of the hallway, and I see that the door to Mom's office is still open.

"Dad's there?" I ask.

She shakes her head. "I came in this morning, and he was sleeping there. I had to wake him up and help him upstairs."

"Thank you, Minna."

"I cleaned up a little. It was a mess. I hope you don't mind. Mrs. Casper never—"

"She's gone," I blurt out without thinking.

Minna murmurs another sorry, then beams at me. "Breakfast is ready, Miss. Your favorite."

Grandma cooked several times when she stayed here. I'm not a fan. Minna's cooking is much better, while Grandma thinks she holds a secret to some magical old-school recipes. No one dares tell her that her cooking sucks just like her attitude.

The house phone rings, and Minna goes to answer the receiver in the living room.

"She has passed. No... Yes... Mr. Casper is unavailable right now..."

She hangs up and walks back to me, shaking her head. "Everyone calls and calls and calls. Solicitors, strange people. Everyone!"

"You should unplug the phone."

Minna laughs. Whether I'm joking or not, Grandma gave specific instructions to answer every phone call.

I throw another glance at Mom's office and make a mental note to snoop around in there the first chance I get. I'm sure I'll find interesting stuff. But before Dad wakes up, there's something else I need to do.

"Hold on to the breakfast," I tell Minna. "I'll be back."

I walk to the office and notice that the spare key is still in the door lock. I pull it out, grab my bag, and, in my sweatpants and hoodie, get in my car and drive five miles to the hardware store. With a copy of the office key, I drive back.

I pull back to the house when EJ calls.

"How's the tenth circle of hell?" he asks, making me snort.

"It's all right." I trip on a flower arrangement as I walk up to the door. It's open, and there are a lot more flowers outside now.

"You have classes today?"

"Not until Monday."

"Your grandparents left yet?"

"Yeah, yesterday."

"Should be peaceful now."

"Tell me about it." I walk into the house and pause between the hallway and the living room where Minna is picking up a giant arrangement of lilies. "Dad is supposed to meet with the lawyers today. He got wasted last night, said some crazy things."

"About your mom?"

"That too. I'll tell you later. But he was... He was smoking and drinking in Mom's office."

I glance at Minna, who stiffens with the flowers in her hands and gives me a brief alarmed look, then starts walking toward the entrance.

"Ooooh shiiiit!" EJ laughs. "Daddy Casper is getting loose."

He knows my family well enough to know that this, indeed, is out of hand.

I grin. This shouldn't be funny. This is like dark comedy spiraling downhill until it turns into tragedy. But my family is ridiculous, and I'm past the point of being diplomatic and lying to myself.

"What I was going to say is... I have a spare key to Mom's office." I glance at Minna, knowing that my words will make her ears curl. "Dad broke into Mom's desk last night."

"Holy shit, Kenz!"

Minna lowers her head as she walks past me. She's always been on my side, so I'm not paranoid about saying this in front of her.

"Yeah. And I think he was looking for something. But that's beside the point. Once he's out of the house, wanna come over and help me go through Mom's paperwork?"

"I'll be there. Yes. Give me an hour or so, and then I'll head your way."

I think Mom kept some secrets in her office. Dad might be searching for something. But I'm determined to find it first, or at least something, anything, from Mom's past.

I hurry to Mom's office, stick Dad's key into the lock, then walk to the living room.

Only now do I notice that most of the flowers are gone.

"What's going on?" I ask Minna.

"Mr. Casper is still in bed, but he asked for coffee and said to get rid of all the flowers. Said he doesn't want to feel like it's a funeral home."

"Good," I say in relief.

Minna pauses in front of a huge exotic arrangement. They are magnificent rainbow roses, black and orange. There must be over fifty of them in a bouquet that rests inside a black marble vase decorated with golden netting.

Minna presses her hand to her chest and shakes her head. "Aye, these are beautiful."

I walk over and read the little black card with golden letters tucked into the flowers:

To the finest woman I've known.

Huh. Must be another crazy fan. Or?

The guy she's been shagging behind my back.

Dad's words ring in my ears. But I agree, the bouquet is extravagant and gorgeous. We'll see if Dad notices it.

"Leave this one," I say to Minna. "The rest can go."

Minna gives me an awkward glance. "You don't mind if... If I take some home?" She nods toward the stack of flowers in the hall.

I smile at her. "You can take all of them. Give them to friends or something. No reason to throw them out. They are worth a small fortune." Then I get an idea. "Just do one thing. Pull all the cards out of the bouquets and save them for me, please."

I'll study them later. You never know what will come across as suspicious. I still don't know who is sending me the letters.

The house phones ring again. Minna hurries to the receiver and picks it up, then writes something on the list tucked under it. It's already marked with dozens of messages. Mom has always been in charge of everything, including bills. Dad? He put his cell phone on silent to keep his peace of mind, and I don't blame him. He doesn't touch the house phones either.

I walk to the kitchen, and Minna is right behind me, already pulling out a plate and serving me fried eggs and bacon with avocado toast.

I plop down on the bar stool at the kitchen island. I prefer eating here rather than being served at the giant dining table. Meals used to be almost ceremonial when I lived here. Breakfasts would be elaborate spreads with multiple utensils, napkins, carafes, pastries, and a basket of fresh fruit that never looked a day old though no one ever ate them.

I like things simple. And I enjoy hearing Minna hum under her breath and tell me about her family dramas rather than her walking around with a fake smile and cold eyes like she often did in front of my parents.

Minna is happy not to have Grandma boss her around and treat her like a servant. Yes, there is a difference between a maid and a servant. Minna could tell you all about it after Grandma left.

"There is a lot of mail for you, Miss," Minna says as I eat. She walks to the mail basket and picks out a big envelope. "But there is this one envelope. Seems important. It was just there in the mailbox this morning. No return address or a stamp."

She sets it next to me.

For Mackenzie Casper, says the printed sticker.

As I chew on bacon, I rip the envelope open and pull out a smaller envelope.

This one makes me stall. I almost choke on bacon as I stare at the familiar words:

From #1 fan. XOXO

LETTER #3

You don't know that glass is broken if you don't hear it break. Even when you see it, it still doesn't fully register in your mind. But when you step on it, oh, then you feel it. That's the moment of truth. *Feeling* is how reality makes itself known. Pain is its ultimate manifestation.

She was everywhere I went. It was like seeing broken glass but from afar.

It wasn't until I saw her one day talking to Ben outside the main campus that I realized she was in Old Bow because of me.

I watched them from afar. Ben laughed, his laughter so loud and happy on that sunny September day that my heart ached. The way it ached in those sad movies you rewatch, seeing the main characters revel in happiness because they didn't know yet—but *you* did—what would happen soon, that the tragedy would rip their lives apart.

I didn't know what she wanted or why she suddenly showed up in my life.

Maybe it was a coincidence.

Maybe it was nothing.

I asked Ben later how he knew her.

"Tonya? Oh, the guys and I met her at the bar one night. She is cool. She's here from out of town, just moved in. Why?"

"Saw you talking to her. I thought I knew her from somewhere," I lied.

I knew then she was targeting him. Not because he was a handsome guy—there were plenty. But because he was mine.

I was never jealous of Ben hanging out with his friends. He liked loud places and crowds—not my cup of tea. But suddenly, I was jealous that *she* was somewhere with him where I wasn't. Where I didn't belong. And I couldn't do a damn thing about it.

I loved Ben, you see. I was dirt poor, and though I managed, he occasionally paid for my things. I was a loner and preferred it that way. He was the life of every party, and he gave me something to write about. I never envisioned a bright happy future. But he often joked that when I got famous and rich with my books, I'd be his sugar mama. He laughed about it. But I suddenly saw a future with him, and it was brighter than it had ever been in my dreams.

I often let him read the new chapters I wrote.

He always praised me. "Jeez, Lizzy, you are so talented. How does this pretty little head of yours come up with this crazy stuff?"

And he celebrated with his friends every week. Holidays. Birthdays. A block party. A Friday. There was always something, while I stayed home and wrote.

Two weeks after I first ran into Tonya, I invited myself out with Ben.

"I could use some company," I said, wanting for once to be out with him.

And there she was, that very night, Tonya, laughing with one of his friends' girlfriend when we walked into the bar where everyone met up.

Among dozens of people there, mostly students, Tonya stood out. Happy, confident, so easy-going that it made me envious.

"Hey, Tonya, this is Lizzy," Ben introduced me. Not his girl. Not his girlfriend. Just Lizzy.

She waved with a smile. "Hi, Lizzy. You look familiar. Have we met before?"

"I don't think so," I murmured, wanting to disappear.

"You remind me of a girl from school, when I was fifteen or so. She liked to play with fire, that one. Check this out, guys, so this girl—"

Blood pounded in my ears when she started telling a story about a barn fire. Told it casually, like it was some tabloid gossip.

"No way!"

"Oh, shit!"

The guys laughed while my blood simmered.

"Crazy, no?" Ben nudged me with his elbow, his eyes never leaving hers.

I knew the story, of course. *My* story. I knew the guys she was talking about and the investigation that followed that fire.

That's when I really felt it—the pain of the past. Like stepping onto broken glass, the shards cutting into tender flesh.

I had a feeling this was just the beginning of a nightmare.

I stayed at the bar for an hour, as long as I could manage, trying to avoid her eyes, embarrassed at being there, with Ben, who barely acknowledged my presence.

I told everyone I was going home and went to the bathroom. On the way out, I ran right into Tonya, who blocked my path.

We stood staring at each other for a short moment, a moment that swallowed me into the past, to my years at the group home, the three boys, and her words back then, "You stay away from Brandon. Understood, little mouse?"

And it spat me back out, leaving me trembling in anger.

"What do you want from me, Tonya?" I asked bluntly, scared of hearing the answer.

She lifted her hand and ran her forefinger along my dark hair as it fell on the side of my face. She did it slowly, like a lover, her cruel eyes roaming my face. "I know what you did, sweet Lizzy. You think you got away with it?"

A sinister smile curled her lips.

I flinched at her words. "I don't know what you are talking about."

"Oh, you do. I have evidence. And I can go to the police." She leaned so close I could smell her perfume and the faint smell of minty lotion. Her lips pressed against my hair as she whispered in my ear, "Any moment, Lizzy. Be careful."

The words made me panic, though I didn't show it.

I wanted to tell her that I had only wanted to scare them. That I had only wanted them to regret what they'd done to me. But I definitely couldn't tell her that I was glad about how it had turned out. With all three of them dead.

THIRTEEN

I'm nervously pacing around my room when EJ arrives.

"Your old man is still here," he says, walking in. "Some guy is clearing flowers out of the house."

He's dressed in his usual jeans, a black hoodie, and Converse sneakers, his tousled hair slightly damp—it must be raining outside.

I hold out the envelope.

"Ohhh," he mouths and snatches it out of my hand. "Another one?"

He sinks onto the edge of my bed as he reads the newest letter while I pace in front of him, tugging at the drawstrings of my hoodie, my eyes never leaving his face as I study his reaction.

When he's done reading, his hands holding the pages slowly drop to his lap, and he raises his eyes to me. They reflect the same thoughts that I had only an hour ago when I read it.

"Oh-kay," he says.

"Oh-kay," I echo.

"There it is."

"I think it *is*."

A confession—there's no other way to call what Mom wrote in the letter.

"Damn," he whispers.

"We need that file, EJ," I say. "The investigation file. I think it will clear things up. Or at least give us more details."

"Yeah, well, my guy will get back to me as soon as he has something."

EJ goes to the bathroom while I carefully fold the letter and put it into the envelope it came in.

At this point, I wonder if I should use gloves to handle this mail. Obviously, I won't snitch on whatever Mom did in the past, unless... No, scratch that thought. There is no "unless." Still, this is evidence. Who knows if the person sending this is a whack job and will come after me. Right now, one thing is absolutely certain—I'm being watched.

I put the envelope with the previous two that are already in a plastic file folder and shove them in my bag.

The bathroom door squeaks open, and EJ appears in the doorway. He loudly shakes a yellow prescription bottle in his hand, his concerned eyes on me. "Are you taking these?"

I roll my eyes. "Occasionally."

"Occasionally?"

"Yeah, whatever. It's not like I'm going to drop dead." Let's hope not.

EJ doesn't move from where he stands. "Oh, come on, Kenz."

I really hate pity from others. There's a boatload of it lately.

I smile at him. "You gonna miss me if I do?"

He shakes his head.

"I'll haunt you, EJ. You'll be having a good time with your next cyber queen, and I'll be moving shit around your house, spooking the hell out of you."

A grin breaks out on his lips. "I like you alive. I'm not into cyber queens."

"Anymore?"

He disappears into the bathroom to put the prescription where it belongs.

"Since when?" I ask louder.

He walks out, his reproaching stare on me.

"I thought that was your type," I taunt him.

"Oh, yeah? You are an expert, Snarky?"

He switched to Snarky again. Kenz is for serious moments. If he calls me by my full name, that means something is seriously wrong.

My phone dings with the entrance gate notification.

I turned the notifications on since Mom's passing, when I temporarily moved back to my parents'. We have multiple cameras on our property, plus the house alarm, plus the sensor for the front gate—you can never be too careful when your mom has crazy fans. That has been our reality for years. The security precautions came in handy several times when Mom was stalked.

I check the camera footage and see Dad leaving in his car.

"Let's go," I tell EJ, meeting his eager gaze. "Time to learn E. V. Renge's secrets."

FOURTEEN

When we get downstairs, the front door is open, and a young guy in a plaid shirt and jeans is taking several flower arrangements at a time and hauling them out of the house.

"Hey, Mackenzie!" he hollers at me.

"Hey, Nick!"

"Sorry to hear about your mom!"

That's Minna's nephew. Through the doorway, I see his pickup truck backed up right to the entrance, its bed half-full of flowers.

Minna is helping. "Is it okay?" she double-checks with me, motioning to the flowers.

"Absolutely. Take them all. Hey." I motion for her to come over. "We are going into Mom's office. Not a word to Dad, okay?"

"Sure." She smiles like a conspirator.

I'm not even surprised to find the office door locked. Just to prove myself right, I walk to the indigenous mask and rummage in its thick mane, but the usual hiding place for the spare is empty.

I knew it.

"Look who is ahead of the game," I murmur, proud of myself,

as I pull out the copy I made earlier this morning from my hoodie pocket and open the door.

It's dark inside Mom's office. The thick burgundy curtains are closed.

"Shut the door and lock it," I order EJ, then walk to the window and pull the curtains open, letting the light in.

"Whoa!" he muses, looking around.

In the daylight, the office looks almost normal. Businesslike, even, albeit with a gothic feel.

EJ has never been inside, and I let him slowly walk around, his eyes wide in awe.

Mom's office does look like an altar of sorts. Veiled lamps, gothic paintings, raised panels with intricate carvings, posters of her books from promo events and accolades.

A massive ashy-black wooden cabinet stretches floor-to-ceiling on one entire side of the room, with multiple shelves and drawers, trinkets and old books on the shelves. In the center of it is a giant fireplace.

A leather living room set is arranged on a plush carpet in front of it. Mom's vintage desk is to the right of it. The window is to the left.

"Are all these special editions or something?" EJ asks, running his fingers along the shelves that display dozens of variations of Mom's three bestsellers.

"Yeah. She has an entire cabinet full of them. Most are professionally printed. A few are custom bound by fans who send them to her as gifts."

"Cool," EJ says.

I might not be a big fan of my mom's personality, but she was brilliant. I don't like being compared to her, but if I'm being honest, I have had many moments in life when I burst with pride when people found out who I was. That was a long time ago.

Being in her office is like stepping into an old castle with a slick modern touch. Thick carpet. Black wood and steel. Anger, hate, desire—that's what she wrote about—all of the darkest human emotions combined into a visually represented cocktail that's in every haunting detail of this room.

"Do you want a little tour?" I ask EJ.

"Hell, yeah!"

I lead him to a giant chest-slash-traveling-trunk. It took three people to bring it in when Mom bought it a decade or so ago. Now, it's full to the brim.

"Is that—" EJ doesn't finish.

"It is." I nod, undo the mock lock, and lift the lid.

Adrenaline spikes in me, making my hands tremble a little. I've never been allowed to touch anything in this office.

The top compartment is full of envelopes and letters, simple, on fancy paper, elaborate packaging—all fan mail.

I push a lever, and the top compartment slides up, revealing the rest of the trunk with all sorts of curiosities in it, courtesy of her fans, too.

"Holy crap." Amused, EJ sits down on his haunches, and so do I, so we can pull one thing out after another and inspect them.

"The famous piss jar?" EJ points at the Ziplock bag with a vial in it.

"Yeah. No idea why Mom kept it."

"Maybe as evidence." He shrugs. "Did the investigators ask for any of this?"

I give him a thoughtful stare. "There's too much of it here. Plus..."

"Plus, they don't really have proof that her accident wasn't accidental."

"Right."

Strangely enough, no investigators ever came to talk to me about Mom. Not since Grandma booted one out of the house.

EJ and I spend half an hour going through locks of hair in little plastic baggies with notes, weird toys, dolls made to look like my mom with needles pinned through them. There's red soil from

Namibia from one fan. There are rocks from a volcano in Iceland from another. A collection of antique cards. A piece of clothing. An antique dagger.

"Wow," EJ says, pushing up to his feet. He throws a last look around and turns to me. "Okay. What are we doing?"

Fans' presents might be exciting, but I know EJ is anxious to investigate. So am I.

I don't know where to start, but one thing is for sure—you don't lock up a room unless you are hiding something you don't want anyone to see. And I'm pretty sure my mom had plenty of secrets.

FIFTEEN

EJ slowly walks by the massive cabinet that occupies the entire wall and tugs at the drawers. When one drawer doesn't budge, he yanks at it harder, but it's locked.

"You have the key to this one?" he asks me.

"No."

"It should be around."

"Mom probably kept the drawer keys somewhere else."

"Nah," EJ argues, going step by step along the cabinet, pressing on the nooks and crannies. "She'd want to be able to get into these even if she left the keys somewhere else. I'll work on this one. Anything that's locked is important."

I let him do his own thing as I step around the giant desk and take a seat in Mom's chair.

I wait for a second for the memories to hit me with grief—no, not happening. But it feels surreal, and instead of crying, I smile—this is where Mom did most of her work. This position lets me look at the office with her eyes.

Did she feel like a queen of the thriller genre when she worked here?

I run my hand along the desk edge, and my heart thuds in anticipation of finally touching her personal things.

I don't need to get into her computer yet. I'm sure it's password-protected. We will worry about it later. The drawers are a different story.

The top of the desk has the usual—the framed first handwritten page, a picture of Mom, Dad, and me taken during my high-school graduation, another picture of her and three other best-selling authors.

There are neat stacks of papers and documents—thanks to Minna's cleaning up after Dad's search last night. The office vaguely smells of cigarillo smoke. It feels like Mom's spirit is already being smoked out, though I can't help but steel my spine—it's as if I expect her to walk in any time and unleash her wrath on me, seeing me at her desk.

More importantly, I feel uneasy at the memory of the last letter. Mom was never an angel, but thinking that she might have committed horrible crimes and buried the evidence somewhere here makes the room feel eerie.

EJ keeps tinkering with the different compartments around the locked drawers. Meanwhile, I start with the stack of papers on the desk.

It's boring stuff, mostly bills and invoices, bank statements and legal contracts. I sift through those quickly and impatiently lean toward the top drawer on the right side of the desk. The lock is broken, of course, but the drawer is empty. This must be where the paperwork came from.

The next drawer's lock is broken too. There are more papers in it and a black box. When I open it, there's a gun inside and a clip with bullets.

"Whoa. Why would my mom need a gun?" I say out loud.

"Everyone has a gun these days," EJ quips from his spot.

True, but everything that has to do with my mom now raises suspicion in me.

I look through the papers. More contracts. I want to set them aside when one name catches my attention.

Evelyn Casper.

"Why would Grandma's name be on legal contracts for Mom's books?" I muse.

EJ looks over his shoulder. "Maybe your grandma was employed by your mom?"

Huh.

I snap a picture of the contracts and NDAs with my phone, then go for the third drawer.

There's a folder there. Inside it is a stack of transactions. One account is clearly Mom's business account. The other one has no names, just the number. The transactions are all outbound, repeated every half a year, like clockwork, going back to seven years ago.

"I think Mom was being blackmailed," I say, studying the papers.

"Hold on. I think I might have figured this out," EJ responds in a strained voice, not paying much attention to me, as he reaches deep inside one of the shelves.

I go through the transactions, noticing that the amounts increase year by year, with the last transaction just this summer. At the end of the stack, there is one piece of paper. It's handwritten, with words that make my blood go cold.

There is no running from your past, E-li-za-beth.

A smiley face is drawn next to it.

"Yeah," I murmur, snapping a picture of that too. "Definitely blackmail."

"Bingo!" EJ shouts, making me snap my head in his direction.

He beams at me, wiggling his fingers like a magician, next to the drawer that's now open.

SIXTEEN

I drop the papers and walk over to EJ.

"A hidden lever opened the drawer." He spreads his arms in triumph. "Ta-da!"

It's a deep drawer with multiple large black boxes in it.

For a moment, we stare at them in silence, then EJ tips his chin toward them, prompting me to open them.

There are three heavy boxes and a document folder inside the drawer. I pick them all up, bring them to the desk, and set them on top of it, then lick my lips, nervous at what we are about to find out.

"Come on." EJ impatiently nudges me with his elbow.

I open the lid to the first box. There's wrapping paper, and I unfold it carefully, wondering if we just found some type of rarity. When I peel away the last sheet, it reveals two identical notebooks with flowers on the binding and a larger writing pad on the bottom.

I take the first notebook in my hand and open it.

Elizabeth Dunn, it says in a neat handwriting in the top corner. *Brimmville, Nebraska. January 1 0.*

My breath catches in my throat. "This is Mom's notebook. From the group home."

I flip through the yellowing pages of notes, quotes, words, and phrases.

"What's in the other one?" EJ prompts impatiently, leaning with both hands on the desk.

I pick up the next one.

They Had It Coming, says the first page in large letters. *By Elizabeth Dunn.*

I hold my breath, flipping to the next page. It's gone, and the next one starts with the familiar words that I just reread recently. It has corrections and crossed-out words, written in ink, with tiny ink blobs marring some words.

"That's genuine ink and a quill that she used sometimes," I say with pride. "Wait-wait-wait," I murmur, putting down the notebook, and pick up the framed first page of Mom's first bestseller sitting on the desktop. When I set it right next to the notebook, the fact is unmistakable—same handwriting, same paper.

"Same notebook," EJ states.

"It is," I repeat in awe. "This must be Mom's very first draft."

"Check the next one," EJ says.

I pick up the larger notebook, and the very first page says, *Lies, Lies, and Revenge by E. V. Renge.*

"The official draft," EJ says, and I nod. "Next," he orders impatiently.

I already suspect what's there, and I'm right. Same wrapping paper, carefully folded to nestle a fancy notebook with a leather binding. The first page reveals the title of Mom's second best-seller, *The Wolfe Whistle.*

"EJ," I whisper, flipping to the next page and stroking the letters on paper. There are multiple corrections in this notebook, scratched-out words. This must have been the first draft.

"Shit," EJ murmurs. "Do you see it?"

"What?"

"It's the same paper as the pages you got from an anonymous fan."

Is it?

The letters I received are upstairs, but I'll compare them to the notebook later.

I open the third box.

This one contains pages of different types and size, from different sources. The things scribbled on them are messy, written without order, scratched out violently, written on top of each other.

"It's a mess," EJ says. "You think your mom was high when she wrote this?"

He chuckles when I elbow him playfully. Though I wouldn't be surprised. Occasionally, Mom had long intervals of dark moods. That's when she would lock herself up in the office for days.

One page immediately catches my attention. "These are the notes for *Angels and Villains*, her omnibus of dark fairy tales."

"She was obviously in a different state of mind when she wrote this," EJ says.

"You don't say."

Dad and I both know that Mom's moods had gotten darker lately. I should know. I noticed during my teenage years. *Angels and Villains* was published five years ago. It was a completely different genre from her previous books but with Mom's unmistakable taste for gore and morally gray characters. They were a huge hit.

Surprisingly, this box doesn't contain a full written manuscript.

"Maybe it's in that last one." EJ nods toward the plastic folder and impatiently picks it up himself.

Inside is a stack of papers. The pages are from some basic notebook you can probably buy in any store. The writing is again more or less even, but nothing much makes sense.

One page has the same words written over and over again like a mantra.

Sharp teeth. Sharp teeth. Sharp teeth. Sharp teeth.
Sharp teeth. Sharp teeth. Sharp teeth. Sharp teeth.

Sharp teeth. Sharp teeth. Sharp teeth. Sharp teeth.
Sharp teeth. Sharp teeth. Sharp teeth. Sharp teeth.
Kill them.

"Is that blood?" I say in a half-whisper noticing dark-burgundy smudges on the page.

I turn to EJ and see the same unease in his eyes that makes my toes curl.

"What does it even mean?" he asks.

"Not sure but Mom's next novel she was talking to Laima about? The working title was, *Sharp Teeth.*"

My phone beeps with a gate sensor notification.

Scrambling, I pull it out of my pocket and see that a vehicle entered the house gate.

"Shit. It's Dad," I say. "Let's get this and go."

I start packing the notebooks and manuscripts back in the boxes.

"You mean we are taking these?" EJ looks at me in surprise mixed with excitement.

"Yes. Otherwise someone else will swipe them."

We grab the boxes and beeline for the door when I notice the picture of a signing event on the wall. I never really paid much attention to it, except now my eyes land right on a person I've definitely seen before.

I stall, staring at it.

"Kenz, come on!" EJ hurries me, holding the door open for me.

There are several dozen people in that picture, aligned in three rows. Mom is at the front, surrounded by people with name tags and smiles, all holding her omnibus in their hands. Dad is there, too. So is Laima Roth. I recognize several PR people.

In the very far-left corner, peeking from behind everyone else, is a man. It's the guy Dad had a fight with at the memorial service.

It could be nothing. But if he is a nobody, then what was he doing at the exclusive invite-only national book award ceremony?

SEVENTEEN

I spend the rest of my weekend at my parents', deciding that I will go back to my town apartment starting next week.

It's mostly quiet in the house except for the never-ending ringing of the house phone. Minna is like a secretary lately, constantly answering the phone and taking messages.

It's raining outside, the fall weather fully settling. I like when it's gloomy outside. It goes well with the mood of Mom's letters.

I know for sure they are Mom's. I took her leather-bound notebook with the second manuscript and compared the pages with the ones I received—the paper is identical.

I spend my entire Sunday rereading Mom's omnibus with the dark fairy tales, comparing the scribbles and notes from the third box, underlining the identical phrases. Some stories creep me the hell out.

There's one person who knew quite a bit about what was going on in Mom's head, and I decide to find out.

Mom has a phonebook in the hallway, with business cards from every professional she's ever needed or was in touch with. I find the number I need—for her therapist. I call the office, but no one answers—it's Sunday, of course. I dial the emergency number, and two rings later, hear the familiar voice of Dr. Pecora.

"Mr. Pecora, hi, this is Mackenzie Casper. I am the daughter—"

"Hi, Mackenzie. What happened?"

His voice is concerned or maybe puzzled. I know what I say next will puzzle him even more, but I need an answer.

"Everything is all right, I think. Maybe. I don't know. I need your help," I say in my most tragic voice to create a sense of urgency. He adored my mom. Hopefully, he will help. "I have a question, and it's important. When was the first time Mom contacted you?"

"Contacted me?"

"I mean, the first time she started having sessions with you?"

"Not sure, Mackenzie. What is this about?"

"It's important. I am trying to put some things together and... I just need to know."

"About eighteen years ago, I'd say. I would have to look in my records. That was around the time her first book hit the bestseller lists worldwide."

"Was she... Did she have issues?"

"Issues?"

"Like, mental troubles?"

He produces a sort of a grunt or a sigh. "You know I can't discuss that with you or anyone."

"Right." I sigh in disappointment. "Just a general question. You were her friend. Do you think... Do you think that fame changed her?"

There's a momentary silence, followed by another sigh. "Fame changes everyone. Hers was like an avalanche. But... Again, I can't speak of her particular case, but I can tell you for certain that with creative people, it's not the therapists who do most of the healing, but art."

"Art?"

"Yes. People like your mother, or creative people in general, find all their answers, all their healing in creative activities."

I wait for him to continue.

"Sometimes, it's a double-edged sword, though."

"How do you mean?"

"The same talent destroys them, too."

A long silence follows.

"I'm afraid I can't tell you much more," he says apologetically. "Would you like to schedule a session with me, perhaps?"

I have to restrain myself from laughing. Of course, he'd try to rope in another client.

I apologize for disturbing him and hang up.

There goes nothing.

The third manuscript is definitely out of whack. I wonder if Mom's darkness wasn't just her imagination. Maybe, it was *her*. That's why fans felt so close to her, their dark disturbed minds seeing something in her work that normal people considered a sick imagination.

It's evening when I pack the manuscripts in their respective boxes and tuck them into the bathroom closet, behind the towels and rags. One day, these will be worth a fortune, already probably are, but I don't want someone else to find them. I'll take them to my town apartment and keep them safe. I'm sure Laima freaking Roth would love to get her hands on them.

When I leave my room, the house is dim and eerily quiet.

Dad is out.

Minna is in the kitchen, making roast chicken.

"Mr. Casper said he'll be back for dinner," she announces. "I'm making his favorite."

"I doubt he'll be back for that. I'm sure he's having his liquid dinner as always."

Minna gives me a reproachful glance and shakes her head.

I notice that the mail basket is overflowing. Mom always took care of that. Dad obviously doesn't feel like picking up the responsibility.

I sift through the mail out of curiosity. There is voter information with my name on it. There's a bank statement from my account, though I don't have much in it. There's a medical bill addressed to my parents and me. I open it to find the prescription receipt for my meds. I rip the letter into pieces and toss it in the garbage bin, then do the same to two more that I find.

Bitterness comes back with a nasty feeling in my stomach. I wonder how long it would take for my dad to ask me about my health. This is a side effect of growing up in the family of a celebrity with plenty of money but little time to care about the basics. I could probably hide a corpse in my room, and no one would care even if it started stinking up the hallway.

Besides Minna. But she doesn't clean my room—I do.

By the stove, Minna murmurs something to herself and shuffles to the walk-in pantry.

The house phones ring, the one in the kitchen next to me so loud I almost jump.

Minna makes a loud racket in the pantry. "Oh, ouch, will you get that, please?" she shouts to me.

Annoyed, I pick up the receiver. "Casper residence."

Landlines should be outdated. But apparently, many businesses still rely on the old technology.

"Hello, I am calling about an outstanding bill. We are trying to locate the payer."

"Not sure, but I can take a message and pass it on?" I grab the notepad and the pen next to the phone. There are already several pages full of messages there. This is a waste of time. Dad will never bother with them.

"I'm calling from Huckleberry Supplies. We gave you a credit line extension for two months, and this is a reminder that it's two weeks past due."

I chuckle at the name. "Huckleberry?" I repeat, writing it down with a smile. If he adds Finn, I'll definitely mess with him.

"Correct. Huckleberry Supplies."

"I'll pass on the message."

I hang up and shout to Minna, "Got it! An overdue bill!"

"Thank you!" Minna shouts back from the pantry.

The phone rings again right away.

Smiling, I pick up. "Huckleberry Finn?" I answer, stifling a chuckle.

No one answers.

I clear my throat and rearrange my face into a serious expression that will reflect in my voice. "Casper residence," I say importantly.

Still, there's no reply, but I can hear heavy breathing on the other line.

"Hello?" I repeat, quieter this time. My heart skips a beat, then resumes louder, beating against my chest. "Hello?"

Still no reply, but there is a chuckle, an unmistakable male chuckle, soft and sinister.

I slam the receiver back and stare at the phone, waiting for it to ring.

Instead, my cell phone in my pocket pings with a text message.

My hands shaking, I pull it out.

Anonymous: Check your mailbox.

It's Sunday night. There won't be any mail. And that's how I know that whoever is doing this is close, too close to me for my liking.

But I can't stop myself.

"I'll be back in two minutes!" I shout to Minna.

It's drizzling outside when I dart out of the house. So, instead of walking, I jump in my car and drive through the gate and to the road where the mailbox is. This will save me five minutes of getting drenched in the rain.

There's no guard in sight.

Dammit.

My heart pounding, I stop myself before exiting the car.

This might be someone's silly game. Or someone wants to bring up Mom's old secrets.

There is another possibility—that person, whoever it is, might be crazy. These letters might be bait. I might be stupid and falling for a sick trick. They might want to hurt me.

But the curiosity gets the best of me.

I veer my car so that the headlights point at the mailbox, scan the dark road, and not seeing anything, dart out of my car.

It takes me several seconds to grab whatever mail is in the box, run back to my car, and slam the door shut.

"Got you," I say in triumph, panting.

A chill goes through me when I look at what I grabbed.

There's just one letter.

From #1 fan. XOXO

LETTER #4

Sometimes I wondered what it would feel like to kill my boyfriend.

Not quickly, no, but the way I do in my books, with months of deliberate bullying beforehand, watching him slowly go crazy.

One night, I watched Ben sleep sprawled on my bed. For hours, I sat next to him and watched his lips move just slightly with every inhale and exhale. I watched his eyelashes flutter as he was dreaming. The way the fingers of his hand, resting peacefully on his naked chest, occasionally jerked in tiny spasms. The way his chest rose, up and down, in deep breathing. His pulse was beating on the side of his neck, in that vein under the thin skin, such a fragile little thing, so easy to snuff out with extra pressure or a quick sharp cut.

I wondered if I could slowly poison him, making him sick. Stir some sedative into his drink, so he stays here, with me, dependent on me, instead of going to *her*.

I wondered if I could poison them both. I pictured the police cars at her house, wherever she lives, whatever slimy place they escape to together, thinking I don't know. A peaceful night, the blue-red police lights slicing across the darkness, bouncing off the house windows as the officers stand inside the house, by the bed where both their bodies are splayed motionless, long cold.

The first time I knew Ben was cheating, I noticed red lipstick on his shirt, right on the bottom hem. I've never kissed Ben with lipstick on. Not down there, anyway. And the shade wasn't mine. It wasn't Chanel, the one that cost me twenty dollars. It was something else. Someone else's. The cheap stuff. The other girl's.

I didn't confront him that time. He was sleeping in my bed, his expression so innocent that I thought I was making things up.

I wrote. And wrote. And wrote. I hoped that once I had my first book published, I'd have the whole world in front of me. I'd have funds. I'd move to the East Coast and make sure your life was nothing like mine, beautiful girl. You'd never have to go through what I did.

The second time Ben stood me up, I went to the bar where he used to hang out with his friends. I stood outside the tavern and wondered if I was becoming one of those pathetic girlfriends who stalked their loved ones.

But here's the wild thing—in months of being together, we never said the words "girlfriend" or "boyfriend." I rarely went out with Ben in public. His friends knew me, nodded to me at lectures, but never, never cared to talk. I was *that* girl, his *thing*, the one he was *with*.

It didn't bother me a bit.

Another girl, though? It did.

So, that dark warm September night, I stood across the street from the tavern. The summer shutters were up. The place was bursting with music and laughter. And among the crowds spilling onto the boardwalk was my Ben, laughing, smoking, chugging beers.

With one little detail that made my skin crawl—there was a girl hanging off his arm. Not just any girl. Her, Tonya.

That little detail marred it all. That snake had charmed her way into his company.

I should've left, should've talked to him, should've told him things about my past, and her past. Maybe, he would've understood. Maybe it would've changed what happened afterward. Maybe, he would've left me, and a lot of bad stuff would've been avoided.

But that night, I stood in the shadows of the mulberry trees and watched, watched, watched. *Her.* I watched the way she laughed so easily and joked with others. The way they looked at her like they never looked at me, accepted her, brought her beers.

And I watched Ben. The way his gaze lingered on her for longer than a friend's would. The way everyone laughed at something he said, and he casually wrapped his arm around her shoulders. The way she leaned into him, easily, perfectly, as if she'd done it many times before.

I should've been writing that night, but instead, I watched for hours from the shadows. Then, Tonya seemed to be leaving, and Ben was trying to follow her, but she stopped him. They talked around the corner. She checked her watch and laughed, and Ben hung his head low in that clowny way of his. She laughed again, then wrapped her arms around his neck and kissed him.

My Ben wouldn't have kissed another girl. My Ben wouldn't have lied to me that he was studying that night.

The truth was—it took me a while to confront it—that Ben wasn't mine anymore or had never been mine in the first place.

The realization hurt.

But it wasn't Ben I was after, it was her, the girl who'd come from the same place as me and who was now taking away something I loved.

When they parted, I didn't go home, no. I followed her instead.

Five minutes later, when she turned onto a dim alley, I did the same but lost sight of her. Angry, I stood under the streetlight, simmering with hate.

"Fancy seeing you here," Tonya said from behind me, whipping me around.

She flashed me a snaky smile as she stood in the middle of the alley, her arms crossed at her chest. "Spying, are we?"

"What do you want?" I blurted out.

She chuckled, amused. "Me? You are the one following me."

"What do you want from me and Ben?"

"Is that even a thing? You and Ben? I wasn't aware. Should we ask his friends?"

She knew how to push my buttons. Bullies grow up perfecting that skill.

"Ben and I are in love, and you know that," I snapped.

"Uh-huh." I hated that calmness of hers. "Does Ben know he is in love?" A mocking chuckle followed. She cocked a brow. "Does he know about your past?"

I knew that would come.

"Do you think he'll still like you when he finds out you are a murderer?" she taunted.

"He won't believe you."

"I have evidence."

My heart stilled, then gave a violent thud. *Can't be.* It wasn't my fault. It was an accident.

But here is the thing about girls like Tonya—they know how to ruin someone's life with a single snap of their fingers. They learn it growing up. They practice it like it's a job. And with years, they perfect it.

True evil is not taught, I wrote in my novel. True evil is natural born.

Tonya might not have been evil, but she was smart and vindictive.

"Leave me alone. Why are you doing this?" I asked.

"Brandon was my first. But then you probably knew that. Everyone at Keller's did."

God, I haven't heard those names in a long time. I hoped I never would. But there stood a girl who knew my past, because hers came from the same place, intertwined with mine.

"He was my first love," she said, taking slow steps toward me. "My first friend. My first everything. And you murdered him."

She smiled then, like it amused her, the effect her words had on me.

"You know what they did to me," I said quietly, feeling anger stir inside me. "All of them. In that very barn."

Her eyes narrowed as she stopped only inches from me. "Maybe if you weren't such a snobby little bitch, they wouldn't have even paid attention to you. You were always a prissy little thing, weren't you?"

"You were always something guys wanted to use and discard."

"Oh, yeah? And you weren't? How did that work out for you in that barn?"

I didn't register myself moving until Tonya's head snapped to the side, and my hand stung from the powerful contact with her cheek. I couldn't curb my anger, gloating at the shock in her eyes.

"Leave us alone," I hissed and stomped away.

It could've ended right there. If only I went home. If only I hadn't decided to sit on a bench on Main Street and mope about what happened.

Not even ten minutes later, I recognized Ben across the street, walking hastily, his head down. But he wasn't walking home or toward my house. He was walking to where I just came from.

I followed him then. Of course, I did. For nine blocks, to an old brick apartment with dimly lit windows.

He rang the doorbell.

I watched again, from across the street, drowning in shameful betrayal, as the door opened and she—*she*—stood right there in front of him. He said something. She laughed in response. And he picked her up in his arms. Her legs wrapped around his waist as he carried her inside, kissing her, slamming the door shut as I stood alone in the darkness, wanting to set that house on fire.

I didn't go home right away, though I should've. I would've

taken my revenge on her. I would've tortured her and made her beg for mercy and would've probably killed her in the end. At least, on paper.

But I didn't.

That night, I stopped at the 24/7 store and bought a bottle of booze, then walked to Poplar Street and knocked on John's door.

He opened with his eyebrows raised in surprise. I'd only been to his place once, for a small party he had during my first year in town.

"Why do guys like girls like her?" I asked right off the bat.

"Who?"

"That girl, Tonya. Tell me what they can possibly see in her? You? Ben? Everyone else?"

He chuckled. "You all right, Lizzy?"

"I'm not. I need you to tell me. Right now. Go."

He gave me a once-over, his eyes lingering on the bottle in my hand, then flicking up to meet mine. "She is cool, I guess. And fun. Why? What's up?"

"Oh, she is. Fun! You think she's fun? That's funny," I spat out bitterly.

"You are being weird."

"I'm angry, John. What's weird is that my boyfriend is in bed with her right now," I blurted, tears welling up in my eyes.

I saw his Adam's apple bob as he swallowed hard. The pity—I wished I never saw it in his eyes. I didn't need pity that night. I wanted an explanation. At the minimum, I wanted to forget.

"I thought you were on my side," I gritted out.

His face fell. "Lizzy..."

That's right. I'd rather take an apology than pity.

I lifted my hand with the bottle and shook it. For once, I needed to forget how much people can hurt. I needed a friend. And I needed to finally talk to someone who'd understand. Me, her, and our past.

He held my gaze for a moment and stepped aside. "Come in."

The best thing about heartbreak is that it often helps you see the truth in all its ugly colors. It hurts, but it teaches you a lesson.

The worst thing about heartbreak is that, sometimes, it makes you do unspeakable things.

I would get to find out about it soon.

EIGHTEEN

They say that genius goes hand in hand with deviation and crime. I think my mother might have done something horrible in the past.

My mom is a murderer. My mom is a murderer. My mom is a murderer.

The awful thought spins in my head, and I can't let it go. It's not the first time dark thoughts have consumed me. I think of my mom's hand-written notes with the dark fairy tales, and now one thing is clear—I am truly my mom's daughter, and my head might have some madness of hers.

I sit on the bed in my room. The letters, all four of them, are laid out in front of me. The pages are double-sided. There's no mistake now that they came from one notebook.

Thunder cracks outside. The vicious rain starts slamming at the windows. I pick up the copy of *The Wolf Whistle* and open the page with one of the bookmarks:

She is evil.
I hate her.
I will make her disappear.

I slam the book shut and close my eyes.

It's fiction, I tell myself. It's a made-up story about two girls, one stealing another's boyfriend, the other setting off on years of masterful revenge. It ends with blood and torture, and I wonder how close it is to the truth.

I stare at the book and feel dirty just having it in my possession.

"*Raw, unapologetic, riveting,*" the critics say.

How many sick fictional stories out there stem from real life events? How many are secret confessions written out as a form of therapy while the readers have no clue?

I call EJ. "Number one, I just got another letter."

"And?"

"Hold on. Two, my dad was a cheater, and a bad one."

"Whoa. Spill!"

"Later. I need to do something. You know how I have the gate security sensor hooked up to my phone? Dad made me do it a year ago, after the incident with Mom's stalker."

"Yeah?"

"I know they have a server, it's a Wi-Fi sort of thing, where you can watch all the house cameras on the phone."

"And?"

"I want to hook them up to my phone"

"Okay?"

"Then I can watch the recordings of anyone on those cameras. Like go back, right? Go back in time and see who came to the house, if anyone snooped around?"

"Well, not until you have it hooked up to your phone. If you are an additional account, you will only have the recordings stored after you activated it."

"Dammit."

I hear him cough. "Care to share?" I ask, knowing he's smoking one.

"I'm not smoking, Snarky. I'm sick."

"Oh. Flu? Virus?"

"Don't know. I feel like shit though."

"Want me to come over and bring hot soup? I can get Minna to whip something up real quick."

"No, don't worry. I'll be fine. I don't want you to catch it, too."

"I won't catch anything. I won't even come close. I'll sit on the opposite side of the room."

He laughs and starts coughing again. "That's not how it works, Snarky. With a virus, I mean."

I shouldn't be upset, but I'm disappointed. "Okay, we'll talk about the letter tomorrow."

"Sure."

"Only if I can be your doctor."

A laughter escapes him. "Are you getting kinky with me, Snarky?"

"Whatever, EJ." I'm glad he can't see me blush. "I'll call you tomorrow after class."

Tomorrow can't come soon enough.

All night, I toss and turn in bed, imagining someone knocking on my window, though my room is on the second floor. I imagine my mother setting a barn on fire, her pretty face distorting into a sinister expression as the reflection of flames and shadows dance across her features. I imagine her main heroine from *The Wolf Whistle* sharpening a knife as she's singing a lullaby to her unborn daughter, but then the lullaby changes into a children's rhyme, a horror one, and the knife sharply slices someone's flesh, blood dripping, dripping, turning into a thick stream, and I wake up with a start, panting, sweat trickling down my neck.

It's light outside. The rain has stopped. My heart is beating hard as I wipe the perspiration on my neck and reach for my phone.

Nine o'clock.

Dammit. I'll be late for my first class.

I scramble out of bed, into the bathroom. Ten minutes later, dressed in jeans, hoodie, and sneakers, I dart out of the house.

It's too cold outside, and I shiver as I get in my car. An hour and a half later, I pull into the university parking lot. I'm late for class, so I decide to skip it.

I walk into the campus with no hurry.

The first thing I see is a giant banner with my mom's face on it.

Celebration of E. V. Renge's life.

There are more stand-up banners announcing that the newly remodeled Pearl Lecture Hall in the West Wing will soon be renamed E. V. Renge Hall in honor of the author.

Great.

I spend an hour at the café on the second floor, checking emails on my laptop. One of them is the copy of the banner announcing the E. V. Renge's event in two weeks.

Fabulous speakers in attendance, including the author's husband, Ben Casper.

Dad, of all people?

I grit my teeth. Why didn't anyone tell me that? It was probably the idea of Laima Roth or one of Mom's PR managers. I definitely need to find an excuse not to attend.

My second class passes without any excitement, except for Alex, who is *in*conveniently in many of my classes, making another jab about my mom. If I read my mom's books more attentively, I could probably get ideas for how to get rid of him, because he's been getting on my nerves too often this semester.

This sudden gruesome joke makes my stomach turn. I don't want to be like her. And I don't have these kind of thoughts. *Didn't.* Until I started reading her diary pages.

After the class, I call EJ right away.

"Still sick as a dog," he says grimly.

"I'm coming over."

"You'll get sick, too."

"I won't. But I'll bring the letters. And you'll help me look for more info online."

"You are not a good listener, are you, Snarky?" He chuckles, but there's no anger in his voice, no reproach.

"I just know better."

"If you do, take your prescription pills before you come, yeah? 'Cause you probably skipped them for the last who knows how many days."

I smile. EJ is the only one who's concerned about my condition.

An hour later, I'm hauling a large shopping bag up the stairs to his apartment. It has the essentials—chicken noodle soup and his favorite fried dumplings from the local café, as well as flu medication, cough lozenges, tea—I'm sure EJ doesn't keep that kind of stuff—and lemon that I got from a convenience store.

When he opens the door and lets me in, I study his miserable face and red nose, then bring the bag to his kitchen. He follows, watching with amusement as I unpack it.

"You clean up nicely," he says.

"I'll punch you," I warn.

He means my face. I barely had any time this morning, so I skipped the makeup altogether. He just quoted my mom, and I used to hate it when she said, "clean up nicely," as if otherwise, I looked like a dirtbag.

"Where's the letter?" EJ asks, sniffling, while I unpack.

"You eat first, then I'll show you the letter."

"Yes, Mom," he says with mild reproach, but when I heat up the soup in the microwave and pour it into a bowl for him, he obediently sits at the kitchen counter and slurps the liquid eagerly with no objections.

That's not surprising. All he has in his fridge is leftover pizza, soda, beer, and sports drinks.

EJ throws curious glances at me as I make him tea.

"What?" I ask. "I'm making sure you don't croak on me. I like having you around."

"Yeah?" He grins.

"Yeah."

"I come in handy?"

"That you do."

"Have something for you."

"What you got?"

He leans back in his chair. "My buddy sent me the file."

"What file?"

"The investigation into the barn fire."

I freeze in my spot. "When? Why didn't you tell me?"

"I thought you'd want me to send it to you, and I wanted to read it together."

I narrow my eyes on him, and there's that grin of his again that makes my heart melt. Freaking EJ, seriously.

"Where is it?" I demand.

"Chill, chill," he quiets me with a self-important mock expression. "I'll eat first, right? Then I'll read the letter, then we figure out the file together."

I wanna strangle him.

When he finishes eating, he takes the medicine I give him, then a tiny sip of hot tea I made. He already looks better. Or so I think, patting myself on the shoulder.

"Thank you, Doctor Casper," he says teasingly.

Finally, I take the latest letter out of my bag.

EJ reads it without excessive emotions, his face suddenly too serious and concentrated. When he's done, he ruffles his hair and looks at me with pity.

I freaking hate pity.

But I realize this look is not for me when he says, "Kenz, I think your parents were seriously messed up."

NINETEEN

"Okay, who is this John guy?" That's the first question I ask.

"Someone who studied with your mom?" EJ suggests as he settles into his computer chair and I take a seat in the armchair that he, again, dragged close to his.

"It doesn't say anything about studying. He worked at a coffee shop. Can we call them and ask?"

"You nuts? About someone twenty years ago? Who remembers that kind of stuff? If it's even owned by the same people. If it's even a coffee shop. If he worked there legally. And without knowing the name? That's a stretch, Snarky. Sorry."

"Right." I feel silly for a moment. "I can ask Dad about him."

EJ snorts. "Number one, there is nothing to ask about. I mean, nothing has happened yet in those letters. Maybe nothing will. Two, it looks like your dad wasn't an exemplary boyfriend."

"You don't say."

"Who knows what else he did. I mean, it seems like your mom got back at him. I mean the dud he mentioned to you while he was drunk."

"Yeah."

"What are you going to ask, anyway? About some random

dude your mom was friends with? Or wait, 'Hey, Dad, who was that chick you were cheating on Mom with in college? At least the one she found out about?'"

I bite my lip. This sounds so much worse coming from another person.

"Sorry, Kenz. It's just... Yeah, messed up."

I try to think logically. "Then who is Tonya?"

"Yeah. Good question. There are a bunch of files in that folder from the investigation. Including her info, because I requested it."

I huff in frustration. "Why are you holding back on me?"

"I'm not. We are going step by step. So, the file, right..."

He turns toward the computer and opens a document.

"Tonya Shaffer. She left the group home the same year as your mom. In fact, she took the GED exam at the same time, too. Get this, she was pregnant when she left the group home."

"What?"

"Yes. She must've been. Medical records state that she had been pregnant for six months when she came to the clinic for the first time."

"Where's the baby?"

"Given up for adoption."

"Jesus."

"There's barely anything about her after she was discharged from the group home. No bank account. No tax records. Nothing. There was a property registered to her an hour from Old Bow."

"In the letters, it sounded like she had a place in town."

EJ shrugs. "Maybe a rental. There's no record of it anywhere. But that property, a lake cabin, belonged to one Mrs. Cavendish, who passed away and willed the house to Tonya. I couldn't find any connection. Maybe a distant relative."

"She still lives there?"

"No, that's the problem. Two years after she inherited it, the property was bought out by Etched Properties LLC. For quite a hefty sum. Obviously, they didn't buy to flip it."

"Huh."

"It still belongs to that same LLC. But Tonya Shaffer vanished."

"What do you mean vanished?"

"Just that. There are no records of her. No activity. No social media. Nada. She dropped off the face of the earth."

"She didn't go to college in Old Bow or anywhere else?"

"No."

"No jobs?"

"Not officially, no."

"Okay. What's with the barn fire file?"

"Oof." EJ clicks on another folder on the screen and opens multiple documents. "So... There are about fifty pages in the file."

"We need to read it."

"I saved you the time and read it last night." He turns to me and winks. He sure looks more cheerful since I came. That chicken soup worked wonders. "I did. I was bored and couldn't sleep. My buddy pinged me at two a.m. with the email."

"Sneaky," I taunt him.

"Okay. So, the barn fire. I'm going to spoon-feed you the facts."

"Please, do. Who needs brain work?"

He smiles, without turning to look at me, and starts talking as he scrolls page by page through the documents on the screen.

"Okay. First things first, the fire started somewhere between eleven and twelve at night, on the property half a mile behind the Keller Foster Care Facility. The fire investigators determined that the source was gasoline that came from the containers found burned at the door. Because there was no trail or pour pattern, the initial fire had a limited spread. The possibility of arson inconclusive. As in"—he turns to me to explain—"the container tipped, spilled over naturally, and caught fire by accident."

"By accident? By what, lightning bugs?" I snort.

"Well, whatever. Who knows. Maybe someone was leaving and threw a match."

"That's arson."

"Right. Maybe the boys were playing with firecrackers. The investigators couldn't prove that someone was there besides the victims."

"Got it."

"Two of the victims' bodies were found by the door, one at a distance deeper into the barn. As per the report, it's not clear if they were trying to get out or passed out there earlier. They did an autopsy, since the victims didn't burn completely."

"Jesus."

"Yeah. A high alcohol level in the systems of all three. Traces of a drug, an unusually high amount of it. It's a prescription drug often used to get high."

"So, they did drugs and drank?"

"Or *were* drugged. Here, this is what was suspicious. The investigators found a partially burned stake just next to the side of the building."

I frown, not understanding. "And?"

"And it was partially burned. Nothing suspicious there. But there was an imprint on that stick that did not coincide with the rest of the burns. Which—one forensic expert argued—that part that didn't match the rest of the stick wasn't burning as fast, because it was pressed against something. That imprint somewhat coincided with the barn door handles. He suggested a strong possibility that someone used the stick to lock the door from the outside, then, when the fire subsided, took the stick out and discarded it."

My stomach twists with unease. "It *was* arson, wasn't it?"

"Well, the initial investigation was inconclusive. Partially, because there were no witnesses, and everyone who knew the three guys had alibis. Including..." He turns to me. "Tonya Shaffer."

"Tonya?"

"Yeah. Our Tonya."

"What about my mom?"

"Elizabeth Dunn wasn't even questioned. Her name is nowhere in that investigation. Why would it be? There's no record about the previous assault on her. Otherwise, she had no ties with the victims."

"And Tonya?"

"Tonya did. She was dating Brandon, one of the victims. The report says that during both times when she was questioned, she was inconsolable. She was close with all three, but she wasn't with them. Her whereabouts that night were confirmed by two other girls from that same group home."

EJ turns to me and spreads his arms. "That's it. The investigation was closed with the official conclusion that the three guys were assholes and basically had it coming."

I cock my head in reproach.

EJ gives me a shrug. "I read some witnesses' testimonials in the file. You know, teachers, social workers. Basically, the guys had shitty reputations, multiple complaints from others in the group home. One had a juvenile record. No one missed them. No one grieved except for Tonya Shaffer."

"Listen," I begin, but EJ lifts his raised finger in a "shush" sign.

"She never even once brought up your mom during the questioning."

"Huh. Strange."

"Isn't it? Didn't even hint at her. If she was so hung up on that Brandon and knew who did that, why wouldn't she throw your mom under the bus?"

"Right."

I take the last letter and reread.

The worst thing about a heartbreak is that, sometimes, it makes you do unspeakable things.

"There," I say, pointing at the phrase to EJ. "What does it all mean?"

He ruffles his hair. "I don't know, Kenz. It's... It doesn't sound good."

No, it doesn't. That's not even the right word. Clearly, Mom set that barn on fire, even if it was supposed to be a prank or a scare. Technically, she's a murderer.

Someone who can kill once, can do it twice.

Tonya was blackmailing her, and Mom threatened her.

I'm not saying it aloud, but EJ and I are both thinking it.

My mom did something terrible. Again.

LETTER #5

Bad people are like prickly burr heads that stick to your clothes and make you itch. Occasionally, when you pull them off, they ruin your clothes.

I had one more run-in with Tonya.

"Either leave us alone, or you'll regret it," I said, and I meant it.

"Oooh. Regret it?" Her eyes mockingly widened as she stood with a coffee cup in her hand right outside the coffee shop where John worked. "Like what, you gonna lock me up in a barn and set it on fire?"

I wanted to slap her again, but I resorted to my usual therapy. That's what I always did—I wrote my feelings down, and then some.

This time, I wrote about my stalker. It was a new novel, inspired by Tonya. See? Even evil people can sometimes help us grow.

My new story was dark and gory, with twists and bloodshed, betrayal and heartbreak. I got obsessive. The next two months were a blur. I wrote for days. I barely ate. I went to classes, then closed myself off from the rest of the world and wrote again.

It was my last year in college. I had potential job ideas after graduation, though I was hoping for a book deal. I was exchanging emails with my agent, who was asking for rewrites and to be patient because—"Things like this, finding the right publishing house, don't happen very quickly. And there's already a bidding war over yours. Just have patience, Elizabeth. I promise you that when we have a deal, it will change your life."

Yes, that.

But patience can be chaotic. Mine was turbulent.

I finally confronted Ben about Tonya. He denied everything of course.

"You want to be with someone else? I'm not holding you," I said, praying that my words would shock him. "I have things to do. Another book to write. Very soon, things will get busy with publishing, and I don't want to keep you from pursuing whatever it is you want in life."

It did shock him. I want to say it changed him.

I gave him time. Didn't call him. Didn't seek him out at school. I did my best in classes, then came home and wrote, day and night.

This time, my revenge was the color black. In the new book, when the stalker ruined the girl's life and everything she loved, the girl took revenge, and it was much worse than in my first novel.

I came home late one night, and Ben sat at my desk. A cigarette burned in his hand. His intense gaze was on me.

He rarely smoked in my place, usually when drunk.

"What is this?" he asked as I put the groceries in the fridge.

"What is what?" I asked without turning around.

After a minute of silence, I finally turned to see my new manuscript in his hand.

My blood boiled in seconds. "Who let you read it?"

"You always let me read."

"Not this one." I stomped toward him and yanked the pages out of his hand.

"What is this, Lizzy?" he insisted, his panicky eyes on me.

Sure, the new story was wild. I knew why his gaze was slightly panicky. The beginning of that manuscript was about us. The rest? Well, the rest could make one's hair stand on end.

"That's not what you think," I said, though I didn't care what he thought.

In fact, it was a good thing he read it. Maybe that would give him clues about Tonya or what I was capable of if someone crossed my path. In theory, of course.

"Lizzy...." He looked almost scared. "How does your pretty head... Jesus, where do you get ideas like this? This is sick."

I locked eyes with him, wanting to pin all my frustration on him. "Everyone is capable of horrible things. It just depends on how bad a day gets. At least, mine stay in here." I tapped my temple.

He stabbed out his cigarette and rubbed his face with both hands, exhaling loudly.

I wanted him back. I wanted him to care. I wanted him to admire me like he did back then, before *her*. And I was angry, so very angry.

I think you changed that, petal. Or at least I hoped you did.

"It's another book," I said quietly. "I'm writing another novel. It will be brilliant."

His gaze met mine, and I saw a subtle change from panic to admiration, one that made him put his hands on my hips and pull me onto his lap.

"You *are* brilliant," he said, nuzzling the crook of my neck, though by then, his praise was becoming repetitive. "I'm sorry, okay? I'm sorry. I love you."

I think it was the first time he'd ever said those words, and it made my eyes burn with tears.

I glanced at the cigarette butt floating at the bottom of the almost-empty beer bottle on my desk.

"You need to stop smoking around me," I said.

He sighed and raised his pretty eyes at me. "Anything you want."

I knew he would panic at my next words.

"I'm pregnant."

TWENTY

It's been two days, and I haven't left my apartment.

Yesterday morning, when I woke up, I saw the new letter by the door, on the floor.

The stalker knows where I live, where I stay at night, where I study, where I drive. I'm going mad wondering what their intentions are. And with every letter I find, I'm sinking deeper into darkness.

I don't want what Mom had—neither her talent, nor her twisted imagination, nor her sickness.

And I never wanted this *knowing*. They say knowledge is power. They don't tell you how powerful it is at destroying people.

I'm staying in town because I don't want to see Dad, look at him, and know what he did to Mom. I don't want to think of Mom and, instead of thinking of how brilliant she was, constantly remind myself that she was cheated on, humiliated, and mistreated. But mostly, that she did some terrible things.

I dread every new letter now. I'm sick of this, but like an addict, I'm looking forward to the next fix. I need to know the full story.

I cuddle up on the couch and twist the latest letter in my hands.

It's unnerving to read it, those words—"I'm pregnant." This all feels like watching a movie, and somewhere down the line, there will be me in the picture. Yet now I know what my parents lived through before me.

I reread the letter again, then text EJ. When he doesn't respond, I call him, but the call goes straight to voicemail.

I'm not angry at EJ, though. He has his own life. I'm angry at myself. There's one person, only one person in my life who knows about these letters. He's also the only one I would trust with something like this.

EJ calls back late at night, loud music blasting in the background. "How are you?"

He means the letters, the investigation.

"I'm okay, I think."

I'm not. I have so many questions and no one to answer them except EJ and his buddies, who help to retrieve documents online that slowly, like a screwed-up jigsaw puzzle, form the story of my parents' past.

I tell EJ briefly about the last letter.

"Make the snapshots and text them to me," he suggests.

"Then you'll have to sign an NDA," I joke.

"You are right," he agrees.

Mom might be gone, but her story is still a secret, something she entrusted only to me.

"Anyway, I'm sure that party you are at is more exciting than my silly letters."

"It's a networking event with a bunch of stuck-up people who think they are too cool for school but latch onto everyone in hopes that they can score an investor for their startups."

"Well, at least there's booze and music."

"You don't even like booze."

"True."

"And you are a bad dancer."

"Oh, shut up."

He laughs. "I wish you were here, though," he says softly, the words so unusual that they make my heart sing. "You should come with me next time, see what this is all about."

I'm not sure I'll fit in with the cool crowd.

"Well, wish you were here, too," I say instead, trying to sound as indifferent as possible. "I'd read you the letter."

He laughs again.

"When are you coming back?" I ask.

"In three days."

Suddenly, that sounds like an eternity. It feels like an eternity since the last letter, though it came only yesterday.

Like I said, addiction.

I do what a creative person would, what investigative journalists do. I pick up Mom's second best-seller, *The Wolf Whistle*, and reread it.

This time, I read it slowly. When she talks about the main heroine, I stop and compare the image in the book with my mom's, latching onto the small details described in her letters. When she talks to the heroine's rival at school, I picture Tonya. When I read about the stolen boyfriend, I cringe and imagine my dad. When I read about the things the main heroine does to the rival to ruin her life, years later, the hairs on the back of my neck stand on end, and I have to look away for a minute because I don't want to picture my mom doing that.

If her first book of revenge is a vague parallel to her real-life story, then so is the second one. She admitted that in her letters. Her heroine does atrocious things. But that only means that in real life, Mom did something less graphic, but did it, nevertheless.

Punishment is white. Revenge is red. Mine is bloody-black.

I constantly check my phone for another message from an anonymous sender.

I check my mail and glance at the floor by the front door every time I walk by to see if anyone slipped another letter to me.

I call the house phone.

Minna answers.

"Any mail for me?" I ask.

She patiently reads every envelope, but none are the ones I'm waiting for.

It's an obsession, I know. But I know there will be more letters. Mom's story is not over. If we go by her books, there is one more story related to her omnibus, but I'm not quite sure how that will play out. Her fans called her stories fairy tales. Those not familiar with her previous books called them "deranged haunting horror masterpieces of a psycho."

I agree with both.

She was working on a secret project with Laima, *Sharp Teeth*, though there was not a single hint at what sort of book that will be. I just hope she hasn't ruined anyone's life to get inspired.

I reread the letters for the dozenth time.

I stroke the word "petal" in the last one and feel tears coming on.

"Beautiful girl," I repeat to myself every time I stumble upon those words in Mom's letters.

You can tell her mental health was slowly failing. I blame Dad for that and that woman, Tonya.

When it gets dark outside, I light a candle by the window, turn off the lights, and decide to write by candlelight. Instead of my computer, I take an unused notebook from a drawer and a pen and sit down by the lit candle.

I have no idea what to write. But for once, I want to talk to Mom and tell her how I feel. At least on paper, instead of having snarky conversations like we usually did.

It's late, dark, and quiet in my studio. The candlelight flickers, making shadows dance on the white blank page in front of me.

This is silly, I think, but this is therapy.

I smile when I write the first line.

Dear Mom,

I want to say so many things, explain how I feel, ask her how she felt back then. I want to hear her voice. And that's the thing with writers—they talk on paper.

Except she can't write back. She can't. Not anymore.

The thought is suddenly so devastating that it clutches my chest in an iron grip.

My smile disappears. My chest grows heavy. My eyes start burning.

At first, I wonder if I should take my pills. But no, this has nothing to do with my condition. It's not an episode. I just really miss Mom.

There is no stopping the tears that flood my eyes and start streaming down my cheeks. The first sob rips out of my chest.

Mom, I miss you.

Twenty-one years living together, and I barely appreciated her.

Several letters, and I finally let grief take over.

LETTER #6

I would've liked to say that pregnancy was a beautiful time of my life. But that's for the books.

The truth is it was a nightmare.

I had six months to tighten my first manuscript.

In my book, my heroine grew up into a confident woman who went on a twisted, masterfully executed five-year revenge tour, ruining her assailants' lives, destroying everything they loved, and eventually killing them off. This was my ode to my past, and Laima thought it was brilliant.

It was luck that I had gotten picked up by her. All thanks to John. He had talked me into submitting my short story for the national competition in my freshman year. Laima Roth had emailed me, asking if I had anything substantial to share. I had sent my first novel to her in New York.

Laima had said I was a genius. "What imagination!" If only she knew...

She said she would make me rich. We just needed to sign the deal, but I was yet to meet her in person.

I was promised an advance.

And now, I was thinking of ending things with Ben.

This was a hard decision. I didn't have a family. If worse came to worst, his parents, who never cared about meeting me, might still help with the baby. Wouldn't they help their granddaughter?

Yes, we were having a girl.

"A daughter," Ben echoed at the news.

I think he was in shock. I was. Just to know that, in a short time, you would be out in this world, with me, made me scared but so unexplainably happy, too!

Until something inevitably ruined my day.

Strange things started happening.

One day, I came home, walked into the kitchen, and screamed at the top of my lungs at the horrible sight. In fact, screamed so loudly that there came a knock at the door.

It was Grunger, the super of the building.

"What happened?" he asked, rolling his lip piercing with his tongue.

I pointed at the kitchen.

"Whoa," he said as we both stared at the dead rat in the middle of the floor. Bile lodged in my throat. My entire body started to tremble. I barely made it to the sink and retched violently, my knees almost buckling.

It had to be the hormones. Or my blood pressure. Or the grueling migraines that knocked me out for a full day at a time.

"It should be an easy birth," the doctor had said. "The blood pressure and migraines? Those we have to observe to avoid complications."

"We don't have these in our building," Grunger said as he helped dispose of the rat. "Never have. I'm sorry, Liz."

The sight of it haunted me for days, among other things.

My mind had been hazy lately. I did bizarre things and didn't even remember doing them.

A week later, I came home and halted at the door, staring at the new rug in the middle of the room.

Ben had never asked me if I wanted to change it. But when he came home, he stared at it too. "Nice rug. Where did you get it?"

"Are you messing with me?" I snapped, glaring at him.

He frowned, confused. "What do you mean?"

Ben was never a good liar. I knew it couldn't be him. But it wasn't me either, was it? I wasn't even sure.

I was gulping prenatal multivitamin juice like crazy. I didn't have trouble sleeping. On the contrary, I slept like I was in a coma. But that made me groggy during the day. Often, I didn't remember things or was seeing things that weren't there.

"Are you taking anything?" the doctor inquired when I complained.

"No. Just the vitamin juice you recommended."

But things just kept on happening.

That same day, when I came home from the doctor, I opened the closet to change into my comfy home clothes and froze— everything in the closet was rearranged. All the garments were in the wrong places.

When you tell them you are pregnant, they always say, "How beautiful." They never tell you how hard it will be. How exhausting life will suddenly become. How much of yourself you will sacrifice and how hard you'll push to get through it.

I was losing my mind.

The memory of the last months would come back to me at odd times, making me teary, happy, sad, or angry at what Ben had made me go through. Sometimes, the memories made me blind with rage. That's when I wrote my darkest chapters.

And then you would start kicking, petal. And my heart would leap in excitement. I reminded myself that what I was doing was for the two of us. And maybe Ben. Maybe...

There was no sign of Tonya anymore, as if she had vanished. Ben didn't say it, but one day, he stopped by in the evening, wrapped his arms around me, and murmured, "It will be all right, Lizzy. We are good. We are so good."

He didn't need to say it, but I knew—he was done with whatever he had going on behind my back. Don't mistake my calmness for weakness—I hadn't forgiven him. Not yet. But I needed him more than ever.

I started talking to John again. I barely saw him in the last months of my pregnancy. I spent more and more time at home, studying and writing.

He was surprised when he learned I was pregnant.

"Why are you even with him?" he asked, seemingly upset.

I shrugged. What could I say? Because that was how things played out. Because I didn't want to be with anyone anymore. Because I was still in love but embarrassed about loving someone who didn't treat me the way I wanted.

I didn't tell him all that. But one day, Ben flew to visit his parents and came back with the best news.

"I talked to them, Lizzy."

"About?"

"They want to meet you."

"That's nice," I said, stroking my round belly.

"*Our grandchild*, Mom said the other day." Ben grinned.

I guess they had no choice.

"I think it took her a while to come to terms with it," Ben added. "I told her you are soon to sign that book deal. She is happy for us."

Ugh, I wanted to throw something at him. It always felt like there was nothing worthy about me or our relationship besides my book deal. It felt like his parents' goodwill was a barter.

When we are born with a talent, it can become a curse. But mine was something to resort to in the moments when everything else failed me.

And so I did it again. I started a new project. I started writing a fairy tale, the first of many to come. For the first time, I was writing not to purge myself, not even thinking about giving it to the world or the readers, if I had any.

Those fairy tales had one reader in mind—you, my beautiful girl.

TWENTY-ONE

I close my eyes, trying to hold back sobs.

I'm still standing by the door of my apartment, where I found another letter slipped under it through the crack. That's the second one in three days. It's the longest one, and I've only read the first part of it.

I hungrily swallow every word. They hurt. The words can heal, but their biggest power is inflicting pain.

Growing up, I rarely saw this peculiar gentleness in my mom. If you asked me a month ago, when Mom was alive, I would've said bitterly, "Never. She was never nice."

But that was my anger, stemming from the years of rebellion.

Mom could be nice. She was, plenty of times.

I remember my sixteenth birthday when she found out I had a secret boyfriend. She got angry.

"Make sure you keep your legs closed," she said.

But later that evening, she knocked on the door of my bedroom, took a seat on my bed while I tried to ignore her, and said something that startled me.

"Sometimes the smallest things in life, so tiny we barely acknowledge them, can change us in the most profound way."

She talked like she wrote, with that sadness and the dark overtone as if she were warning me.

She looked somehow older, without all that makeup she usually wore every day. Sadder, too, when she studied me. She smelled of wine, having just come back from a party. She smiled, though it wasn't a cheerful smile, nor her well-practiced cold one either.

"You are beautiful, you know," she said then. "And smart, Mackenzie. It's a dangerous cocktail. Learn how to use it, or it might one day ruin you."

Here we go.

There was always that warning in her tone like the world was about to end.

But that night, she smiled again, then cupped my face and kissed me on the cheek. She didn't pull away but stayed for a short while with her cheek pressed against mine, then said, "Beauty and talent can be as much of a blessing as they can be a curse. An apple doesn't fall far from the tree."

I feel tears streaming down my cheeks at the memories. Those words never made sense until now.

But one thing bothers me. She said she wrote the first fairy tale for me. But if you read the omnibus of her fairy tales, you'd know that those weren't written for a child. They are macabre. They are dark. They are violent. And I'm wondering if something happened in Mom's life that turned her fairy tales into horror stories.

I keep reading the next part of the letter. At least, it starts on a cheerful note:

Petal, your grandmother is a bitch.

LETTER #6

PART 2

Evelyn Casper, Ben's mom, didn't come to our graduation, mine or Ben's. Neither did his father. They'd planned a trip to the Keys a long time ago, she said. I wanted to tell her that we had planned to graduate four years ago. But who was I to tell her what to prioritize?

Ben's graduation was nothing to be proud of—he made it by a hair. No internships, no job offers, while I had three.

Evelyn did make a courtesy call. "Very good, dear. I am proud of you. Ben is lucky to have you."

Ain't that the truth.

And yes, we were talking. Twice we did. Your grandmother asked me if we would come and stay with them on the East Coast and maybe, just maybe, consider moving there. She asked me about the book deal, of course, and ended the conversation with, "You two take care of each other."

I'm pretty sure I was the one taking care of Ben. His apartment lease was up after graduation, so he moved in with me. He'd spent so much time at my place before that it felt like he'd lived there all along. Just without the mess that he brought with him.

He had started to fly out to his parents every month even before graduation. That was a good thing, I think. Though he said his mom wasn't feeling well.

After graduation, I was only glad for the weekends of privacy without him. I'd take him to the airport in his car, then pick him up several days later, and he was happy, so happy to see me, like a new man.

My water was about to break. My first novel was edited and ready to go. I was finishing the second thriller, about a stalker. I was ready to take this world by storm.

One weekend, when Ben was out with friends, his mother called.

"Maybe when you have the baby and your book is out and you have more time, we could all go to Greece," she said, making my heart flutter at the words. Finally, finally I would have a family!

"We just came back. It's beautiful out there."

"When?" I asked, puzzled. Ben was just visiting them two weeks ago. He never told me about Greece.

"We came back last week."

"And Ben...?"

"What about Ben?"

"Ben didn't mention that."

"Yes, maybe you should talk to him about it. You two should come soon. We haven't seen him since winter."

My heart skipped a beat.

"Winter?" I echoed.

"Yes. It's been half a year."

My head started spinning, blood pounding in my ears.

Ben had been lying for months, spending time somewhere else.

"Dear, I have to go," Evelyn said and hung up.

I stood with the receiver in my hand, staring at nothing, and felt the unexplainable rage starting to build inside me.

I wanted to confront Ben when he came home, but when he did, that evening, there was something off in the way he looked at me. Slowly, he walked to the armchair and took a seat. He stared down at the rug for some time, chewing on the inside of his cheek, then finally looked at me.

"What happened to you and the three boys at the group home?"

I knew then that *she* was back. In fact, I was slowly realizing that she'd never gone away in the first place. Who else would've fed him the story he wasn't supposed to know? Where else was he spending the weekends he'd said he'd spent with his parents?

"I was assaulted," I responded to Ben. "You read my novel. You know, Ben."

"And then?"

Ah, that's where that bitch worked her evil charms.

"And then they got away with it," I said bluntly, staring Ben down. "And I wrote my own version of the story."

I didn't tell him about my talk with his mom or that I knew he was spending weekends elsewhere. I had to know for sure. I needed proof.

Because the next thing Ben said almost made me laugh. "I am going to see my parents next weekend."

"I'm due in two," I replied with a smirk.

"I know. I will be home for that. Obviously. But Mom is really not feeling well."

While in Greece, I wanted to add but swallowed my poison.

I couldn't even look at him that night. I took my shoulder bag, shoved my diary in it, and left.

What could I do? I needed to man up and finally do something I'd been dreading but that needed to be done, once and for all. I was going to take matters into my own hands, and it wasn't going to be pretty.

Tonya was back. As always, she was bringing out the worst in me.

This was what my latest manuscript looked like.

She is evil. She is evil. She is evil. She is evil.
She is evil. She is evil. She is evil. She is evil.
I hate her.
I will make her disappear.

Sometimes, just sometimes, fiction becomes reality...

TWENTY-TWO

"That's dramatic," EJ responds, handing me back the letter and leaning back in his computer chair.

He's been away for four days, and his absence was excruciating. Not that I will ever tell him that.

I fold my legs under me as I get comfortable in the armchair next to his computer desk. "Do you think she was going crazy? Mom?"

"Honestly?"

I don't respond, only stare at him, waiting.

"Her novels were dark. Like, dark-dark." EJ raises his eyebrows for emphasis. "Things her heroines did? I mean, that's some dark stuff. Mrs. Casper... Well, she came across as someone who could..." He clears his throat. "Dude, don't freak out, but she did occasionally come across as someone who had *experience*, you know what I mean?"

There it is, the truth that friends and family never admit. And the truth is that Mom felt off quite often. Off in an unsettling way.

"I wonder..." Something dawns on me so suddenly that I almost laugh at how I didn't think about it before. "I wonder if Mom was bipolar."

EJ's eyebrows crawl up.

"Wouldn't that make sense?" I ask.

He nods, staring at me. "Actually, it would. Totally."

"Maybe she had a personality disorder. Or a multiple personalities disorder."

"Whoa." EJ's eyes go wide.

I think back on the letters and wonder. "You think she made it all up? What she wrote in her letters?"

"Nah."

"What if she did?"

EJ only stares at me in shock.

I exhale through puffed lips.

It never occurred to me that being a good writer, she could make up anything with unparalleled cleverness. If she had some type of mental disorder—even more so. But I've never heard anything like this mentioned by her or Dad.

"I think I'm being crazy and just... Yeah, I'm making up crazy things."

But when I meet EJ's eyes, he doesn't look at me like I'm crazy. He looks at me like someone who just discovered an awful truth.

"Why didn't she ever give those letters to me?" I ask.

EJ tilts his head back against the chair and studies the ceiling. "Maybe, she was going to, and... the accident happened?"

"You are saying she might not have finished her letters?"

"I don't know."

"What if we never find out how the story ends?"

"Maybe, she did finish the story, and someone was asked to give it to you in case something happened to her."

Shivers go down my spine. "Wait, wh—" I stall as another realization hits me. "You mean, she knew that something might happen to her? And she deliberately wrote this down for me?"

While I'm in shock, EJ seems calm. "Maybe?"

"Then... Okay, okay, okay. Whoever is sending these letters— why not send all of them at once? Why send them as clues?"

"Maybe so that you uncover the truth slowly, do some digging. I mean, if someone came to you and said, 'Listen, your mom killed three guys at a group home, then potentially disposed of some chick your dad was cheating on her with, and she's been cleverly writing this all out in her novels'—would you believe them? No," EJ responds for me, echoing my thoughts. "But now that you are doing some research, you realize there are some stories that are in fact true."

"Huh. Okay."

We sit for a moment in silence.

"I think I need to talk to someone who knew Mom back at the group home," I finally suggest. "Maybe, someone who knew Mom *and* Tonya."

"If you can find those people."

"Right. I think I need to go to Keller Foster Care."

I don't have much money saved up to buy a ticket, but I can always ask Dad for some cash. He'd give it to me easily, now that Mom is gone, and I won't even have to explain what I'm spending it on.

I raise my eyes to meet EJ's amused gaze, his lips curled in a half-smile.

"What?" I shrug. "I need to find someone who knew what happened first-hand, a primary source. They won't discuss this sort of thing over the phone. And maybe, at some point, I can go to Old Bow."

"I don't think you'll find anything in Old Bow."

"Dad had buddies there. I'll get their names, see if anyone still lives there. Many of his buddies knew Tonya. She hung out with them, right?"

"Dude, twenty years ago, yeah. Who will remember some random chick who hung out with them for several months when they were in a permanent state of intoxication?"

"That's how private investigators work. They find things just like that, clue by clue."

"You are not a PI, Snarky."

"Gah. I know. I wish I had money to hire one."

"I have money."

I give him a glare. "Oh, piss off, EJ. I don't want your money. I'll figure it out."

"I'm gonna say something, but don't get mad, okay?"

I give him a suspicious side eye.

"Promise?" he asks with a charming smile.

I roll my eyes. "Promise."

"I will go with you to Brimmville."

My heartbeat spikes. "Really?"

"But only if you let me buy us both tickets and pay for the trip."

I narrow my eyes at him, knowing he's trying to have his way.

Truth is, EJ has plenty of money. Me, not so much. But somehow, I'm relieved that he's offering so I don't have to dig into my meager savings or ask Dad.

"Okay," I say, nodding, looking away. "Thank you."

EJ does a fist pump in the air with a barely audible, "Yes," then asks, "Okay. When are we going? Tomorrow?"

I laugh nervously at his crazy idea, but my heart starts beating like a war drum in anticipation.

TWENTY-THREE

The next day, as soon as I'm done with my classes, I go to EJ's place.

"You'll be disappointed," he tells me when I walk in.

I drop my shoulder bag by the door, then grab a Fizzy out of the fridge and get comfortable in my usual armchair.

EJ spins back and forth in his computer chair. "Or maybe not. Depends."

"Spill," I tell him, excited about any new information.

EJ turns to the computer. "You know there is no way to hide these days." His fingers start flying over the keyboard as he opens multiple browsers and doc files on the screen. "Everything you do leaves a paper trail. Even if you are not online, there are records."

"Unless, of course, they are dead."

EJ clears his throat. "The foster care facility was shut down fifteen years ago. I figured since your mom didn't have friends and didn't mention anyone close to her, there's no point spending time tracking the kids from her graduation year. I pulled out the records, tried several names. There are cross-references on White Pages with dozens of people with the same names and ages across the country. I'd say, it's a waste of time. The smarter way is to see which employees were the closest to the barn fire case."

"How do you figure that?"

"Well, the police file. There are teachers, social workers, therapists. A lot of them, actually. The interviews from the criminal investigation into the fire mentioned a number of them, but only three people were questioned more than once. The first one was the facility therapist, but she passed away two years ago."

"Tsk."

"A group home middle grade math teacher, but he also passed shortly after the group home closed."

"Great," I mumble. "And the third?"

"The third was Dianne Jacobson, the housekeeper. Strangely, she was questioned several times during the investigation. She worked the night shift at the group home that night." EJ gives me a meaningful stare. "According to the lead detective, she was called the godmother among the foster kids."

"You know what's interesting? In Mom's *Lies, Lies, and Revenge*, there was a character, the only nice one, a housekeeper the main heroine turned to for help."

"There you go."

"Okay, spit it out. Where is she now?"

"She actually worked in that group home until it closed down, then retired right after. She is seventy-three years old. According to the records, she owns a property about two hours away from Keller's. I called the number multiple times—it's a landline—but there was no response. No cell phone number is registered to her name either."

"Who doesn't have a cell phone these days?"

"You'll be surprised. She might have a burner phone or something. I checked the DMV records. She has a vehicle registered to the same address. She has no family members, not that I could find."

"You think she lives there?"

EJ leans back in his chair and spins around to face me. "I don't know. But if she never answers the phone, there's no way to find out, unless—"

I cock a brow at him. "Unless?"

"Unless we pay her a visit."

I purse my lips to hide a smile.

"So." EJ drums his fingers on the chair armrest. "Considering it's Friday, and you have no classes for the next several days, I'd say let's fly to Nebraska."

I hold still so as not to scare away the exciting thought that EJ and I might travel out of state.

"Only"—he points his forefinger at me, imitating a gun—"if I pay for the trip."

I hold my breath, trying not to blurt out some stupid joke or come across as ungrateful, though I feel slightly ashamed that EJ is paying for me. "Yeah. Let's do that."

"Cool."

"I'll owe you."

"No, you won't."

He turns to the computer again and starts typing. In a short while, he has booked us two roundtrip tickets to Nebraska the next morning and a motel for one night.

"You okay with one room, Snarky?"

I swallow. It might be awkward, but I crashed on EJ's couch many times. "Yeah. Two beds, right?"

He turns to give me a mischievous grin. "Of course."

I'm so excited and nervous that I can barely eat any of the pizza EJ orders as we discuss the logistics of how and when.

It's late evening when I finally get back to my place. But I can't sleep. I toss and turn the whole night, wondering how the trip will go.

It might be a failure, and we won't find anything interesting.

But maybe, we will find the person who knew my mom. Knew her before she was a celebrity. Before she was independent and wealthy. Knew her when she went through a horrible thing that changed her life.

TWENTY-FOUR

EJ picks me up at seven in the morning.

"Good makeover," he tells me when I hop in the car.

I roll my eyes. *Whatever*.

I barely put on any makeup this time. Well, for one, I don't want people at the airport to stare. Two, in case we talk to someone who knew Mom, I want to look approachable. A goth look is not quite friendly, especially with old folks. Instead of a hoodie, I'm wearing a long-sleeved shirt with a button-up sweater over it and jeans. I put a short parka in my backpack just in case.

Our plan is quite simple.

The Keller Foster Care Facility is only half an hour out of the city where we will land. We'll get a rental car at the airport, drive there to see the facility, or what's left of it, then take a ride two hours west to the housekeeper's residence, then get back to the city the same evening, spend a night, and fly out the next morning.

It's still murky outside and too warm for mid-October as we drive to the airport. We stop at the gas station to fill up and walk in to get snacks. The airport is on the outskirts of the city, and we have plenty of time to get there. So, we nerd out at the arcade kiosk for ten minutes. EJ is a fan of old-school games. He never misses an opportunity to play when he sees one.

When we walk outside, the gas station parking lot is full of cars, people pumping gas, someone walking a dog. A family of five is rearranging their SUV packed to the brim next to EJ's car.

I'm giddy with a sense of adventure. Despite Mom traveling a lot for her book tours, she rarely ever took me with her. I've never left the US and didn't really travel that much, except for occasional trips to the Keys with my parents and grandparents. Not exactly my idea of a fun time.

So this is exciting.

An older couple parked on the other side of our car smiles at EJ and me and asks how we are doing. I wonder if they think we are a thing. For a second, I wish we were, then embarrassingly shoo the thought away.

"Wait," EJ says when I open the passenger door, about to get in.

I glance at him and notice his eyes boring into something inside the car.

"What?" I follow his gaze, look in, and my jaw drops.

There, on my seat, is an envelope.

Frantically, I look around to see if there is anyone watching us. But there's no one close to us besides a family busy rearranging their entire house packed into an SUV.

I meet EJ's worried gaze. "Did you lock the car?" I ask him.

His silence tells me he probably forgot and left it open while we were inside the gas station.

I lean over to pick up the envelope, and I don't need to be a psychic to know what it will say:

From #1 fan. XOXO

LETTER #7

Two weeks until you will be in my arms, petal.

I'm sitting at John's. My belly is the size of a watermelon. The doctor said I'm a perfect mother. I've never thought I'd be a mother in the first place, let alone perfect. Giving birth should be easy, they said. What's not easy is what I'll have to do afterward.

Today was the last straw—the fight between Ben and John.

I don't know what Ben was even doing at John's place, but I decided to stop by and saw them fighting right outside the entrance.

"You don't deserve any of this," John hissed at Ben.

Ben laughed and—my Ben, charming, funny—lunged at John. Drunk, of course.

I screamed. I shouted for them to stop when they both toppled onto the ground. I don't know how it happened, but Ben had a broken bottle in his hand, and he slashed John with it.

There was blood, so much blood. John sat on the ground, holding his forearm, blood seeping through his fingers in tiny streams as I tried to console him.

Ben sat across from him, murmuring curses and apologies until the ambulance arrived.

John lost a lot of blood. The vein on the inside of his arm was damaged. I came to John's after the ER.

So, here we are.

One thing I realize is that Ben will never change. But I am going to change things for you, beautiful girl. I am going to take us on a different journey.

You are going to be a beautiful, beautiful girl. I can already feel it. Soft dark lashes, fluffy hair, the breeze catching in its strands as the sun glistens in your eyes. Your sunshine smile—I can see it in my mind.

You deserve all the best. Don't let anyone tell you otherwise.

You might want a father like Ben. He'd be a good father, I suppose. But I don't want a husband like him. Not if *she* is around.

Even John is part of this story now. The doctor said he'll have a scar left from the fight with Ben. It's a big crisscross pattern on his forearm in the shape of a star. He calls it his unlucky star, with a smile. John and I, we could've turned out differently if that one day, Ben didn't talk to me about my lipstick.

Right now, while I'm writing this, John is making us dinner. He's throwing awkward glances at me. I know he has questions, but I'm not ready to answer them. I don't tell him about my plans. Not yet.

It *is* a dilemma—it's either Ben or Tonya. I don't know how it came to this, but she destroyed me and Ben.

That leaves me with a terrible decision to make.

It's dark outside, but my thoughts are darker. As it often happens lately, I don't want to go home. I want to write here, at John's place. I want change.

Moreover, I'm afraid that if I go home, I won't stop myself.

If Ben lies to me again, I'll snap.

It's either *she* is gone, or he is. Ben will have to make that choice himself. But—

TWENTY-FIVE

"But what?"

I frantically turn the page in my hands looking for the rest of the sentence, but it's not there. It's not there! "Argh!"

EJ yanks the letter out of my hand. "Let me see."

My mind is spinning.

Someone is constantly following us, and it's creepy to say the least. Most importantly, Mom was planning something bad. I want to know what so badly, but whoever this sadistic fan is who sends these pages, he knows how to edge me.

One more thing finally dawns on me. It's probably the most important.

"This last letter is written in present tense, unlike the others," EJ says, finishing my thought as he looks up from the page and passes it back to me.

"Right. Which means, Mom wrote these letters when she was pregnant."

That in itself is important. The letters were written before she gave birth to me. Before she and Dad did something bad, though I'm not sure what it was. And that was twenty-one years ago.

"Damn," EJ says on an exhale, scanning the parking lot in suspicion.

"Right? And that's not the last one, because—"

"*But*," EJ continues.

"Right, it ends in the middle of the sentence. We are yet to find out what happened."

"Okay. We will when we get back."

He veers the car out of the parking lot and toward the airport.

I stare at the beautiful fall colors, but my mood is muddy. Just the thought of going to a place that hurt my mom when she was growing up makes my stomach turn.

But I have no choice. Sometimes, to understand your present, you have to look into the past.

And I have a feeling my mom's past was uglier than I could've ever imagined.

TWENTY-SIX

"Stop jittering," EJ says, glancing at my knee.

"I'm not jittering."

He shakes his head, unbuckles his seat belt, and powers on his phone as the plane taxies to the gate.

Yes, I am jittering, and I can't help myself. The Keller Foster Care Facility was closed fifteen years ago, and I doubt that seeing it will give me any insight into what it was like for Mom to grow up there. Yet I'm nervous and excited.

"Welcome to Nebraska," a sign says as EJ and I walk through the airport.

I can't help feeling like I'm part of some gloomy mystery movie. Mom never talked much about her years in foster care.

"Nothing to write home about," she used to say. "Your father and I did a lot to make sure you never felt the way I did growing up." Those words would always be followed by a meaningful look. "And I mean, *a lot*."

This all makes sense now. It has always felt like my parents didn't want to be together, didn't even get along all that much, yet they were thick as thieves, as if something held them together.

I'm finally starting to realize why. After the anonymous letters with Mom's diary pages, her every word in the past acquired a somewhat sinister meaning.

"Hey, hey, snap out of it," EJ says, pulling me by the arm toward the exit to the baggage claim that I almost missed.

He always senses how I feel, even when I try to hide it. At some point, I should tell him how much everything he's done for me lately means to me. But he knows that. I would do the same. I mean, who spent three days by his hospital bed when he had severe food poisoning? No, not his cyber-queen ex or any of his hacker friends. It was me. As always. But then, none of them know EJ like I do. On second thought, no one knows me like he does. Not even my parents.

"It's gonna be all right, yeah?" He slings his arm around my shoulders as we walk, and for once, I don't brush it off.

"Yeah," I murmur, pushing through the well-practiced fake resentment at his too-friendly gesture.

Lately, I find comfort in it. That's what friends do, right? They help each other through the tough times. It's just... friendly.

This time, a thought flickers in my head—how would he react if I wrapped my arm around his waist in response? Would that be too much? Yeah. Probably.

Half an hour later, we are driving a rental Honda out of the airport and toward Brimmville, where the foster facility is located. I always put a moody playlist on for my road trips. But this time, EJ is in charge, and I'm glad he's put on Matchbox Twenty. The music is cheerful, keeping my spirits up as I sit back and stare through the passenger window.

The graying fall colors unroll all around us as we drive along the windy road through the countryside. It's colder here, in Nebraska. Fall is at its final stage. Though it's not raining, the sky is mousy gray, and so is the leafage. Everything seems to be decaying. I hate this transition from late fall to winter when the leaves are almost gone and everything looks like a depressing washed-out painting.

I wrap the flaps of my open sweater tighter around my middle, though it's warm in the car. EJ is humming the half-assed lyrics to the tune. He doesn't start any conversations, like he feels that I want to immerse myself into what it's like living here, in this part of the country where Mom grew up.

An hour later, we pull into a small town and park at the simple chain-link fence surrounding a long, two-story Prairie-style brown building with a protruding entrance and dark-blue door. A sign over the entrance is graffitied out. *HELL*, it says in black capital letters dripping spray paint.

"Charming," EJ says, looking at it through the car window, then turns to me. "Wanna get out?"

I shrug, then decide that I should at least take a picture of this shithole, for my records. I grab my parka from the back seat and step out into the cold.

"It's depressing," EJ concludes as we both come up to the fence and stare at the gray grass, overgrown and littered, and the brown walls of the foster care facility marked with chaotic graffiti all along its front. The holes in the windows from what looks like thrown rocks make the scene even more disturbing.

Add to this the bits and pieces that Mom mentioned about this place, the boys and what they did, the articles about the barn, and this place feels outright repulsive.

"Wanna have a minute by yourself?" EJ asks.

I roll my eyes. "What, like I'm gonna touch the walls and find some meaningful connection to my mom? No, thank you. I don't like this place."

I pull my phone out of my parka pocket and snap a picture. Just like my mom, I plan on never coming back again.

"Let's go," I tell EJ and, without waiting, turn around and walk back to the car. The building feels somehow contagious, as if being close to it infects you with sadness and misfortune. Inside the car, I feel safe and shake off the tension.

EJ gets in shortly afterward. "Wanna go see the barn?"

"I think I've seen enough," I say, fastening my seat belt.

The barn should be only half a mile or so behind the facility. But it's a walk through the woods, and I definitely don't want to spend more time here, let alone see the place where orphans used to entertain themselves with sick stuff.

Small droplets of rain start falling onto the windshield, and I have an urgent feeling to get out of here as soon as possible.

"Type the housekeeper's address into the GPS?" EJ prompts me.

I do, then place the phone back into the holder and press the sound button. Matchbox Twenty is back on, and I relax and sink into my seat, feeling the overwhelming relief when EJ pulls back onto the road.

I throw the last glance in the side mirror and catch sight of the abandoned building getting smaller and smaller as we drive away.

HELL.

The word still echoes in my mind. I don't know what it was like growing up in a place like this, but I don't blame Mom for never talking about it. With what happened there, I would want to forget about it too.

The only person who might have answers about what happened here is Dianne Jacobson, the housekeeper. I just hope that she hasn't disappeared off the face of the earth like everyone else who knew my mom.

TWENTY-SEVEN

On our way out of town, we stop at the gas station and eat hot dogs, then continue the trip.

The address takes us deep into the countryside, along roads that are clearly not driven on much. It's been half an hour since we saw the last car, a pickup truck with a horse trailer.

The forest towers above us on both sides of the country road. The sky has turned several shades darker, and it's murky outside, though it's still only early afternoon. It's drizzling too, and my mood has changed from gloomy to outright depressing.

"I want to get out of here," I tell EJ.

"What, like, now?"

"No! I mean, we'll see if we find anyone at the address. I just meant..." I sigh, not finishing my sentence.

The truth is, every little bit I find about Mom's and Dad's past gets me closer to something I'm not sure I can come back from.

EJ keeps glancing at me in question.

"I don't know if it's the weather or what, but this whole area is just... creepy," I finally find the right word.

He chuckles. "You love shitty weather, Kenz. Always did. It's your inspirational weather, remember?"

He's right. "Yeah, when I'm inside. This is different."

"Listen, don't stress."

"I don't stress."

"You are stressing right now," he argues calmly.

Gah, it's like he can read my thoughts.

"Okay, I am stressing out," I admit and go quiet for a moment, expecting him to taunt me about it. He doesn't. So I go on. "I feel like... I don't know. What if I shouldn't know some things about my parents? You know what I mean? Like... Maybe some things should stay a secret."

"Your mom wanted to share them with you."

"Well, maybe I don't want to know. I was fine with how things were until those letters. Now I know about her group home. A possible gang rape. A possible... crime, I don't know. Other creepy things. A stalker. Being knocked up. My dad cheating. Her getting paranoid. Contemplating murder. Not sure if she was just contemplating. I mean..." I exhale through my puffed lips. "What if she actually did something, she and Dad, something that..."—I swallow hard, feeling slightly sick—"something that will make me hate them," I finish in one go and take a deep breath.

"Listen..." Without taking his eyes off the road, EJ finds my hand on my lap and squeezes it gently. "It's going to be fine, okay?"

I don't answer, just stare out the window, acutely aware of his hand that holds mine, his thumb brushing against mine.

"Kenz, hey, look at me," he says.

I turn my head to meet his eyes—not taunting or cheeky like they often are but understanding and comforting. I wish he would stop looking at me like that. I wish he joked and made fun of me, because then it's easier to tell myself that I want to be just friends, like we have been for years.

He glances at the road then at me again.

"I'm here, okay?" He looks at the road again.

I nod.

He looks at me again. "We are doing this together, okay?"

"Okay," I say on an exhale.

He keeps looking between the road and me, his hand still holding mine on my lap while his left hand is on the wheel.

"Whatever you need, Kenzie, I'm here. If, at some point, it's too much, we'll just bounce. Back on the plane, back home. You say stop, we stop, and we'll never talk about your mom's letters again. Anything you ever need, I'll be there."

Suddenly, my chest feels too tight.

"Yeah," I say, turning away, because I can't explain how much this means to me.

But I do need to get through this. This is my mom's past and, by default, my origins. I've never understood her better than now. And I've never been more confused about myself or how I feel about my family.

I feel EJ's hand shift, and his fingers intertwine with mine.

My heart pounds against my chest, and for a second, I forget about why we are here and only become acutely aware of our locked hands, his thumb still brushing mine.

"Thank you," I croak, holding my breath as I try to fight a sob. "Thanks for doing this."

"Anytime. You know you can always rely on me, yeah?"

"Yeah." An awkward beat of silence passes between us, and I say the only thing that will break it. "Except when you are preoccupied with your crypto Barbies, right?"

He blurts out a laugh, and his hand lets go of mine, leaving behind an empty feeling where it has just been.

"You are so jealous, Snarky," he taunts.

I snort, giving him a side eye, and slap him on the shoulder, making him chuckle again. "You wish."

I am, and there's not a chance in hell I can tell him that.

EJ murmurs something like, "Yeah," then clicks his vape pen, takes a puff, and exhales thick smoke.

The milky cloud smells like mint and lingers in the air for several seconds until he cracks the window open, and it's sucked out.

I crank up the rock music on the speaker, anything to kill the awkward silence that follows between us.

Again, my thoughts drift to Mom and her books. They were praised for being immersive and atmospheric. I get it now. Try growing up as an orphan in the middle of nowhere in Nebraska.

We pass some sort of handmade sign with elk horns nailed to it on a pole.

"First sign of life," EJ says. "We are almost there."

I bet this atmosphere can really screw with your head. Never mind seasonal depressions. I can't even imagine winters here.

Two minutes later, the GPS takes us onto a wide dirt road that spits us out of the forest and into the fields. Another mile later, we run into a cattle gate.

EJ pulls the car to a stop right in front of it.

"It looks closed but definitely well-kept," he says, leaning on the steering wheel and squinting through the windshield.

"What do we do now?"

He turns his eyes at me. "What do *you* want to do now?"

I look at the closed gate, then at him again. He cocks a brow in question.

Isn't it strange how easy it is sometimes to break the law? Just a several-second decision, a brief, "Oh, hell, why not?" and you are on the wrong side of the law. Which trespassing would be if we open that gate.

"Let's do it," I blurt out. "We might just run into an abandoned property. At least we'll know we tried."

"Yes, boss." Without hesitation, EJ gets out of the car. "Not even locked!" he shouts, pushing the gate open.

Two minutes later, after driving through a field and turning into another dirt road, we pull up to a two-story country house.

"Are we breaking the law?" I ask as EJ kills the engine and we stare at the house that looks abandoned. "I mean, are we trespassing?"

"Not if it's abandoned. If someone is here, we'll apologize. Remember, it's easier to do things without permission and then apologize than—"

"To ask permission and get rejected," I cut in and add, "Unless we are arrested."

"Stop it, negative Nancy. Let's go."

We get out of the car and walk toward the house's porch.

I was wrong in my first assessment. It's not abandoned. There is a tub of fresh Brussels sprouts sitting on the edge of the porch, a raincoat hanging over the porch railing. Muddied rain boots stand by the doormat at the entrance. The place doesn't smell like moth balls and decay. It vaguely smells of the fall harvest and chimney smoke, though I didn't notice any. Yet, there's no light in any of the windows, no sound, no vehicle parked by the house.

Both EJ and I step up to the door, and he knocks loudly.

We glance at each other as silence weighs around us and I feel disappointment sinking in. This is possibly the only clue to my mother's past before her college years.

"No one's home," I conclude, disheartened.

"Just wait." EJ knocks again, louder this time.

He scans the porch, then walks to the nearest window and cups his hands on each side of his face as he presses them to the glass, trying to look inside.

"Someone definitely lives here," he says.

"We can wait," I probe, wrapping my arms around my middle and shivering. I left my parka in the car, and though it's not cold, there's an uneasy feeling in the pit of my stomach. I can't explain it.

"Yeah, we can. Inside," EJ says as he walks up to the door again and turns the door handle.

It gives in without effort, and the door opens just a crack.

EJ goes rigid and looks at me in surprise, then cocks his brow.

"Stop!" I protest in panic. "No, we are not gonna just walk into someone's house."

Suddenly, the sound of a trigger cocking clicks behind our backs, and an elderly female voice says, "You take one more step, and I shoot."

TWENTY-EIGHT

If it wasn't for the voice, I'd think the figure pointing a shotgun at us was a man.

"Thinking of looting the place?" the woman rasps, definitely a she, though, again, it's hard to tell by her looks.

"N-no," both EJ and I say at the same time. "No, no, we are—"

"Think twice. Let go of the handle. Now."

"Let go of the handle," I whisper to EJ, and we both raise our hands in the air as he steps just a bit in front of me, shielding me.

I peek from behind him.

The figure is dressed in canvas bib overalls over a flannel shirt, work boots, and a duck jacket. A baseball hat is low over her face as she leans over the rifle raised at us.

"We honked at the cattle gate," EJ lies.

"No, you didn't," the woman says sharply. "I watched you. On camera."

Shit. How could we have known someone in the middle of nowhere would have a camera?

"We came to talk, ma'am," EJ says. "Apologies for driving right through. But we are not from here. We don't know the rules."

"The rules"—the woman sucks her teeth—"are that you don't walk into a stranger's home without an invite."

"Sorry," EJ says again. "We are desperate though." Nice try. "We flew in from the East Coast. We are here about the Keller Foster Care Facility," he says fast so he doesn't get interrupted. "You worked there, right? You *are* Dianne Jacobson, the housekeeper?"

I can tell by EJ's voice that he's trying to be nice. He can be friendly and insistent. That's why everyone always likes him, and no one ever really likes me. I don't kiss ass.

"Why is she hiding?" the woman asks, tipping the shotgun barrel just slightly at me. "You, behind him, step out so I can see you, and your hands, too."

Though I appreciate EJ shielding me, I have a feeling this woman won't harm us. The most she can do is kick us out.

I slowly step from behind EJ to stand next to him.

The woman lowers her gun just a bit. "I'll be damned," she says, her gun lowering even more until it's at her side, and she's staring at me, her eyes narrowing. "Isn't that a déjà vu..."

She spits on the ground and takes slow steps toward us, her lips curling into a smirk, her eyes never leaving me. "What's your name?"

"Emerson, ma'am," EJ says.

"Not you. Her." She tips her chin at me.

"Mackenzie. Mackenzie Casper," I say quickly. "My mom is Elizabeth Dunn. Was..."

"I see that," the woman says, visibly intrigued. "Like seeing a ghost. Carbon copy, you and her." She stops at the porch. "What do you want here?"

"To talk about her," I say, lowering my hands. "We have some questions that no one wants to answer. Well, we don't know anyone who can."

The woman nods and looks around. "I bet you don't."

With a heavy sigh, she walks up onto the porch and steps

between us, giving EJ a once-over, at which EJ flashes her a charming grin.

"Come on," she says and walks into the house. "Take your shoes off at the door," she adds sharply without turning to look at us.

The place is definitely not abandoned, I conclude when Dianne Jacobson turns the light on and invites us into the kitchen. It might look shabby from the outside, but inside, it's pristinely clean, though the smell of old wood and chimney smoke are unmistakable.

Dianne Jacobson takes off her jacket and shoes, then her hat. She has shoulder-length gray hair gathered in a ponytail at the back. Her hands are rough and callused but quick as she puts a tea kettle on the stove as EJ and I take seats at the table and look around.

The kitchen is simple but neat, with wooden cupboards, wooden walls, wooden floors, everything wooden. A woven carpet is under a small kitchen table, and deer antlers and pictures decorate the walls.

"What did you want to know?" Dianne Jacobson asks.

"You remember her, Elizabeth Dunn?" I ask.

"Of course. She was always trying to stay away from everyone's eyes. But there was something about her that... that just stuck with you."

I smile. That was my mom.

Dianne Jacobson takes several mismatched cups out of a cupboard, puts them in front of me and EJ, and one in front of an empty seat, then takes a seat. She never asked if we wanted anything. I'm not a tea drinker, or whatever it is she is about to make, but I don't want to reject the offer of a woman who knows how to handle a shotgun, and, most importantly, who is my only clue to Mom's past.

She sets her locked hands in front of her and stares at me. "Like a ghost from the past," she says, studying my face. "You are the spitting image."

I personally think that the only things Mom and I had in common were dark hair and hostile facial expression. At least, that's what EJ says.

Nevertheless, I politely smile at the woman's comment. "I'd appreciate anything you can tell me about her, Mrs. Jacobson."

"Dianne," she says. "I'm not a housekeeper anymore."

I nod. "Dianne."

"Your mama was special," she says, her hands resting on the table, thumbs rubbing together in contemplation. "I mean, different from the other kids. You see all kinds come through foster care. Damaged, angry, cruel. But her? Huh." She pauses for a moment. "She was something else. Talented, always writing in her diaries or sitting outside in the garden, sketching. She never cared for hanging out with the others. Not Lizzy. I liked her, your mama. The other kids didn't like chores, you know. No kids do. This one, you ask—she'd do it. No arguments. Discipline." Dianne raises her eyes at me. "Discipline is what we tried to teach them. 'Cause when they got kicked out into the real world, that might've been the only thing they took with them."

Dianne's gaze is intense but somehow commanding. The sort of gaze that can order you to drop and do a hundred pushups, and you wouldn't dare disobey. Gray bushy eyebrows, square jaw, wide mouth, weathered skin.

"Why did you come asking about her?" she asks.

"She passed. Recently," I say.

Dianne doesn't flinch. "My condolences."

She rises from her chair and spends a minute filling the teapot, then brings it to the table and takes a seat.

"Mom was a bestselling author," I say in case Dianne doesn't know.

She chuckles through her nose, her eyes studying me in a way that makes me too self-aware.

"She was always making up stories in her head," she says. "Writing. Writing. Strange things she wrote, too. She let me read them sometimes. Hmm."

"Were you close?"

"You can say that. The kids at Keller's needed guidance. Not that they wanted it. Not all of them, anyway. We had too many of them over the years. It was hard to get attached when it was like a conveyor belt of them going through."

"I understand."

She chuckles. "Do you?" She stares at me again, then shakes her head. "God, the resemblance... It's uncanny."

And maybe now that the woman has warmed up, it's a good time to ask about the incident.

TWENTY-NINE

This is not going to be easy, I know it. But that's what we came here for.

"Something happened to Mom during her years at the group home," I say hesitantly. "She was... assaulted, maybe? Anything you know about that?"

Dianne's gaze on me hardens. She looks at EJ, then back at me, then looks at her hands as she clasps them together in front of her and leans back in her chair.

"She was, yes. In tenth grade."

"So it's true."

"Oh, it is. Though they made it look like it was just good old bickering among the young lovebirds."

"Who are *they*?"

"The board, when I brought it up. I knew something happened from the get-go. You work long enough in a place like that, you notice everything. Who is bullied. Who is in charge. Who is popular. Who is failing to cope. The long-term ones were the undesirables, you know. Those who didn't get adopted, didn't get picked up by foster parents or were sent back. The system is full of kids who can't be *placed*. That's what the official documentation said. You get to know them all. Generation after generation after generation. History repeats itself. Accidents. Scandals. Fights. Crushes. Heartbreaks. Jealousy. Betrayal. When I saw your mama shriveling into herself for days, I pulled her aside and asked. That's when she told me what the boys did to her in that damn barn."

Dianne gives me a meaningful look, but there's no pity in it. Like it wasn't the first or the last atrocious thing that happened on her watch. Like she was used to that type of thing.

"I knew the story. Knew the boys. Who they ran around with. And Lizzy, well, she wasn't popular, wasn't running with the popular crew. But... She was fifteen, turning pretty. Weird, they called her. But the boys, you know... They couldn't take their eyes off her. She couldn't hide that kind of pretty, either. Not from the boys bursting with hormones. They were all rejects, and they didn't take rejection too well."

"Did you report it? What they did?"

A smirk curls Dianne's mouth downward until her eyes narrow in what looks like pure hatred at the memory.

"I did. I did," she says quietly. "There was an internal investigation. They questioned the boys. The boys denied everything, of course. If Lizzy told me right away, we could've sent her to the hospital for an exam. But it was two weeks or so later. And then there was another witness."

"A witness?"

"That girl who ran with the boys, one of the girlfriends."

I exchange glances with EJ but keep quiet, waiting for Dianne to continue.

"Tonya was her name."

I feel my stomach churn. "How was she a witness?"

Dianne shrugs. "She said that Lizzy was friendly with the boys. Too friendly, in fact. She said Lizzy flirted with them, flirted with her boyfriend, was openly suggestive with them. That type, you know."

"Was she?"

163

Dianne snorts. "Lizzy? No. Not by a mile. I was around those kids six days a week, morning 'til night. Tonya? That one was sneaky, jealous, too quick for her own good. And she could spin a story, too, and she did. But the board didn't care. They believed everything she said because it was easier and didn't require further investigation. Case closed."

"Just like that?"

Dianne gives me an indifferent stare. "Just like that. They had too many of those kids, too many problems, and the last thing they needed was to have authorities involved. The state funding for places like that was dismal."

"Did the boys do anything else afterward?"

"Nah. They wouldn't dare. I took them aside the day the board dropped the complaint and told them they ever touch Lizzy again and I would make sure they didn't get a penny after the graduation. That was a big deal. Bitch, they called me. But who cares."

"So, Tonya. Why would she lie about my mother? Because one of the three boys was her boyfriend?"

"I don't think that was the case," Dianne says.

"What else could it be? She was in love with one of the boys. The boy liked another girl. She got jealous."

Dianne shakes her head and leans toward me, locking eyes with me. "That's not what it was about."

I frown, not understanding.

"I don't think she was obsessed with her boyfriend," Dianne says. "I think Tonya was obsessed with Lizzy."

THIRTY

Two hours later, we are still talking and having tea. Thunder crackles, and it has started pouring outside. But inside the house, it's surprisingly cozy.

I'm looking for the chimney, and Dianne notices.

"Baseboard," she says and laughs at the fact that I thought she had a fireplace that heated this place.

"But the smoke..." I sniff the air.

"A smoker, for deer jerky, in the barn outback." She tips her head in the direction behind the house.

We only meant to stop by for several questions. But then, Dianne asked us if we were hungry, and of course, EJ shamelessly said he was, and she made us sandwiches and more tea.

Dianne is not as hostile as she first comes across. Maybe, the opportunity to talk about her life makes her humbler.

She told us more about the foster facility, about my mom, what her habits were.

Of course, I bring up the barn fire.

Dianne knows all about the police report and the investigation details.

I hesitate telling her about my mom's role in it, then decide against it.

"Did you have any suspicions? Something that never occurred to the detectives?"

"Kids talked, you know. They wouldn't spill the beans or rat each other out to the detectives. But they talked to each other. I heard some stuff."

"Like what?"

She brushes it off. "Gossip. The investigators said that the barn door was boarded up then un-boarded before the police got there. But that wasn't conclusive in the report."

"We read the report."

"The fact is those boys did wrong to a lot of people. And even if they didn't, there were many who would do something like that as a sick joke. Teenagers, growing up without parent figures, can be like lone wolf cubs—harmless until they learn how to bite."

"Did any of them keep in touch after they left Keller's?" I ask, hoping that maybe Mom did.

"I never wanted children. Never gave birth to any but had too many of them in my life. Some of them still send me Christmas cards." Dianne smiles. "Only a few. Most try to forget about their years in the system."

Understandable. "And my mom?"

"Lizzy? She called for several years on my birthday and on Christmas. Then she stopped. I always thought that the fire in the barn made her turn for the worse."

"Worse?"

"No, not the right word. She got quieter. Angrier, maybe. She withdrew into herself. She didn't want to have anything to do with that place. I don't blame her. She'd applied to colleges and universities around the country, I know. Got a grant to several. Picked one in Old Bow. I knew she'd take care of herself."

"She graduated with honors and a degree in creative writing," I say.

Dianne nods with a soft smile and an intense gaze on me like none of this is news to her. "Good for her. Good for her."

"She wrote three international bestsellers and became pretty big in the book world."

"Good."

"And then she died."

"Uh-huh." Dianne doesn't ask, but she stares at me as if she wants to coax the answer out.

"Slip and fall."

Dianne's gaze hardens. There's a flash of regret or disappointment in it, I'm not sure. "That's unfortunate."

She tips her chin at me in some sort of contemplation, staring at me for so long that it makes me uncomfortable. Then her face suddenly relaxes as she takes a deep breath. "Well, I hope you are as talented as your mama."

"What about the other girl? Tonya?"

Dianne sucks her teeth. "What about her?"

"Do you know what happened to her when she left Keller's?"

Dianne shrugs. "Like I said, rarely did we follow up."

"Did you? With her?" I press on, and Dianne gives me a hard stare again. "What happened to her baby? She was pregnant, wasn't she?"

Dianne's mouth ticks in a bitter smile. "Some women are not meant to be mothers. Tonya wasn't. She gave the child up for adoption. Privately. No mutual consent registry. Nothing. I heard she got money for it, too. How? Don't know, but I'm not surprised. It must've been too much work, to be pregnant, I mean. Otherwise Tonya would've turned it into a continuous enterprise."

I shiver. Tonya wasn't just a stalker. It sounds like she was evil.

THIRTY-ONE

Dianne takes a deep breath. "Well?"

She slaps her palms on the table and starts getting up.

It's already getting dark. I could've stayed for hours and asked more questions, but Dianne is seemingly done with the conversation.

It's still raining outside. EJ and I have to drive back into the city and stay at the motel overnight to catch the morning flight back.

I thank Dianne for the information. EJ thanks her for the tea and food and apologizes again for trespassing but with that same charming smile that can melt ice.

Dianne gives him another once-over as he puts his shoes on and turns to me. "Your boyfriend?"

I chuckle. "No, no, just friends."

But the word "boyfriend" is already out and lingering in the air, making me blush when EJ glances from under his eyebrows at me while he laces his sneakers.

Dianne glances between us. "You be safe."

EJ, the sassy ass that he is, straightens up and wraps his arm around my shoulders. "I always keep her safe, don't I, babe?" He winks at me, and I turn scarlet.

Dianne only chuckles. "Uh-huh."

Right now would be a really good time to change the topic. "Would you... In her first book, Mom wrote about what happened with her and those three boys," I say to Dianne

She narrows her eyes at me.

"Fictitiously, of course," I add. "There's a character in her book, a housekeeper, the only nice person and the one she turned to for help years later."

Dianne's expression doesn't change.

I shrug with a smile. "I think you inspired that character. Anyway. Would you maybe like one of Mom's books?"

I brought several copies for this very purpose—to butter up someone who'd want to talk about her. Of all people—scratch that, the only person around here—Dianne deserves to have one.

"Sure," she agrees.

"I'll be right back," I say, excited, and run to the car.

I wonder if Mom would've been proud to know that someone from her past read her book.

I grab *Lies, Lies, and Revenge*. Maybe, Dianne will read it and find comfort knowing that Mom took revenge on the boys in this way.

I bring the book to the house and hand it to Dianne.

"It's signed by her," I say proudly. "That's her pen name."

Dianne studies the cover.

"E. V. Renge is an anagram for revenge." I smile.

Dianne turns the book in her hands and looks at the author picture on the back cover.

It's a several-year-old updated picture of Mom, with her signature slick raven hair and bangs and red lipstick that matches the red roses in the background. She looks Gothic, probably a change from her foster years.

Dianne's eyes narrow at the picture. Somehow, she doesn't look too excited about my present.

"That's Mom. About five years ago," I explain.

Still, the silence is awkward. Dianne suddenly seems a little too hostile. "Huh. Of course, she had those."

"What?"

"Flowers. She loved roses."

"Oh." I never heard of that. "Really? Funny. Mom was allergic to most flowers. They were probably fake anyway."

Dianne keeps staring at the picture in dead silence as EJ and I raise eyebrows at each other but don't want to interrupt her. Dianne Jacobson had known my mom before anyone knew my mom. *Before* Dad.

Suddenly, I wonder if she wants to see more pictures of Mom since she left Keller's. I don't have phone reception to check my social media, but I'm pretty sure I have at least one in my picture folder. I open the slideshow file from the memorial service—Grandma included the pictures with Mom, Dad, and me as a baby—and hand the phone to Dianne.

"That's the earliest picture of her I have. I was probably around one year old," I say as we both look at the screen.

Mom wasn't big on pictures, unless they were taken multiple times until her face was captured perfectly. Even then, it had to be retouched or photoshopped.

But that one was taken by Grandma. I'd never seen it until the funeral. In the picture, Mom is holding me in her arms. Her hair is in a ponytail. No lipstick, no makeup. She looks tired as she sits next to Dad who has his arm around her shoulders. He is grinning at the camera while Mom looks like she got caught off guard. She looks very young, in her early twenties, so different from her usual meticulously dressed, pristine self than on other—

"I thought so. Shame," Dianne murmurs.

My eyes snap up at her in confusion. I frown, the word not registering in my mind right away.

"Mom is much younger in this picture and with no makeup," I explain in hesitation, not sure what she's referring to.

Dianne shakes her head, tonguing her cheek. She lifts her eyes at me, her gaze almost angry. "You'll think I'm crazy. But this just won't do."

A nasty feeling is gathering in the pit of my stomach.

Without touching the screen, Dianne taps the air above it with her curled forefinger several times.

"I know her. And I know Lizzy Dunn. That"—she motions with her eyes to the screen and meets mine again—"is not Lizzy. That's Tonya."

PART 2

TWENTY-ONE YEARS AGO

THIRTY-TWO

BEN

"She knows about us. Dammit!" I grunt as I pace around the kitchen of Tonya's lake cabin.

"Well, she isn't stupid," Tonya says, crossing her arms at her chest. "That means that you weren't smart enough."

"I did everything you told me, Tonya."

"I hate to break it to you, but if you did, she wouldn't have any suspicions."

I grab a beer out of the fridge and take a big gulp, trying to drown my irritation.

To be fair, I didn't plan on being a father at the age of twenty-two. Or living with a girl I didn't want to be with. Meanwhile, being in love and having an affair with another girl, who has some bizarre plan of revenge to get rich by using the girl I'm living with.

I didn't plan to get married this early in life either. But then, Tonya says it will be necessary and the baby is going to be our trump card.

Tonya is smart. This plan is screwed up. But then, I hate thinking about what Lizzy did to Tonya back at the group home. Maybe, she does need to share her future success. Tonya deserves justice. She calls it reimbursement.

If only I didn't have to live in that small studio in town. It's depressing.

Tonya's lake cabin is much better. We've been meeting up here weekly for about half a year. She said some distant relative lived here, and she moved in right after the group home to help out. The relative died and willed the cabin to her.

It's lovely here now that it's summer. Driving here in the winter to see Tonya during snowstorms and whatnot was a bitch. But then, I still had my dorm. It was easier to have an excuse for going MIA for several days. With graduation off my plate and having to move in with Lizzy, I have to use my mom as a cover to spend weekends here.

Usually, Lizzy uses my car to take me to the airport. Then Tonya comes and picks me up. Weekends at the cabin are a breath of fresh air, and then it's back to Lizzy's.

I know, I know, it sounds shady, but, hey, I'm not the only one who lives a double life. I support Lizzy morally and with the money my parents send me. She should be grateful. And I do want to take care of my daughter in the future.

It's just that I want to be with Tonya. In the summers, it's a quick one-hour drive from Old Bow to the cabin. I'm tired of hiding.

This whole thing with Lizzy and Tonya has gotten out of control. It would all be fine if Lizzy didn't get knocked up. When I found out, I cautiously asked her what she wanted to do about it. I would've been fine with anything, emphasis on *anything*. She said she wanted to keep it.

No surprise.

I was angry, but who was I to be angry at but myself? I used protection every time to avoid this exact situation. Well, maybe most of the time. Except maybe a handful of times when I was drunk and didn't even remember having sex with her, though I knew we did.

But that's beside the point.

I told Lizzy I would help with the baby. Of course. I mean, if I had funds. I didn't plan on staying with her, but Tonya insisted.

Tonya. Tonya. Tonya. This girl is fire—I watch her watch me as I take gulps of beer and still think that despite this whole ordeal with Lizzy and the baby, Tonya and I will figure it out. She says so, and if this girl says so, man, I'll follow her like a sheep to a slaughterhouse.

When we found out about Lizzy being pregnant, Tonya disappeared for several months.

"You need to focus on Lizzy. And I need to think," she said before she left, and I hated every minute of her being gone.

I tried to make things work with Lizzy. God knows I tried. But Lizzy became unbearable. I only planned on staying with her for the baby. And also because of her place. Brady was dating Monica, so I had to get out of our dorm every time Monica visited. That had lasted for half a year already. That was the reason I hooked up with Lizzy in the first place. She was easy. She had her own apartment. She let me do anything I wanted. She let me show up any day of the week, any time. Of course, I wasn't dumb enough to tell her that I needed a place to crash.

I mean, Lizzy is talented, no doubt about that. The first time she read me some of her stories, it was a no-brainer that she would go places.

But then came Tonya. Fire. Fun. Cool. No jealousy. No strings. Even when I told her about Lizzy and said that I'd stop seeing her if Tonya gave me a chance, she said, "Hold your horses, captain."

I was in love. Tonya was the one. I mean, when you meet a girl like that and feel all sorts of feelings, you just know.

But then I had to go and tell her about the stories Lizzy wrote.

Damn Lizzy and her stories. It's like Tonya fixated on them. Especially, when I snuck out Lizzy's manuscripts and gave them to Tonya to read.

"Brilliant," Tonya said.

I knew that. Everyone did. Lizzy had an agent at that point already, who promised her some sort of advance.

"She'll go places with this stuff," Tonya said, reading the manuscript of *Lies, Lies, and Revenge.*

I knew that too.

When Tonya reappeared after several months, she said simply, "You can't leave her now."

We got in a fight that day, our first fight ever.

"You don't want to be with me—fine," I lashed out. "But I'm not gonna stay with a girl I have no feelings for just for a fucking baby. I'm twenty-two, Tonya. I'm about to graduate, move the hell out of this town, to the East Coast, and get a job. I want to live, not babysit."

"It must be nice," Tonya said in a way she never talked before. Her eyes welled up with tears.

"What?... Nice? Nice what?"

"To be able to let go of the past. Not think that someone who gets to have everything once upon a time took everything from you."

I frowned. "What the hell are you talking about?"

That's when she told me about the barn fire.

"Yes, we knew each other," Tonya said grimly. "I mean, she doesn't remember me these days. Why would she? I was a nobody. And she took the only thing I had—my boyfriend. She was jealous because he was a popular guy, handsome and smart, and he chose me over her."

"She never told me that."

"What would she tell you, Ben?" Tonya snapped, tears rolling down her cheeks, and I'd never seen Tonya cry before. "That she was a psycho? A creeper? With some deranged ideas in her head? And because she was jealous of one boy and me, she followed him and his two friends to a barn and set it on fire, killing them? You think she'd actually tell you that?"

I stared in shock. This couldn't be. Not my quiet, naive Lizzy.

But then...
I was still staring at Tonya in shock.
"There. I knew you wouldn't believe me."
She held a newspaper clipping out.

BARN FIRE AT GROUP HOME PROPERTY KILLS THREE.

THIRTY-THREE

BEN

That's when I understood a different side of Lizzy. She always seemed so quiet and mysterious, but her novels told a different story. I could never understand how someone like her could come up with the twisted, gory revenge plots she wrote about.

Now it all started to make sense.

"Hey, hey, baby." I walked up to Tonya and held her in my arms. "Shh, I believe you. It's okay. It's okay."

She sobbed for a while, then raised her tearful eyes to me. "Do you understand now?"

"Yes, I will leave her."

She closed her eyes, pursing her lips. "No, Ben." Her eyes snapped open at me. "You can't."

"I don't get it. What do you want then?"

"She owes me, Ben. Those stories. That pain. Everything she's writing about, using my grief and capitalizing on it. And guess what? When she publishes those books, she will get rich, too."

I still didn't understand.

"You," Tonya said, "you are the only one who can get part of it."

"H-how?"

"You are the father of the baby."

"And?"

"You will stay with her until the baby is born. You will marry her, too, before the book is published. And then..."

My head spun at what she was suggesting. It was unfair to me and to Tonya. "And then?"

"And then you will get every penny from her."

"But... What about *us*?"

Tonya wiped her cheeks with the back of her hand. "I'll have to sacrifice. Us."

"Not a chance—"

"Listen!" she shouted angrily, then closed her eyes to compose herself and opened them again. "Listen to me. I can. I will. And I know you can too. For me. For our future." Her lower lip trembled, her pretty eyes shedding tears again. "We just have to be patient, baby." She cupped my face so sweetly. "You will do as I said. And I will be right here, next to you. Just not in public. And in a way she doesn't know. And then,"—she bit her lip and batted her eyelashes at me in a way that made my heart race—"and then, baby, when we get what she owes us, you will leave her, and we will finally be together. And rich."

"But—"

"You, me, and your daughter."

"My daughter?"

"We will get your daughter, too. You know what Lizzy's capable of. Your daughter will be better off with us. Safer, too."

Only Tonya was capable of such love.

It all proved true in the next several months.

I never mentioned the barn fire to Lizzy, of course. Not then. I mean, I'm not dumb. I didn't want to freak her out or anything.

But Lizzy was becoming crazier. She was getting suspicious. She was saying angry things and throwing threats that didn't make sense. She was doing crazy stuff around the house then accusing me of it.

I thought she might be just overreacting. Until I found her second manuscript.

I snuck it out of Lizzy's place so I could show it to Tonya.

I stand on the pier and listen to her screams from the boat. The screams of the woman who is losing her mind. The woman who doesn't yet know why this is happening to her. The woman whose life is slowly falling apart. Who is watching her husband drown, unable to help.

A woman who deserved it.

Desperate. Panicky. Clueless.

Clueless, because this was all my doing. Including her husband's death.

She had it coming.

She should've never crossed my path.

"Who in their right mind writes that?" Tonya asked through tears as she peeled her eyes off the manuscript and stared at me in shock.

"I mean..." I pinched the bridge of my nose. "It's fiction, right?"

"Fiction?" Tonya yelped. "Sure, babe, fiction. Except"—she frantically flipped through the pages—"there, there. The two main heroines were rivals in school. Then one stole the other's boyfriend. And years later, the other"—Tonya's panicked eyes were on me—"sets up the first girl's husband for drowning, then burns their house, and steals their baby. Is this what you want to happen to you?"

"To me? Wait-wait-wait—"

"Are you blind, Ben?" Tonya's brows furrowed in pity. "She is an awful person. She destroyed my life once. I won't let her do it again. She needs to pay."

Her chest shook in a sob.

Ugh, women and their theatrics.

182

But this was Tonya. And I couldn't help it, not when she was like this. I hugged her again and cradled her to my chest.

"Shh, it's all right. It's all right."

"I-I-I can't d-do it without you, Ben. But I n-need it. I n-need this to feel normal. I d-don't want to lose you. But I need help to make her pay. Please?"

She lifted her beautiful eyes to me, and there was nothing in the world that could make me say no.

"Four more months," she said.

It seemed like a prison sentence. A graduation that wasn't so jolly. Lizzy, who was getting more eccentric and paranoid. My parents whom I eventually told about Lizzy.

"Couldn't keep it in your pants, could you?" Mom snapped.

But then I told them about Lizzy's publishing deal, and they asked to talk to her. Lizzy talked on the phone with them for some time, and by the end, she was glowing, and they were content.

I promised her the world, of course. What else could I do?

I was still in love with Tonya.

But then it was two months *until*... I moved in with Lizzy, because my dorms had to be vacated. My friends dropped off the face of the earth, one after another, because they had jobs, scattered across the country. I had nothing but a useless degree.

Then it was one month *until*.

Tonya and I had a plan, though I wasn't quite sure how to make it work.

Marrying Lizzy? Wild. My parents said we could stay with them for some time. Until we got back on our feet. Until Lizzy's books were published.

Tonya said she'd move, too, closer to us, without anyone knowing.

So, here we are—only days *until*.

My parents are nagging. My girlfriend is about to pop a baby. The girl I love lives outside town in a log cabin by the lake. I am a cheater. I am in love. I'm tired of lying.

And I am about to lose my mind.

What do they say? When it rains, it pours.

Ain't that the truth.

In less than a week, I'll be a father. The fact still doesn't quite settle in. I am soon to be a co-parent with the girl I'm supposed to marry.

Lizzy dropped me off at the airport an hour ago. When she left, Tonya swung by to pick me up.

As I'm taking swigs of beer, everything suddenly feels wrong—all these lies just to spend one night a week with Tonya.

But I can't stay away.

"What's with the sour face?" Tonya asks.

"Just..." I don't know how to explain it. I'm not sure if this is the last weekend we get to spend together for a while. When Lizzy gives birth, I might have to help out with—

"Fuck! I really don't want to do this," I blurt out.

Tonya stares at me. "Do what, Ben?"

"The whole parenting thing."

Her expression softens, then she laughs, not cheerfully but in that way that makes me uneasy. "It will all work out. You'll see."

It's already getting dark outside, so when the headlights of a car shine into the window, both Tonya and I notice right away.

"Who is that?" Tonya muses, looking out the window.

I don't care. I shut my eyes tightly, trying to figure out how my life turned into this soap opera.

That's when Tonya says, "It's your car, Ben."

I snap my head in her direction.

She's still staring out the window. "It is," she says. "Guess who is here?"

She doesn't need to say it. I know.

It's Lizzy.

I think we are fucked.

THIRTY-FOUR

BEN

"Look who the cat dragged in," says Tonya cockily as she walks out onto the porch.

I'm standing behind the door, holding my breath, and praying that Tonya sends Lizzy away.

"Where is he?" Lizzy snaps.

"Who?"

"That coward and cheater. Ben. Where is he?"

Tonya chuckles. "What makes you think he's here? And how did you find this place anyway?"

"I followed you. Both of you. Yes, from the airport, so spare me your filthy lies, Tonya."

I close my eyes, cursing on repeat in my head.

Maybe that's the sign that I should finally sort this out *my* way, tell Lizzy how it is, and break things off. Tonya and I can manage. We love each other, and we don't need whatever potential money Lizzy can make with her books. Tonya doesn't understand that all these lies are not worth it.

"I know this has been going on for a while," Lizzy says. "No need to try to weasel your way out of it."

Determined, I pull the door open and step out onto the porch.

Lizzy stands in front of the car headlights, her face the angriest I've ever seen. Her body, with the protruding belly, throws a giant shadow over the porch, reaching my feet. Her eyes bore into me with so much hate that I forget what I was trying to say.

"Lizzy..." I mumble. "It's not what you think—"

"Oh, cut it out, Ben!" she shouts. "I talked to your mother. I know you haven't been home in half a year. Stop lying."

"I can explain."

I was going to say something different, but she is so angry, so full of spite that I can't bear it.

Tonya crosses her arms over her chest and cocks her head, staring at Lizzy. She doesn't say anything. And I don't know how to say things without hurting Lizzy's feelings.

"Lizzy," I start. "Let's just talk like grown-ups—"

"I don't want to talk!" she spits out. "You know what? I should've done it a long time ago. But I was a coward. Just like you. I thought things would work out. They are not. They haven't been in a while."

"Lizzy, calm down." I can see her chest rising and falling rapidly. She's losing her breath and holding on to her belly. "Let's just—"

"No, Ben!" she shouts so loudly that her voice gets raspy. "Let's not! I don't want you. My baby doesn't want you. *We* don't want you!"

I think she's crying. Oh, man, she is.

I put my arms up in front of me, with my palms out. "Just relax, Lizzy, okay?"

"No!" she screams, her voice high-pitched. "Don't touch me! Don't come close. We are done, Ben! We! Are! Done!" she screams at the top of her lungs.

Suddenly, her expression contorts in pain, and she screams and bends into herself, holding on to her round belly.

"Lizzy?"

"Aah." Her mouth opens widely but barely any sound comes out this time. Her eyes bulge at me in shock.

"Lizzy?" I take slow steps toward her. "What's wrong?"

Panic starts taking over me.

She stumbles. A meek whimper leaves her mouth as she looks down at her sweatpants. I can't see very well in the dark, with the headlights blinding me.

"Ben?" she whimpers helplessly, staring at her legs.

That's when I see it. Her light sweatpants are getting wet.

She raises her alarmed eyes at me. "Ben?" she whispers.

"Holy shit," Tonya says from behind me. "Her water just broke."

Lizzy's eyes dart to Tonya, then to me, then to her legs.

"Aah!" she rasps in pain, and her knees start buckling.

I surge forward and catch her in my arms.

"We need to get her to the hospital!" I shout to Tonya.

I can't hold Lizzy up, and we both sink onto the grass.

Tonya kneels next to me and looks into Lizzy's pained face.

"We have to go. We'll drive my car," I pant.

"No," Tonya says.

I snap my alarmed gaze at her. "What do you mean no? She is giving birth. We need to get her to the hospital."

Tonya turns to face me, and her expression is determined but somewhat cold. "We don't have time. She'll just have to do this here."

At these words, I feel like I'm about to throw up.

THIRTY-FIVE

BEN

I wish I could turn back time.

Not even to the days I used to crash at Lizzy's. I wish I could turn it back to an hour ago.

Lizzy is in the bedroom, on the bed, curled up in pain. She's moaning and occasionally screaming, the sharp pleading sound of it making my stomach turn.

Blood pounds between my ears as I watch Tonya go in and out of the bedroom, checking on Lizzy, while boiling water in the kitchen and tearing an old sheet into rags.

She constantly tells me to do this or that. She makes me give Lizzy a pill—I don't ask what the pill is.

"We need to go to the hospital," I keep repeating, my own voice like an echo.

"She wants to leave you, Ben, don't you understand?" Tonya hisses as we go back and forth from the bedroom to the kitchen, bringing "supplies," as Tonya calls them.

"So be it," I say.

"Don't be stupid. She can't leave you. Once she is in the hospital, forget about the future or the books."

"Forget about the books, Tonya!" I shout.

She fists the front of my shirt. "No," she snarls with so much viciousness that it makes shivers run down my spine.

"We'll help her here, at the house," she declares. "It's not rocket science. Many people do home birth. Then we'll help with the baby. She is not leaving this place or getting her baby until we make a deal with her."

I gape at her. "Are you insane?"

Lizzy's moan comes from the bedroom. "Help."

Tonya widens her eyes. "It's too late. We have to do this ourselves. Toughen up, Ben."

"H-how? H-how do we even know what to do?"

"I know." Tonya grabs a bunch of clean towels from a closet.

"H-how?"

Tonya shoves them into my hands and pauses for a second to stare me in the eyes. "I don't think you want to know, Ben. Go."

I've never wanted this. No guy ever wants to witness this—a girl giving birth. I don't know how they do it. I can't look.

For an hour, Tonya and I are with Lizzy, trying to calm her down as she thrashes all over the bed.

"Okay," Tonya finally says. "She is ready. Are you going to help me with her?"

"No," I plead, staring at Tonya.

"I need to undress her. Go wait outside the room. I call you— you come in. I ask for things—you do it in a second. Understood?"

I nod vigorously, stumble out of the room, and stand in the hallway. Panting, I try to come to terms with what's happening.

There's one remedy that works like a charm.

I run to the kitchen, take a bottle of whiskey from the cupboard, and come back to the hallway and take a gulp. Then another. And another.

The bright lightbulb hanging from the naked ceiling is blinding.

Tonya's voice inside the room is like an echo from horror stories. "I need to strip you. Help me out."

There are more of Lizzy's grunts.

I take a gulp of whiskey in hopes of drowning them out.

"You have to help me, okay? Now you have to push."

There is a scream, then another.

More orders.

More grunts.

I take another gulp, the liquid burning my throat and making me slightly dizzy.

Then comes a horrible roar that belongs to Lizzy but sounds almost man-like.

"Okay, okay, okay. Ben! I need more sheets! She's bleeding!"

I set the bottle down and grab more sheets from the closet. When I walk into the bedroom, I stall.

Again, I wish I could turn back time. I wish I could unsee what I'm seeing. There's Lizzy. There's Tonya. And there's blood. So much blood that everything on the bed looks red.

"Come on!" Tonya shouts, her bloody hand reaching for me. There's skin, so much naked skin on the bed, and it's all colored red like a murder scene.

I drop the sheets and stumble backward and out of the room.

Shaking my head doesn't make the horrific image go away. Neither does closing my eyes.

Bile comes up to my throat. I take a deep breath and hold it. Until I'm dizzy. Until I know I won't throw up.

Some things leave an imprint for life. Some things just can't be unseen.

I take a gulp of whiskey.

Then another.

And another.

One more.

I want to drown in whiskey until I'm sick. Sick from booze and not the horrible sounds coming from the bedroom.

The burn of the whiskey in my throat mixes with the screams from the room that sound animal-like, Tonya's orders and angry shouts lacing through them, more screaming, grunts, moans, whimpers, more whimpers.

Soon, I lose track of time. I sit on the floor, my back against the wall, and the bottle is empty, though I wish I had more whiskey, much more, so that I could pass out and forget about what's happening in this cabin. No one is around us for miles, no one to help, and no one to tell me that this is wrong, so horribly wrong. I feel it in my gut.

I don't know how much time has passed. An hour? Two? Three? I doze off.

It's almost like a dream when I hear an unfamiliar sound, a sound I've heard in movies, the joyful moment that somehow feels eerie right now—the sound of a baby crying.

Tonya comes out of the bedroom, cradling something to her chest. "Do you want to see it?"

I can't even lift my head. I shake it. I don't want any of this.

"I see you took to the bottle," Tonya reproaches. "So much for helping."

I don't answer.

Then come the words I never wanted to hear. "Something is wrong with her."

That's when I lift my head. "Wha' you mean?"

"Something's wrong with Lizzy. She doesn't make sense. She can barely talk. And she lost a lot of blood."

Tonya disappears in the bathroom. I hear the water running, the sound of it like a distant waterfall. The baby is not crying anymore. The cabin feels dark, even though the lights are on in every room. It feels like a horror movie, though it's suddenly peacefully quiet.

Tonya walks back to the bedroom. The next time she comes out, I lift my head.

"Where's the baby?" I whisper.

I'm still sitting on the floor, unable to summon the strength or courage to get up and go *there*, into that room where Lizzy is. Where the blood is.

"The baby is fine. It's sleeping. It's not the baby I'm concerned about."

A heap of sheets in Tonya's hands is soaking red, bloody red. The blood drips onto the floor as Tonya carries them to the bathroom.

I stare at the red drops on the wooden floor, the drops that look almost black in the sharp light of the hallway, and realize that we messed up. I think I made a bad call. And I think we just did something horribly bad to Lizzy.

Except, I know I can't turn back time.

It's too late.

THIRTY-SIX

BEN

I don't know if I like them or loathe them—these sounds that come from the little creature wrapped in a torn sheet lying on the couch between me and Tonya. It sounds like a baby-pterodactyl.

They say you can tell the baby's resemblance to its parents. This one looks just like any baby. A little mohawk of black hair. Scrunched-up face. Puffy mouth.

It's been mostly sleeping for two days now. Because of the state Lizzy is in, we have to heat up store milk and give it to the baby. Tonya tells me it's not good, but that's all we have for now.

"It needs to be fed soon," Tonya says, studying the baby without much interest. "Babies need to be fed every three or so hours."

How would she know that?

For another minute, we sit in silence and stare at the little bundle between us. It needs a mother. But its mother has been as helpless as the baby itself.

Lizzy has stopped bleeding. She's been in bed since *that* night, with a vacant expression, occasionally murmuring something. She refuses to eat, but Tonya seems to have force-fed her a couple of times.

Lizzy doesn't talk. She makes inaudible sounds and sleeps mostly, except when she lies in bed, staring in front of her and rarely responding to Tonya or me when we walk in.

The room has been aired out multiple times, but there's no way to get rid of the blood smell. Every time I walk in, I have a flash of what happened *that* night.

We need an air freshener.

We need help.

We need some freaking professionals to handle this.

But Tonya won't hear it.

"What do you suggest we do?" she argued yesterday. "If we take her to the hospital and she gets better, you can say goodbye to the baby and to everything else. Who knows what she tells the doctors. What if she doesn't get better and they take your baby for what you've done?"

Horror washes over me. "Me?"

"Me, you, irrelevant. What if they say you are incapable of taking care of the baby? Then you lose everything."

Tonya is right. She's smart. We just need time to figure this out.

"We need baby supplies," I finally say, looking at Tonya and willing her to look back at me.

I don't know what to do with the baby, really. Does it want to play? To move? It sleeps an awful lot. Tonya is the only one who acts confidently as if she knows how to handle babies. Odd, really.

We don't have anything for the baby in this cabin. Back in town, though, we have a stroller with a removable bassinet we got some time ago, diapers, toys, and baby clothes—all that stuff Lizzy bought.

"I need to go to town for baby stuff," Tonya says.

And for more beer and liquor. I need to have a drink to get my mind straight.

"We need baby formula, too," Tonya adds. "I tried to make her feed the baby, but it's not working well. Like I said, something went wrong in her body."

Her words make me cringe. Suddenly, I feel bad. Not for Lizzy —it is what it is—but for the baby. It's so small. All this is not its fault. This baby is... mine.

"Mackenzie," I say quietly.

Tonya gives me a puzzled look.

"Mackenzie," I repeat. "That's what Lizzy wanted to call her."

"I don't care."

"Mackenzie it is," I say, and the little creature moves its tiny hands and makes a slurping sound.

I think as soon as I give it a name, it becomes real, though it's been real for two days.

"You need to learn how to hold it," Tonya says. "For when I'm not around."

"Why won't you be around?"

"Tsk. Because we are not going to sit in this cabin for the rest of our lives, Ben. Right? And you have a baby."

"*We* have a baby," I correct her.

"Yes. But it's *your* baby. Don't forget that. So learn to be a father."

As if sensing that it's being talked about, the baby starts waving its hands in no particular direction and making those pterodactyl noises again.

Tonya carefully picks up the little bundle, but instead of cradling it, she passes it to me with a nod. "Come on. Take it."

Awkwardly, terrified that something will snap in the baby's body, I take it in my arms.

"We need to feed it," Tonya says. "Come on."

"Her."

"What?"

"Her. We need to feed *her*. Mackenzie." I give her a weak smile.

Tonya responds with a smirk, and I'm pretty sure she rolls her eyes a little. "Right. Mackenzie."

THIRTY-SEVEN

TONYA

If Ben gives me one more of those dumb sheepish stares of his, I swear, I'm going to bash his skull in.

God, I am tired of playing mommy. To both of them. Three now, actually. The last two days have felt like for-fucking-ever.

Lizzy is the worst problem. She might do something stupid, like running away, and then we can say goodbye to the book deals. Except, right now, she is pretty much a zombie.

"You stay here with the baby and her, and I'll go into town, grab some clothes, and buy baby formula," I tell Ben. "I'll stop by her place and get that baby stuff she's been hoarding for months. Anything else?"

"Why don't I do that?" Ben asks miserably, cradling the baby in his arms.

It suits him. That's pretty much all he's capable of at this point.

He's irritating, seriously. If he gets on my nerves and I snap, his Lizzy will end up exactly how the previous owner of this cabin did —with a sudden prescription overdose.

I take a deep breath to calm myself.

"I am better at navigating a potential crisis," I reason.

"I can navigate," he says.

"You can't. And I need to do research, among other things. I have fewer chances of running into someone I know in town. What if you stumble upon your friends or professors? What if they ask about the baby? About your girlfriend?"

His stupid eyes are on me again. I can't stand this puppy expression. If only the guy took himself seriously for once.

Don't get me wrong, Ben is fun. Charming, too, the life of every party. If only life were all about partying.

He barely graduated. To be fair, I never went to college, but some of us don't have to get a degree to prove themselves to the world. Just like I didn't need to go to a nursing school to know how giving birth works. Some of the hardest life experiences come from the worst mistakes. Getting knocked up is one of them. I should know. Been there, done that. This is one of the many things Ben will never find out about me.

"Don't talk to anyone in town," Ben warns.

He is annoying. Cute, but, god, is he stupid. He is lucky I like him, because he is not even good in bed. His only gift is his talented girlfriend who is slowly becoming a vegetable.

"Ben, baby—" I take a step toward him and cup his face. "We got through the last two days, didn't we?"

He nods, his expression already softening. He's so easy.

"We'll get through the next. Just trust me," I say in the sweetest voice my current mood allows me to conjure.

It's important to keep Ben—I want to say happy, but screw that —mentally stable. I need him.

"What about *her*?" he asks.

I want to punch him. I swear, it was easier to take care of this mess the last two days than to practice patience with Ben. He might feel bad about the whole Lizzy thing, but it's not my problem. I'm tired of weak people.

But being angry will only spook him and upset him. He might just do something stupid and ruin this whole enterprise. So, I need to keep playing my part.

I push hard to tear up. Oh, yeah, the tears are coming. Here we go, that will make it more believable. I bite my lip, sniffle, and feel my eyes finally well up with tears.

"She took everything I had, Ben," I say in a shaky voice. A little whispery, a little bitter—perfect. "You don't get it. We were orphans. That boy, my first love, was everything. And she took it. Just like that." I snap my fingers. "She ruined my life." I swallow intentionally hard and fake a tiny sob. "And she owes me. Yes. I'll take it with money."

It doesn't hurt to remind Ben for the gazillionth time why we are doing this.

I can see pity starting to take over his face. *Good.* He shifts the baby into one arm and with his other, pulls me into him.

"It will be all right," he says quietly as I press my forehead to his shoulder for a moment and, knowing he can't see my face, roll my eyes. He needs to feel manly and supportive? Works for me.

"Okay, I have to go," I finally say, pulling away from him.

"Hey, don't forget the beer." When I meet his eyes, he shrugs apologetically. "It's been stressful the last couple of days."

He doesn't know what stressful is. Try growing up in a group home.

But I don't say that. Experience is subjective.

I give him a quick kiss and check the baby.

Mackenzie, he said Lizzy wanted to name her. Not that I care. The baby is cute. It's not the baby's fault that its mother is losing her shit. Again, not my problem.

I don't bother checking on Lizzy. She's quiet, in a permanent state of half-asleep, half depression. She only has herself to blame. In fact, this issue with Lizzy might just be working well for us. She has to stay here, at the lake, at least for a while, until I think of a different plan of action.

I want to comfort her. Really, I do. But not out of compassion. It's more like pity, what you feel for an animal you are about to put down.

I can probably tell her that I envied her back then, at the group home. She was smart, mysterious, pretty. Even my boyfriend had a crush on her, and so did his friends. She had it coming. Shouldn't have batted her lashes at them.

It didn't take long to coax them into thinking that pretty Lizzy was a slut and liked boys and talked about them all the time.

They'd been nice to her, they said. I heard Bobby and Danny talk about it, what they'd done to her in the barn, that she'd even enjoyed it, they'd made sure she had. Except Brandon shouldn't have been there. He said he'd only watched. Not that I believed him. He even secretly left roses on her bed afterward, as an apology. Pathetic. And all that while dating me.

I was shocked when I saw her one night, weeks later, creeping up to the abandoned barn where the boys got together for a party. I was on my way there, angry at Brandon, who couldn't shut up about Lizzy. For weeks, the boys had been discussing their little tryst with her like it was the best thing they'd ever done. Earlier that day, I had slipped prescriptions I'd stolen from a nurse into the bottle of moonshine they had gotten in town. Just to teach them a lesson. That was my revenge. I was on my way to the barn to watch them get high out of their minds and gloat over it.

But then I saw Lizzy outside the barn. She poured liquid from a gas can in front of the barn door and set it on fire.

Seriously, who sets a building with people inside on fire out of spite?

But look at that—a brave little thing. I was fascinated with her. I wanted to stand next to her, watch the blaze, see the shock on the stupid faces of those three, plastered drunk and probably peeing in their pants in fear.

But Lizzy ran off. A pity, really.

Then I had another idea.

I could confess to precious Lizzy right now that when she ran off that night, I came to the blazing door, took the pole propped on the side, and shoved it into the door handles so that the door could never be opened from the inside. Fuck those three. They liked her better than me. I was bored with them, anyway.

I could tell her all that now, but she is already losing her mind.

There is clearly a difference between being smart and being brilliant. Lizzy lacks common sense. I mean, I told her I knew what she'd done that night. When I told her I had evidence, she only blinked those pretty eyes at me and believed me.

Seriously? What evidence could I possibly have years later?

Like I said, stupid. If you are that stupid then you might as well take up the guilt for what happened, right? Smart people know how to get away with crimes.

I did.

THIRTY-EIGHT

TONYA

I exhale with relief when I step out of the house, get into my car, and drive off the property. As soon as the house disappears from my view, it's like a stone has been lifted off my chest. I crank up the radio and start singing to the music.

I'll get through this. I'll figure this out. Some of us are given opportunities. Some of us take them. If I had half the talent that Lizzy does, I would've been a celebrity by now. That girl? Jesus. A useless degree, a shitty apartment, and Ben. What a package!

When I first met Ben, knowing that he was sneaking around with Lizzy, I was charmed by him. He *is* a charmer, I'll give him that. I even had a crush. A tiny one. For like a week. But then, crushes are for teenagers. Brandon was a crush. As soon as I realized that the only thing Ben had going for him was Lizzy, I knew I needed both of them.

If there had been a chance to get to Lizzy without him, I would've done so. Ben became helpful. So did that baby. I am not even surprised Lizzy got herself into more trouble with a boy.

Well, her troubles might just be my jackpot.

I veer the car onto the main road and glance at the giant fish sign that signals the turn to the lake cabin.

We call it the "gar" turn, and I hate that sign. The fish on it looks like a monster with sharp teeth. Apparently, it's called a garfish, and they inhabit the lake in large numbers.

When Mrs. Cavendish told me the local legend about it, it made my skin crawl. I saw that sign daily for over a year when I was taking care of Mrs. Cavendish. That old hag was annoying. But at least she left me her house before she croaked. With a little help. Everyone these days needs a push to get what they deserve—a crappy relationship or a grave. At least, that's my experience.

As I drive toward Old Bow, I'm trying to work out the next plan of action.

If Lizzy follows through with her threats and takes the baby and moves away, Ben can say goodbye to the money she will potentially make with her books. And goodbye to me, because I don't need him without Lizzy.

Me? I will have to start fresh, follow Lizzy again, blackmail her —and that's annoying. I wasn't born for petty blackmailing. Or for a shabby house by the lake.

My first stop in town is the public library.

First things first, I check out several books on postpartum complications and read for several hours, trying to figure out what's wrong with Lizzy. Clearly, something is.

Two hours later, I'm left with several options. Cardiac arrest with severe oxygen deprivation that results in neurological damage. Hypovolemic shock. A stroke resulting from high blood pressure— that's most likely—that can lead to brain damage.

It all sounds sort of gruesome, but it's not my fault. Many people give birth without the help of doctors. Complications are a given. We'll just have to give Lizzy some time and then decide what can be done. She's clearly out of it right now. Not just out of it. It's not just some postpartum depression. And not just the sedatives I spike her liquids with, which Ben doesn't know about. She doesn't remember things, doesn't seem to register me or Ben. Just the baby.

Next, I go shopping. There's a store closer to the lake cabin, in a small village just ten miles up the road where we can get more supplies later if I miss anything. That depends on how long we stay there. But right now, I pop into a big department store and load up on essentials, food and baby stuff. We need baby formula, for sure.

It's my crappy luck, of course, when I hear a voice behind me. "Tonya! What's up?"

It's Garret, from Ben's crew. I didn't know he was still in town after graduation.

"What's up?" I ask, stepping in front of my cart so he doesn't see that it's loaded with Pampers and all sorts of baby stuff.

"All good. What's up with you these days? Haven't seen you in ages."

He does steal a glance at my cart, and I smile coldly, annoyed at him being snoopy.

"Just the usual. Work. House. Helping out a friend," I add for credibility in case he wonders why I have baby stuff in my cart.

"Talked to Ben lately? Haven't seen him around much."

I keep a straight face. "No. Not for months. Someone said he and his girl left town."

Garret frowns. "Really?"

I shrug. "Gotta go. See you around."

I pay for the stuff and get the hell out of the store.

I can only imagine Ben doing this and trying to explain to Garret where Lizzy is and why he is the one shopping for the baby. Ben is not smart enough to navigate tricky conversations.

Next, I go to Ben and Lizzy's apartment.

It's clearly not my lucky day, because as soon as I get to the second floor, I see Grunger, the super of the building, leaving his apartment.

I halt and take a step back before he can see me, but it's too late. His eyes lock on me, and his lips spread in his usual sly smile.

"Well-well, look who's here."

He shifts his eyes to Lizzy's apartment deliberately slowly, then returns his gaze to me.

He does a once-over that reminds me what I had to do to get into Lizzy's apartment a year ago.

I'm sure that's his first thought too at the sight of me. His smile becomes suggestive, and he wolf whistles as he takes slow steps toward me.

"Hey, beautiful. Long time no see."

I really *really* don't want to deal with him right now. But I might not have a choice.

Crap.

THIRTY-NINE

TONYA

Ten minutes later, I get off the couch, fixing my skirt, while Grunger zips up his jeans. There's a satisfied smile on his face.

Yes, we did it on Lizzy's couch. This is only fair, considering she's had Ben for months while I have lived by myself in the stupid lake cabin. And, well, Grunger is much better at sex than Ben.

Grunger was my first connection to Lizzy when I came to town a year ago. Messy dark hair, tattoos, and more piercings on his face than I can count on the fingers of both hands.

I learned that he was taking care of the building for his uncle, the owner. That he was Lizzy's neighbor and, as a super, had keys to all the apartments for emergencies.

One night, I followed Grunger to a bar. One thing led to another, and we ended up at his place that very night. Six beers in, and I knew quite a bit about Lizzy and the keys, and I had access to her apartment whenever I wanted. Whether that was legal or not wasn't my concern.

Right now, Grunger is a nuisance. He spreads his arms along the back of the couch, lustfully studying me. He'd better not be planning on extending this surprise encounter.

"You have to go," I tell him.

"And what exactly are you doing here?"

"Helping out."

"Uh-huh." He's suspicious, rightfully so.

You see, Grunger is sneaky. I thought I'd get what I wanted from him and be done with him. But he's just too observant. Our encounters have become quite frequent ever since our first night. Most of them were quite pleasant, despite having to sneak into his place without anyone in the building, especially Lizzy, seeing me.

I set my hands on my hips and feign tiredness. "Listen, it's just... It's complicated," I say. "I'm helping out friends, and there's a lot on my plate."

I sigh theatrically and chew on my bottom lip, studying him with seeming longing so that he feels wanted.

He doesn't answer, only watches me with a half-smile.

"I need some time to sort things out, and then..." I purse my lips, as if trying to hide a smile, and lock eyes with him. "And then maybe we can get together for a drink or..."

I cock a brow.

"Or?" he echoes, his smile growing.

"Just not right now, Grunger. Maybe in a couple of weeks or so," I tell him. A guy has got to have some hope. "Right now, I really need to figure some things out. Alone." I give him a meaningful stare.

"Point taken," he says and gets up slowly.

"Also..." I step up to him, pluck a loose thread from his shirt, and gently set my hands on his chest, giving him a seductive look from under my eyebrows. "I wasn't here. In case anyone asks."

"Uh-huh." Grunger's hands take my waist, pulling me closer. His eyes drop to my lips.

"But you gotta go," I whisper, studying his lips like I want to devour them. "I'll give you a call."

I kiss him quickly. "Bye," I say as I walk off and into the bathroom. "Close the door behind you!"

As I clean myself up, I hear the front door shut.

Phew, good.

I need to get rid of Grunger. Considering he sells drugs on the side to make extra cash, I have a pretty good idea of how to pull it off.

Grunger once told me he had run-ins with the local police. Having been in his apartment plenty of times, I know where he hides his stuff for sale, in a small compartment attached to the outside AC unit. The cops would never find it. Without a little hint, that is.

I make a mental note to use the street payphone later to give the local law enforcement a courtesy call that hopefully will make Grunger go away for a long, long time. He knows too much, especially about my key copy to Lizzy's place.

Grunger has been helpful, sure. He's not educated, but he's street smart. Thanks to him, I've been in Lizzy's apartment plenty of times. First, when I left that note for Lizzy a year ago. That was fun. I can only imagine her face when she found it.

The next several times, I left a dead rat in her kitchen, rearranged her clothes, switched the rug in the living room, slipped powdered hallucinogens into her bottled drinks. Where did I get it? Again, Grunger and his secret stash. Driving Lizzy insane was precious. Given that she was pregnant, her hormones probably caused a riot.

Now, her apartment looks like a mess. I'm sure it's Ben's doing.

When I come out of the bathroom, the old antique writing desk by the window draws my attention first as always. It's old cherry wood with chipped golden ornaments. There's a lamp, candles, and dried flowers on it. I run my fingers along the edge and feel the goosebumps on my skin.

That's what always attracted everyone to Lizzy—the mystery about her. She is like that pretty witch who lives in an old gothic mansion that everyone whispers about. Like a wizard who knows some magic spells. That's how she always came across—from the way she dressed, in shabby clothes that felt retro and stylish, to the way she talked, in a timid seductive voice you couldn't get enough of, to the way she looked like she could see through you, with a smile that was endearing or a vicious anger that seemed possessive.

Lizzy Dunn was a mystery. Only Ben's dumb crew never appreciated her.

Now as I touch the things she owns, that she uses to write her haunting stories with, I can't get enough. I want to be that person who sits here, who uses the old quill, even if for fun, who pulls out drawers and rearranges the stacks of old papers.

The sudden ringing of the phone on the kitchen counter jerks me upright.

"Jesus," I murmur, shaking off the thoughts.

I stand still until the phone goes silent. Then, I open one of the drawers and pull out thick leather notebooks. One is titled, *Lies, Lies, and Revenge.* The other one is *The Wolf Whistle.* I smile picking up the latter—clever Lizzy wrote a book inspired by me and her. Cute.

I clear out the drawer, then the second one. If someone comes knocking, looking for her, some landlord or, God forbid, police, I don't want them to find the manuscripts.

I jerk when the phone starts ringing again. Maybe I should pull the cord out. But then someone who urgently wants to get ahold of Lizzy or Ben might really come knocking if no one answers for days.

I breathe in and out slowly, staring at the phone and waiting for it to shut up.

When it goes silent, I set the tote with the manuscripts and documents at the door and go for the chest of drawers.

There is only one suitcase in this place—probably Ben's, when he moved in here after graduation. I shove some clothes from his drawer into the suitcase, then go for Lizzy's drawer. Hers is half-full. The girl was really money-savvy.

When the suitcase is full, I zip it up and roll it to the door, where the tote bag is. I search under the bed and in the closet, but there are no other bags around. So, I grab several trash bags from under the kitchen sink, intending to use them for whatever baby supplies Lizzy bought for her baby.

I round the kitchen corner when the phone rings again. The sudden loud ringing makes me jump, and I press my hand to my chest, catching my breath.

Dammit.

It won't stop ringing. This is the third time in a row. I wasn't planning on answering the phone while being here, but now that the ringing is so insistent, I think maybe I should.

It could be Grunger, teasing me. He'd do that. But what if it's Ben's parents? They only talked to Lizzy once, or twice, as far as I know. Maybe they are worried. What if it's the college? Ben said Lizzy had several job offers. It could be someone looking for them both. Doctors? Neighbors?

Jesus, my head spins with the options, and now I realize one simple thing—we can't hide forever. At some point, someone might come looking.

As the phone keeps ringing, I finally give up and answer it.

FORTY

TONYA

"Hello?" I say in my most miserable voice. Then, just for credibility, I cough a little and, trying to fake a rasp, repeat, "Hello?"

"Hello? Oh, hi! I didn't think I would get an answer, and there's no answering machine," the cheerful female voice says. "May I speak to Elizabeth Dunn?"

Crap. Now I am in a pickle. Is this a random call or someone who knows her and knows her voice?

"Who am I speaking to?" I check just in case.

"This is Laima Roth, the literary agent. Is this Elizabeth?"

I hold my breath, trying to remember everything Ben said about Lizzy and her agent. I know they emailed each other. Lizzy sent her manuscripts, too. Though I don't know what the full extent of their interactions was.

"Yes?" I say meekly, hoping I can work around this if I get caught lying.

"Oh, my goodness! Elizabeth! Hi! It's so, so lovely to talk to you! I just hope it can be in person soon! I emailed you several times in the last week and never got a response."

Double crap.

Lizzy doesn't have a computer, but she does go to the college internet café. I didn't even think about that.

"I... I was busy."

"I have great news, Elizabeth!"

I hope so, because things have been falling apart lately. I just need to figure out how to spin this.

And I am eternally grateful to literary agents, because apparently, they never shut up.

Laima Whatever starts chirping away about the manuscript and the second one and the publishing house that finally offered the highest bid. But it's somewhat all a blur after I register her words, "Fifty thousand copies first print run."

While she keeps talking, I do the math. It doesn't seem like that much, but what if the book becomes a bestseller and runs multiple prints?

My mind spins at the numbers as I answer in curt "yes," "I see," "sure."

Laima Something doesn't stop talking a mile a second. "The publication will be scheduled for somewhere around the end of next year."

My heart sinks into my stomach. "Next year?"

"Right, just like we discussed. But! I explained your situation to the publisher, the baby and all. Considering the second manuscript, the publisher is willing to give you a hefty advance. That's the biggest one in years for a new author. I'm working really hard on your behalf here, Elizabeth."

She laughs proudly and finally shuts up.

I think I can hear my heartbeat. "When?"

"Oh! Well, that depends. I mean, it depends on how soon you can get here to New York. I know you are due sometime... Oh, my goodness! I didn't even ask! It's somewhere around this time, isn't it? That you are due?"

I swallow hard, my brain running different scenarios of how to play this.

"I am."

"When?"

"Two days ago," I blurt out without having figured out what to say next. At least, that's the truth.

"Oh, my goodness! Congratulations, Elizabeth! That is wonderful!"

I murmur thank you and answer some other questions when Laima Chirpyhead gets back to business.

"When do you think you will be up and running and can fly to New York?"

"I can't do this via email?" I ask hesitantly.

She laughs. "You could, but, well, considering the hefty advance, I'd like to do this in person," she says in a patronizing tone. "We will sit down with the publishing house representatives, go over the contracts, and seal the deal. There is no hurry. I understand your situation, the baby and all. But of course, we'd like to do that as soon as possible. We will, of course, pay for all the expenses."

There's silence again.

My head spins. Suddenly, a wild scenario unfolds in my mind. In fact, it's so ridiculous that it makes me laugh.

This lady doesn't know Lizzy in person. What I have in mind shouldn't be complicated. I know one thing for sure—never in my entire life has my heart beat as wildly as it does now. I've always wanted to have something special, something of my own. And I've never had an opportunity this big. No, no—this is giant! This will change my life. This will be my *new* life.

"Can we do it next week?" I ask, amused at myself.

"Oh... Oh! Well, absolutely! As long as you are... Yes, absolutely. Let's jump right on the hot train!" Laima-the-hustler laughs happily. "I just need a copy of your driver's license to book your ticket."

"I'll email you. Can you give me your email again? I seem to be having trouble with my login."

"Sure."

I grab the pen and paper next to the phone and write down what she dictates.

"All right, Elizabeth, we are all very excited to finally meet you and get your books into the hands of millions of readers."

The word "millions" rings in my ears, and I catch myself smiling.

"I will see you in New York next week, Elizabeth!"

Yes, I think to myself. Next week. In New York.

I will fly there. I will be Elizabeth Dunn. I will even stay with this doofus Ben until I can get rid of him. I will take care of the baby, too, if needed. I will do whatever it takes to get that money and the publishing deal.

There's only one problem.

I need to get rid of the real Elizabeth...

FORTY-ONE

TONYA

When I get back to the cabin, Ben's eyes light up with glee as if he just saw Santa Claus.

"Finally," he says, wrapping his arms around me.

It actually makes me smile. I like when he's affectionate. Also, I'm in the best mood ever.

"Go get the stuff from the car, and I'll check on the baby," I tell him.

He runs out of the house, as if happy to be anywhere but here.

I don't blame him. The baby is cute, sleeping. Tonight will be family reading night. I brought some baby books from Lizzy's place so we could learn new things about babies, because, yeah, we have a baby on our hands.

Lizzy is non-responsive. She doesn't even react when I walk into the bedroom. She is huddled on the bed, watching her own forefinger as it strokes and strokes and strokes the same tiny spot on the pillow fabric. It looks like the sedatives I gave her are working great.

I walk out, thinking that I will send Ben to feed her this time.

"We can't keep her here. She needs a doctor," Ben says

glancing at me from under his eyebrows as we unpack the groceries.

"She isn't bleeding. I checked. I will give her another bath and check again. She's eating liquids, so that's good."

"She needs help."

These annoying conversations never end.

"So, what do you want us to do, Ben? What if we take her to the hospital, and they blame us for the way she is? What then? I mean, what if they charge us?"

Ben almost drops the carton of eggs in his hands as he stares at me in horror. "What do you mean, they'll *charge* us?"

"Like, with non-premeditated harm or something, I don't know. What if it's illegal?"

"What is illegal?"

"To give birth like this?"

"You said it was fine."

"I said it," I say in a raised voice, "because we didn't have a choice, Ben. She was ready to pop out a kid. And then she was tired. And we were confused. And then she wasn't well. And... Now it might be too late."

"Fuck," Ben whispers and starts pacing around the kitchen, clutching his hair.

I wish he would man the fuck up.

"Smarten up, Ben. We need to go through that book deal. But first, we need to do something about the baby."

He stops, and his head snaps toward me. This time, he looks horrified.

"Do *what* about the baby?" he asks in a whisper.

It suddenly dawns on me, the realization so shocking that I start laughing. I laugh for a good half a minute then meet his eyes. "Register the baby, Ben. What else?"

He exhales so loudly that his entire body sags. He's clearly relieved, and I suddenly realize that his thoughts went in a totally different direction.

I step closer. "What was it that you thought, Ben?" I taunt him.

He doesn't think I'm that twisted, does he? I mean, Mrs. Cavendish who owned this house is one thing. She was old and a bitch. Plus, Ben doesn't need to know about that. But a baby is different. I mean, unless things go way south and we have to take extreme measures.

He shakes his head, looking around bewildered. "I... crazy thought... I ... I mean, this is already crazy, the baby and her... I..."

I step even closer, gently setting my hands on his shoulders. "We are not monsters, Ben. We are just desperate. And that's your daughter. We need to register her."

"But how are we going to bring Lizzy there and explain?"

"Lizzy will walk in and provide the medical records of her pregnancy to prove it. The baby was born at home, in an emergency situation."

Ben chuckles. "Yeah, okay. How is she going to walk in?" He tilts his head at the door of the room where Lizzy is. "She can't even put two words together."

"*That* Lizzy won't," I say, pointing at the same door. "But another Lizzy will."

I only smile when he looks at me bewildered, with that stupid sheepish look.

"You need to feed the baby," I prompt. "I got baby formula."

"How do I do that?"

"Read the instructions, Ben. There's something else I have to do."

Without another word, I walk to the bathroom and open the cupboard where I put one of my purchases. It's black hair dye, the shade called "Ultimate Intense."

Perfect.

An hour later, after I wash my hair, dry it, and straighten it, I take the scissors from the drawer and cut the front strands in one swift snap.

I stare in the mirror in satisfaction, smiling at the new bangs.

How did I not think of that before? The look suits me, it totally does. I just need to sharpen my brows. And—

I dig in the drawer and pull out something I only used at home, in moments like this, thinking what it would be like to be a femme fatale.

I apply the red lipstick to my lips, smack them together, and step away from the mirror to give myself a once-over.

A stupid chuckle escapes me, and in seconds, I can't stop my ridiculous laughter.

This is uncanny.

This is wrong.

And this feels so good.

Because the face staring at me from the mirror is a copy of Lizzy Dunn.

No, not a copy. It's the *new* Lizzy Dunn. The clean, confident, smart Elizabeth Dunn, ready to take the world by storm.

FORTY-TWO

BEN

I stay away from the bedroom as much as possible. Walking in there reminds me that despite this seemingly peaceful last week, something went horribly wrong there.

Lizzy is not Lizzy but an empty shell of a human. I'm not a doctor, and I don't know how to put this in words, but it's not just depression or tiredness. I think something glitched in her brain that night she bled for hours.

She never looks at me when I occasionally walk in to give her the baby or bring food. I'm glad she doesn't. Her vacant stare is haunting and creeps me out.

While I'm miserable, Tonya seems to be taking this complication quite well. She goes to town now and then, and I'm not even sure what she does there. I spend most of the time anywhere but in the room with Lizzy. I started taking the baby away from her more often. I don't trust Lizzy anymore.

It's been days of hell, mental and emotional.

"This is wrong," I tell Tonya one evening as we have dinner in the kitchen. This is one of many such conversations lately.

Tonya gives me a reproaching stare. "Should've been more

careful around Lizzy. If you hadn't gotten caught, she wouldn't have been here."

"Oh, it's my fault?"

"What, you think it's mine?"

"I didn't want to stay with her."

"Neither did I, Ben. But guess what? We need to live on something, and you don't have a job, and I'm not working as a waitress all my life while she"—she stabs her finger in the direction of the bedroom—"gets to live it up, write books, and make millions. She's a murderer. She killed Brandon and others."

I don't need a reminder of what Lizzy is capable of.

I glance at the baby in the bassinet. Mackenzie has been mostly quiet so far, sleeping, eating, sleeping, eating. I hate the smell of diapers. And the smell of the baby. But none of it is the baby's fault.

I turn my gaze to Tonya.

She looks different with her hair dyed raven black. There's quite a startling resemblance to Lizzy, if you look from afar—same hair, same body build. It's uncanny, and that feels wrong, too.

Tonya gets up from the kitchen table and goes to heat up the baby formula. "I'm taking the first shift with the baby tonight. So you can take a nap."

She says it with so much indifference, like this is our new normal. It slowly starts sinking in that maybe it is.

I hate this. The house, Lizzy in the bedroom like a zombie, the living room with two beat-up couches where Tonya and I sleep, the baby bassinet that we keep dragging around the house to keep an eye on little Mackenzie. I never wanted any of this.

But we just have to pull through, I suppose.

The next day, early in the morning, Tonya tells me that we are going into town.

"Both of us? What about—"

"The baby is coming with us."

Confused, I stare at her.

She meets my eyes. "What, Ben? We need to register the baby and the home birth thing. Surely, you don't think you can walk into the baby clinic with a baby but no mother. You suck at lying."

Before we leave, Tonya spoon-feeds Lizzy. I'm not looking, not even going into that room. I hear a muffled whimpering from Lizzy, but I don't want to see what's happening. This is wrong. But maybe Tonya is right. We messed up, and there's no way of fixing this except for going forward.

I take the baby outside, onto the porch, and watch her sleep until Tonya comes out.

My eyes widen at the sight of her. "Whoa."

She's quite a sight, all dressed up and wearing red lipstick. To anyone who didn't know Lizzy well, Tonya could totally pass as her.

We lock the house, then prop the door with an additional panel in case Lizzy tries to escape, though I don't think she's capable.

Before pulling away from the house, I throw another glance at the boarded-up door. Suddenly, it dawns on me that we are not simply waiting this out. We are keeping Lizzy prisoner.

FORTY-THREE

BEN

We stop by the college, and Tonya goes to the internet café to check her email. She comes back beaming. "I'm flying to New York in four days. Got my tickets."

Excitedly, she shakes the printouts in the air.

I don't respond. This is insane, but Tonya might be the only one who can pull off the fake identity with the publishing people she's flying to meet.

Next, we pull into the back street of our apartment building and run straight into a bunch of police cars.

Instantly panicking, I slam on the brakes. My first thought is that we are caught. Someone is looking for Lizzy and the baby.

"Drive slowly," Tonya orders calmly. "Drive past the entrance and look normal."

As we do, we see Grunger, our super, handcuffed, being dragged into a police car, while officers and a K-9 unit swarm the entrance.

"I guess, we'll have to stop at the apartment a little later," Tonya says, craning her neck to see what's happening through the back window as we drive off.

"Why would the K-9 unit be there?" I muse, uneasy.

"Drugs, probably."

"I thought there was something iffy about that super. Never liked him."

"Well, I guess he finally got caught."

I can't help but notice a gloating smile on her lips. Tonya has a good sense of people, and she doesn't like criminals.

To avoid someone recognizing Tonya or me, we drive for over an hour to the next town to register the baby. The Vital Records office asks for Lizzy's medical paperwork when she was pregnant. Tonya brought it all with her. How she knows all these things is beyond me.

Don't ask me what people think when they look at two twenty-two-year-olds who had a home birth. There are questions. There is more reproach than suspicion. There are tips and lectures, of course. An elderly lady at the Vital Records registry coos to the baby and tells us what to do next, that the baby has to be checked by the doctor, and so does the mother.

Obviously, Tonya will never go for any checkups, though she stops at the local baby clinic to make an appointment.

When we stop at the apartment later that evening, Grunger's apartment door is taped with police caution tape.

"Tough luck," Tonya says.

I personally think that luck is definitely karma. How we didn't get caught yet is beyond me.

I call my parents and tell them the news about the baby.

"Lizzy is a trooper," Mom says, excited about the baby.

I tell her about Lizzy—and that's when I almost say Tonya's name then correct myself—flying to New York. Mom asks to speak to her. That's certainly a good sign. An even a better sign is that they talk for half an hour while I'm feeding and changing the baby.

Tonya sounds deliberately tired and exaggeratedly timid to confuse Mom with her voice. She is a good actress. This should feel wrong, but I'm happy Mom is talking to the girl I love.

When Tonya hangs up, satisfaction is written all over her face. "I think we should move to the East Coast as soon as possible," she declares.

I agree. We already discussed that.

"Your Mom said she will help with the baby and everything. I think it's a good idea."

What she doesn't say is what exactly is going to happen to Lizzy. The *actual* Lizzy.

I don't ask. I'm afraid of the answer. But I know something will have to be done about the lake cabin and Lizzy and Tonya and me and the baby.

On the way home, Tonya cranks up the radio and sings. There's a smile on her face, the one I fell in love with—so damn confident like the whole world belongs to her. She looks gorgeous, and I wish we didn't have that *Lizzy thing* hanging over our heads.

"How long are we doing this?" I ask Tonya cautiously.

She shrugs. She always does, with that ease as if nothing is a problem.

"Forever," she replies, leaning over and wrapping her arms around me. Then she turns to the back seat and coos to the baby.

I can't look away. I wish Tonya and I were a family.

But there's an unanswered question here.

"What are we doing about Lizzy?" I insist. "What's happening next?"

"Who?" Tonya lifts her innocent eyes at me, and for a second, I stall.

But she bursts out laughing. "*I* am Lizzy."

"Well, yeah, right now, but—"

"Ben." Her expression changes into a slightly angry one. "Don't be stupid. *I am* Lizzy, okay? You better learn that and be able to say it in your sleep."

"Okay, but..." This is messed up. We can't possibly keep this up for long. "What about her?" I nod in the vague direction of somewhere up the road, by the lake.

Tonya's expression changes into one that I don't like. Sometimes, it makes me think twice about ever crossing her path.

Her face looks somewhat sinister. Her smile is gone when she says, "We need to get rid of her."

FORTY-FOUR

BEN

Four days later, I take Tonya to the airport.

She looks stunning.

"Wish me luck." She kisses me so passionately at the terminal that I almost believe that everything will somehow work out. Until she adds, "When I come back, we'll deal with her."

There goes my good mood.

I get home later in the afternoon but stand by the porch for some time, holding the baby bassinet and unable to force myself to walk in. This cabin used to be our happy getaway. Now it feels like a prison.

A crazy thought crosses my mind—I should bring Lizzy into town, to the hospital, tell them what happened, and deal with what may come. Whatever Tonya means by "getting rid of her" scares the shit out of me.

Eventually, I unboard the front door of the cabin and walk in.

Every time I do, my knees are weak as I expect to see Lizzy dead. But when I enter the bedroom, she's still where we left her, this time sitting with her one arm wrapped around her knees brought close to her chest, rocking and drawing invisible patterns on the sheets with her other hand.

She doesn't react to me or Tonya anymore. Only when she hears Mackenzie squeak, she turns her face in her direction. When I let her hold the baby, in her most present moments, Lizzy cradles her and murmurs something, some word on repeat that doesn't make sense. I think the word is "petal," whatever that means.

What Tonya contemplates doing with Lizzy scares me. "Get rid of her" doesn't mean a hospital.

I stay in a gloomy mood for several hours. It's so quiet in the house that it kills me. I hate being here when Tonya is gone. Guilt eats at me every time I think about why Lizzy is the way she is.

Then paranoia sets in.

First, I think about what might happen if Tonya leaves me. What if she never comes back from New York? I'll be stuck with Lizzy and the baby by myself, having to deal with the consequences.

Then I realize that Tonya would never do that. She loves me. She sacrificed a lot by letting me live with Lizzy while we were trying to work out a plan. Plus, Tonya can't pretend to be Lizzy unless I'm by her side.

I go to the kitchen and take a bottle of whiskey from a cupboard. I pour myself a glass, then another, and before I know it, I'm feeling pretty good.

That's when terror suddenly kicks in, making my thoughts go in circles.

We can't get rid of Lizzy. We can't. That's just... horrible. We can't.

I convince myself that nothing bad will happen if I take Lizzy to a doctor. After all, she might never come to fully, right? I should do this. That's the right thing.

By the time I finish another glass of whiskey, I have fully settled on the idea that I'm taking Lizzy into town.

I barge into the bedroom and pull Lizzy by the arm.

"Come on, Lizzy."

Her eyes snap to the part of her arm where I touch her, then shoot up at me in panic, and she starts yanking her arm away.

"We gotta go. Gotta go to town. Now!" I insist and grab her harder, trying to pull her up, but she starts fighting me off, making that bizarre, muffled sound like a cornered animal.

Nothing I do makes her get off the bed, so I give up.

She's crying. I bring the baby, and she sets her eyes on her, and finally the emptiness in them somehow morphs into tenderness as I let her hold Mackenzie.

Fucking fuck.

After some time, I take the baby away from her, put the baby into the bassinet, and leave the house.

The house suffocates me. For the first time, I feel bad for Lizzy, for what happened to her while giving birth. And I really can't go ahead with whatever Tonya suggested. No way.

This time, I don't board up the door, don't even lock it. I carry the baby with me to the lake that's only a two-minute walk from the house, set the bassinet some distance away from the water, and walk into the lake, just like that, in my clothes.

I dive into the water, then choke a little as I pop above it.

I should've brought the bottle of whiskey with me, because I'm drunk but not drunk enough. I can't wipe away Tonya's cheerful smile and her sinister words, "We have to get rid of her." I can't unsee the bloodied bed from when Mackenzie was born. I can't unhear the animal whimpers Lizzy makes when I touch her.

I can't undo the mess that we created.

I dive in again, and this time, I wish that some giant nasty fish would attack me and end my life.

Tonya told me about the local legend once.

Turns out, this lake accommodates a permanent community of garfish, which are rare. They are ugly-looking creatures that can grow up to 300 pounds. Monsters with sharp teeth like the one on the stupid turn sign by the main road.

There's a story behind it.

As per the legend, centuries ago, there used to be a small Native American settlement here with just several dozen inhabitants. Marauders came by and raped women, beat up men, killed the stock, ate and drank for two days, then, drunk, went into the lake for a night swim. None of them were seen again. Only the villagers fished out their clothes in pieces for days afterward.

The garfish, they said, were protecting the lake and those who lived off it. But garfish don't eat or attack men. Except for those in the legends.

I wish they did now. I wish a vicious gar would come upon me and chew me up with its sharp teeth and put an end to it all.

I dive again and hold my breath under the water. I wish I could drown. If I drink more and swim far enough, I probably could.

When I can't hold my breath, I finally swim to the surface, cough and spit out water, then hear a meek sound.

It's the baby, Mackenzie. She can barely open her eyes, but she's smiling at me, I think, from her bassinet.

I listen to her helpless cooing, and I can't hold back anymore. Tears start rolling down my cheeks. I lift my face to the night sky and roar like an animal.

I've let Tonya be in charge this long. And I'm going to let her do what she wants. Because, at the end of the day, it's me, her, and Mackenzie, and that's all that matters.

Lizzy? She is the unfortunate one. I wish I didn't have to hurt her. But sometimes, life requires sacrifices.

FORTY-FIVE

BEN

Two days later, I pick up Tonya from the airport.

She's beaming when she flings herself into my arms at the terminal.

"Whoa." She pulls back, studying me in surprise. "You smell like you drank everything we had in the house."

But she smiles again instead of lecturing me.

It's raining. The summer air smells like acid and blooming trees, and it's sweaty as hell.

"You should've seen it, Ben! The city! The lights!" Tonya tells me as we get on the road. "The building? Their office was on the twenty-first floor! Twenty-first!"

She motions the number with her fingers, her eyes wide in awe.

I can imagine. For a moment, I'm happy that she's happy. Where she just came from sounds like a different world.

Then I remember that it's all a scam.

"The whole pregnancy thing worked out perfectly!" she says. "There was something in the manuscript that they wanted to change, and I had no clue. I apologized and blamed it on the fogginess of my brain because of the pregnancy and giving birth, blah, blah, blah." She laughs cheerfully. "You should've seen their faces! They were so apologetic like they wanted to sink through the floor. Come to think of it, I can probably use that pregnancy excuse for months. In case, you know, we have any irregularities in our story."

My mood instantly falls.

Months?

She talks about it all like it's nothing.

"We have two book deals," she continues. "And then we'll think of something. If anything, I'll just have writer's block for the next decade."

She thinks that this will actually work?

"Decade?" I murmur. "Tonya..."

As much as I want to be with her for the rest of my life, I thought this New York publishing stunt was a one-time thing.

"They say the money will be transferred to our bank account within ten business days or so." Tonya doesn't even pay attention to me. She takes a pocket mirror out of her purse and checks her lipstick as she keeps talking. "Which means, as soon as we get it, we can move to the East Coast. And we don't have to live at your parents'. We'll rent something. Something nice."

Tonya keeps chirping as I drive, while I feel my insides turn the closer we get to the gar-sign turn. If she's talking like we are already together, then...

What about Lizzy?

"Tonya," I say louder.

She turns to me, her eyes blinking innocently as she cocks her head.

I mean, this is already bad. Lizzy needs professional help. I was a nervous wreck in the past two days thinking of how this will all turn out.

"What about Lizzy?" I finally say.

Tonya keeps staring at me as I glance between the road and her. She doesn't say anything, doesn't look away, and I can see the minuscule second-by-second changes in her face that eventually turns into a hard mask.

"We talked about it, Ben," she grits out. "I told you"—she punctuates every word—"that we will have to get rid of her."

"Tonya—"

"Don't Tonya me. Forget about that name. You know what has to happen."

The next time I glance at her, she's still staring at me, but there are no emotions in her eyes, just that intense stare, cold and calculating, that makes my skin crawl.

There is no reasoning with her. The first time she came to the cabin from town, right after Mackenzie was born, she brought books from the library. She even showed me the articles that talked about irreversible brain damage after complications with birth.

Now, her words ping in my head like bright red flashes. I'm already a criminal for going along with what she did. A criminal for lying about who she was when we filled in the birth info for the baby. A criminal for being in the bank with her while she put some cash into Lizzy's—now her—account.

"She is a looney-tune, Ben. She's not Lizzy. Not anymore. But someone has to be, because someone has to take care of the baby."

She motions to Mackenzie in the back seat, for the first time bringing her up during this ride.

"If you don't want to go to prison and want this to work out and have a good living that you deserve—we *both* deserve it—then man up," she snaps and looks away out the side window. "She has to disappear," she adds.

I feel like screaming in helplessness. When I spot the gar-sign and turn into the lake road, dread comes back again with a vicious thud of my heart against my chest.

When the car rolls onto the clearing in front of the cabin, I think I might be having a panic attack.

I've felt this for days, and that same nasty feeling twists inside me when I take Mackenzie out of the car seat, transfer her into the bassinet, and Tonya and I step onto the porch.

Bile rises to my throat when we walk into the house. Soon, another crime will be committed, and I don't know how to stop it, don't know if I can go through with it, but I know for certain that Tonya will.

When we step into the kitchen, I immediately spot an unfamiliar piece of paper on the kitchen table.

"That wasn't here before," I say, setting the bassinet down and walking over to pick up the paper.

It's some nonsense, scribbled words and phrases. I can make out sentences, but they are nothing more than quotes from some fantasy books.

"What is this?" I murmur.

"Ben!" Tonya calls from the living room.

When I walk in, Tonya is reading a piece of paper she holds in her hands. There are two more on the couch, another one on the wooden coffee table.

Where did these come from? Did someone break in?

Tonya lifts her eyes at me, and they burn with that same awe as they did when she read Lizzy's first manuscript.

"Someone has been out and about," she says with a little snarl in her voice. But it's not angry. It sounds... excited.

She walks toward the bedroom and throws the door open. "Holy shit..."

I walk up from behind and stall, looking around the room.

There are dozens of pieces of paper lying around. Books are pulled from the bookshelf, pages ripped out of them, the blank ones written and scribbled on.

Lizzy is crouched on the bed, scribbling something on another piece of paper.

"She went nuts, completely nuts," I whisper.

My heart squeezes hard at the sight, then thuds in panic when

232

Tonya starts taking steps toward the papers on the floor and picks one up.

"I think she's writing some bits of her memories of those fairy tales she started some time ago. Except"—she frowns—"these are some dark things, Ben. Yeah, I think she's going mad."

Horrified, I refuse to meet Tonya's eyes. Now, Lizzy definitely doesn't have a chance.

My knees grow weak. I want to run away. I don't want to see what happens or what sick plan Tonya will come up with for Lizzy.

Except, when I finally raise my eyes to Tonya, she is smiling. One by one, she picks up the papers, carefully reading every single one.

"You know what? This is good," she murmurs.

My eyebrows start crawling up. "Wh-what?"

"This is very good." Tonya chuckles. "She is not so useless after all." She walks to Lizzy and strokes her hair. "Hey, Tonya, this is good, very good," she says.

Tonya?

Lizzy doesn't respond.

A sick feeling gathers in the pit of my stomach at the words. She calls Lizzy Tonya. This is messed up.

"This is very good," she repeats. "Can you write more? A lot more?" She pets Lizzy's head like a puppy. "Good girl. I'll get you more paper and stuff. This is brilliant."

Tonya lifts her eyes at me. I can tell she is already thinking of something. And I've never felt so sick at the realization of what she has planned for us for years to come. But what she says next is somewhat of a relief. At least, in regard to Lizzy.

"Ben, I think we've found our golden goose." She smiles. "I think we might just have to keep her for a while."

PART 3

NOW

FORTY-SIX

MACKENZIE

My parents' past is like cancer that eats me out from the inside and poisons my thoughts.

Dianne Jacobson invites us to stay overnight at her house. We can't stop talking. There is too much to discuss, the revelation about my mother, or two of them, too shocking for me to process.

We talk about what could've gone down twenty-one years ago. I show Dianne Mom's letters.

"What can you do?" Dianne asks after reading them. "Who will believe you that the woman who raised you is not the actual Elizabeth Dunn? Whatever they did with Lizzy can't be proved."

"This is so messed up," EJ keeps saying.

We are about to go to bed, crash in Dianne's spare room, when she calls out to me.

"About that barn fire." She looks uneasy, like she regrets she said what she did, but is about to say more.

I've come to believe in the short day we've spent here that Dianne is a woman who knows a lot more than she leads us on to believe.

"The night of that barn fire, I was working the night shift," she says. "I saw Lizzy sneaking back in around midnight, shaking like a leaf, looking over her shoulder like she was being followed. Lizzy wasn't the type, though. Not the type to hurt anyone. Now Tonya —that one was a different story. She was trouble, through and through. There was something dark about her, right to the core. They have a fancy word for it nowadays—sociopath. No regard for right or wrong. That's her."

I don't need to know more about Tonya. I already know what she was. The thought that she raised me makes my stomach turn.

"About an hour after Lizzy came in," Dianne carries on, "I saw Tonya creeping back into the house from the direction of the barn. That one wasn't scared. She was slick, like an eel. That one knew what she was doing. When we found those three boys, I knew both girls were mixed up in it somehow. But I couldn't tell on Tonya without telling on Lizzy, and that sweet girl didn't need any more trouble. Not over those three bastards. So, I left it at that."

I feel the weight lift off my shoulders. I needed to hear that.

Dianne nods repeatedly. "If you ask me, whatever went down, your mama wasn't the one to blame."

"Thank you," I say, but then my feelings get then best of me, and I walk up to Dianne and give her a hug.

I barely sleep that night. We don't say a word when Dianne sends us on our way in the morning. I barely talk to EJ on the plane. The pity in his eyes when he looks at me is now permanent. So is the cautious undertone in all his words, like I'm a cancer patient dying.

Two days later, I am at EJ's apartment. We order takeout from a Thai place. We talk about trivial stuff, anything but my parents. My thoughts are getting darker and darker. I can't stop thinking about Mom. My *real* mom.

I poke a piece of curry chicken on my plate with a fork, wondering how they did it, where, when. *They* being my dad and the woman who raised me. How could a person simply disappear off the face of the earth, and no one cares?

"Kenz, you need to eat," EJ prompts me.

"I'm not that hungry."

"You've said that for two days. But you—"

"EJ, just don't, please..." I shake my head, drop my fork onto the plate, and lean back against the couch.

EJ sets his plate on the coffee table. "Listen. Dianne was right. There's not much you can do right now. Your mom, I mean, the woman who raised you, she is dead. Your biological mom is gone. If you—"

He ruffles his hair, thinking what to say next as I watch him.

He's trying hard to be supportive, and I appreciate it. He has more logical ideas than me. He agreed with Dianne that this is a situation not easily resolved, if resolved at all.

"She was cremated," Ben says. *She*, that's what we call Elizabeth Casper, the one who pretended for over twenty years. "Still, there are traces of her in your house that can work for a DNA exam. The only thing it will prove is that she is not your biological mother. There's no way to locate the remains of your real one."

I flinch at the word remains.

He notices. "Sorry. But that's the problem. If they were to... I mean, police, they might try to determine if Elizabeth Casper was not Elizabeth Casper. There would be an investigation. But if your dad doesn't crack, and he denies everything, they can't prove shit. That will only create chaos. The whole world will be after you. You realize this, right? It will ruin your family and probably your future. Paparazzi will be all over you. At the end, it might just become a giant nightmare for you with no way to turn back time."

For the longest while, I just stare at him.

I want to say thank you for being here for me. But mostly, that I am so-so sorry I dragged him into this. There is no way to cut EJ loose from all of this. He'll have to keep it secret, and that's a lot to ask from a person who has nothing to do with my family.

"So, we just leave it at that?"

His expression becomes pained. "I don't know, Kenz. I don't know. I'm sorry, but I just don't know what to do."

I bring my backpack to the couch and pull out the letters. I've reread them so many times, I think I know them all by heart. For weeks, I tried to reconcile the girl in the letters with the woman who raised me, picking the writing apart, marveling at the wording, cherishing the little words she called me. *"Petal."* No wonder I've never heard it from the woman who raised me.

I unfold the last letter page.

"Listen to this," I say to EJ as I start reading it out loud. *"You are a beautiful, beautiful girl."*

Tears well up in my eyes that very instant.

"Kenz," EJ whispers. "You are torturing yourself."

I smile bitterly but can't stop. *"I can already feel it. Soft lashes, fluffy hair, the breeze catching in its"*—I pause to hold back a sob, and the page gets blurry as I blink and tears starts spilling—*"in its strands as the sun glistens in your eyes."* I sniffle and sob, then continue in a shaky voice. *"Your smile that shines onto others."* I lift my eyes to EJ. "She wrote this to me. I wasn't even born yet, and she wrote this to me. My *real* mother."

Another sob escapes me.

"I'm sorry, Kenz."

"You know what the worst part is? I realize she didn't write those to me. She didn't mean to tell me her secrets."

"What do you mean?"

I shake my head, staring at the letter. "No, she didn't. She never meant for these pages to see the light of day. She was talking to me while I was inside her. Because..." The thought makes me so sad that I sob and blink, and the tears drop onto the page. "Because she went through so much. She fell in love with a man who betrayed her. She was with child, scared, losing her mind. But in the end, she was lonely, EJ." I lift my eyes to him, and I don't even care that he sees this mess of me as I'm about to lose it. "She was so lonely that the only way she could cope with it was to write letters to her unborn child and have a conversation that way."

A loud sob escapes me, and I finally break down crying.

In a second, EJ is next to me, his strong arms wrapping around me and pulling me close to him, tightly, rocking me like I'm a helpless child.

And I feel it, the helplessness so profound that I want to scream and lash out and break things and yell at those who were part of this betrayal decades ago.

"If you ever need to talk to someone, Kenzie, you know I'm always here for you, right?"

Another sob rips out of my chest.

"Right? Say that you know that."

"Y-yeah," I blurt out.

I cry for the longest time. EJ doesn't say a word, only keeps me tightly against him.

Finally, I pull back and look away, wiping my wet face. "Sorry," I murmur. "I had a little breakdown."

"It's all right."

EJ leans with his forearms on his knees so he can look into my face.

I smile through tears. "Got your hoodie all wet." I sniffle.

"Any time. It's at your service."

We both chuckle and sit in silence for a minute until I know I can talk without sobbing.

I roll my lips between my teeth as I finally look at AJ. "I think I am going to confront my dad."

EJ looks at his hands he rubs together. "I think it might be a bad idea, but if that's any type of closure, sure."

"Yeah."

"Just... Just make sure you don't sound too crazy when you talk to him."

There's a warning in his voice that makes me suddenly too uneasy. "Why? What do you mean?"

He looks at me hesitantly. "I mean, I watched plenty of documentaries and whatnot. When someone starts wild accusations..."

He doesn't finish but slowly raises his eyebrows at me.

"And?" I prompt, still confused.

"And they get locked up in a psych ward or a rehab center."

"Are you kidding me?" Shocked, I get up, wiping the rest of the tears off my cheeks.

"I just don't want anything crazy to happen to you."

We both stare at each other for a moment, and I let the realization sink in—my dad might be capable of anything.

"I'll be all right," I say, though now I'm not sure. "You are a witness. You know the story. I'm just going to drive home and see how many lies Dad can pull off until he cracks."

EJ throws his head back in resignation, but he knows he can't argue.

You are strong-headed, Dad once said. *Like Mom*. Oh, the irony!

You are talented just like your mom, they said. Finally, the words make sense.

But only that liar, my father, knows the true meaning of those words. It's time to confront him.

As I walk out of EJ's apartment, his warning flickers in my head, "Be careful."

I'm so nervous that I want to vomit. At this point, I clearly understand that I might be in danger.

FORTY-SEVEN

I'm getting into my car when my phone beeps with an alert for the house gate entrance.

I ignore it. If my dad is not home, I'll wait for him. I'll wait until he comes back, probably drunk, and then I'll find out what I want. In fact, going into my mother's office with what I know now is a good idea. I'll be able to look at her paperwork with fresh eyes.

I am only five minutes into the drive when the same notification beeps on my phone.

Another minute goes by, and my phone beeps again.

Then, two minutes later, it beeps once more.

That's too frequent in such a short time, and it's suspicious.

Feeling impatient, I pull over at a shopping plaza and fish my phone out of my pocket.

The "events" folder in the motion recordings app shows multiple recent activities.

It's not my dad's car but my grandmother's that goes through the gate the first time.

"What the hell..."

Grandma never comes to town without letting me know.

The next recording shows a car leaving. It's an old Volkswagen

—Minna's. Strange, considering my grandma likes to be waited on, but apparently, she dismissed Minna early.

The next car, a red Lexus—and there is no mistake here—belongs to Laima. I've seen it many times before. What the hell is she doing there?

The next one is a pickup I don't recognize, so I switch to the main entrance camera.

8:01 Grandma arrives at the house, by herself, without Grandpa.

8:08 Laima Roth strides in.

At 8:14, a man parks the white pickup and enters the residence. Despite the fuzzy recording and his face hidden by the baseball hat, I recognize that hat—it's the man from the memorial service, the same one from the picture in Mom's office.

Odd.

I don't know what's happening, but it's suspicious. Why would my dad, grandmother, a literary agent, and a man who potentially had an affair with Mom have a meeting at our house?

I drive as fast as I can to my parents'. An hour later, I walk into the house that's quiet except for the strained voices in Mom's office.

I know an argument when I hear one. It sucks that the office is well soundproofed, so I have to press my ear to the door to actually make out what they are saying.

There's Laima's high-pitched voice, "What does it even mean?"

There's Grandma's, "No need to be—"

"This is fucking outlandish!" That's Dad. "You are a scumbag!"

"Stop! Just... Calm down!" Grandma snaps.

"You can all go fuck yourselves," an unknown male voice says.

"Pardon me?" Laima is almost screaming. "Who do you think you are?"

"Especially you, Benny-boy. You're fucked. It's only a matter of time. All of you! Trust me!"

"Get out of my fucking house!" Dad roars.

I've never heard Dad roar.

There's the sound of a muffled struggle, then a woman's squeal, and devilish laughter, so cheerful and careless that it's garishly out of place.

The footsteps approaching the door from the inside are so quick that I barely have time to dash toward the corner and hide behind it when the door flies open.

"Bye, Felicia!" the man says with a cackle, and when I look from behind the corner, I see the guy with the baseball hat walking toward the entrance door. Without turning, he sticks both middle fingers in the air. "That's the new deal."

When the door slams behind him, I tiptoe toward the office and bump into Laima.

"Jesus!" Her glare at me is far from friendly. So much for diplomacy since her cash cow, E.V. Renge, slipped and fell.

Laima marches toward the door, her high heels viciously clicking against the parquet floor.

"Sort that out!" she shouts, not turning back. "Whatever that is! I'm not coming back until that animal is out of the picture!"

Where did all the manners go?

I would've mused and laughed at whatever just happened if I didn't have more pressing things to discuss with Dad.

I walk into the office slowly. And there's a surprise sight.

Grandma is sitting in Mom's chair. I mean the chair that belonged to the woman who used to be the queen of the house. But it seems Grandma is very comfortable, like she is in charge, like she belongs in that chair.

Dad is sprawled on the couch, both hands rubbing his face.

Grandma's head snaps in my direction. "It's a bad time, dear. Please, leave us."

What happened to "hello"?

"I didn't know you were in town," I say, taking slow steps forward.

"I had business to sort out." She gives me a fake smile. "Your dad and I still need to talk. Please, give us a moment."

She dismisses me with a careless flick of her wrist that makes me angry.

I don't budge. "Who was that man?"

She exhales in irritation, tapping a pen on the desk. "Mackenzie, some things are none of your business."

"Oh, I think they are," I argue, walking up to the couch and pausing in front of Dad. I cross my arms over my chest, trying to subdue the nervous tremors in my body. "That was the same guy you argued with at the funeral, wasn't it?"

Dad slowly lowers his hands from his face and raises his eyes at me.

"He did no such thing, dear," Grandma intervenes.

"Actually"—I turn to look at her—"I wasn't talking to you, Grandma. I need to talk to Dad. I'd like to know who that man is. And while at it"—I turn to look at Dad again—"you can tell me what happened to Mom."

The confusion on Dad's face is unmistakable.

"My real mom," I add.

Dad's face changes so drastically that I want to laugh at how easy it was to catch him.

When I flick my eyes to Grandma, she sits with her eyes closed, her lips pursed in that way that I know all too well. My super-composed, super-diplomatic grandma is about to lose her shit. And it won't be pretty.

"I know the woman who raised me wasn't my mother," I say, watching both their faces.

"Oh, dear." Grandma sighs, gets up abruptly, and walks out of the office.

Dad helplessly watches her like an abandoned puppy, then turns his eyes to me, and I swear, I've never seen him so scared.

"Talk," I order.

FORTY-EIGHT

"Kiddo, you are finally grieving," says Dad with a weak smile.

I almost choke at his answer. "Are you kidding me?"

Not that I didn't expect him to try to weasel out of this conversation.

"Listen, Mackenzie, we have some issues right now, and it's not a good time for crazy accusations."

"Oh, really?"

"Yes. We have some... Let's just say there are people who are trying to take advantage of our grief. They are making outlandish accusations, spreading nasty rumors and whatnot. This—" He points vaguely around.

"Go on, Dad. This what? Who is the man who just left?"

"No one."

"Didn't seem like no one. He was at the memorial service. He is on that"—I walk to the shelf with the picture I saw him on, but it's not there. I stall for a second, then whip around to face Dad. "You know that man. Don't deny it. He was just here. What did he mean by '*You are fucked*'?"

"Mackenzie!" Dad gives me a reproachful stare, but it's fake, all so fake, this trying to draw attention away from the topic.

"I heard him, Dad. What did he mean?"

"He is one of the people who tried to blackmail us."

"For what?"

"Just... An absurd accusation against your mom. And your mom was an exceptional woman, a brilliant talent—"

"Stop it, Dad! You are clearly trying to avoid the topic."

"Mackenzie, please."

The sound of the heels clacking against the floor makes me turn around.

Grandma is walking in with two wine glasses filled with wine. She offers one to me. "Here, dear, have some."

"I don't drink, Grandma."

"It's just wine. It will calm your nerves. Sit down and relax."

"I don't drink," I repeat angrily. "I just need to talk to Dad." I turn to him. "Back to my biological mom. Talk."

He sheepishly looks at Grandma, then back at me. "Mackenzie, I don't know who told you lies and where you got this—"

"Shut up, Ben," Grandma snaps from behind me so angrily that Dad flinches.

I turn around and come face-to-face with her. She stands so close to me that I shiver at the coldness of her eyes that are suddenly too hostile. Her mask just slipped, giving me a glimpse of who she truly is.

Grandma always reminded me of a hyena. Have you ever seen a picture of one? They look cute. Grandma is like a friendly hyena with snow-white short hair, red lipstick, meticulous makeup, all grace and elegance.

Have you seen a hyena bare its teeth? Its teeth can crush bones.

That's Grandma, again, whose kind smile can turn into a vicious scowl in the span of one second.

I've only seen it a few times. Once, when she argued with Mom. I felt bad for Mom then. Now? I think she deserved it, but that's not even the biggest revelation.

The biggest one is that Mom might have never been the queen in the house. Grandma was.

FORTY-NINE

"Take the glass, Mackenzie," Grandma says sharply. Her eyes bore into me as she pushes the wine glass into my chest. "Let's have a drink and a talk if you want to talk like an adult."

Fine.

I take the glass from her hand.

"Cheers." She clinks it with hers, then takes a sip.

I take one too. The wine is sweet and bitter. I don't care for booze, don't like it much, but I'll play along if it gives me the answers I'm looking for.

"Sit down, Mackenzie," Grandma orders and takes a seat across from Dad, elegantly crossing one leg over the other. In her dark woman's suit and turtleneck, she looks like a retired CIA agent. No wonder Dad always acted like a schoolboy around her.

I take a seat next to Dad.

"Have a drink." She raises her glass in the air. "You'll need it. I want to have a calm, serious conversation instead of you spitting out accusations."

She takes another sip, then another. I mimic her. *Fine.*

"I know the woman who raised me wasn't my biological

mother," I say, staring at her, trying to figure out what effect my words will have on her.

One corner of her lips tilts slightly. "Who told you that?"

I snort. "Does it matter?"

"It's nonsense. Whoever said it was just trying to mess with you, dear."

I force a chuckle, then take another sip of wine. Suddenly, it tastes so good. And it calms my nervousness. Especially from what I'm about to ask.

"Right. Then who is Tonya Shaffer?"

Right when I say it, I look at Grandma, not Dad. I wish I could get him alone. He's not a good liar. Grandma is a different beast altogether. I really need to know what she has to say. I wonder if she has a clue what happened in Old Bow twenty-one years ago.

Surprisingly, Grandma's lips tick in a smile. She shakes her head. "Tonya Shaffer was a nutcase."

The words surprise me, but I stay quiet, waiting for her to continue.

"She was a stalker. She was obsessed with your father and mother. And she did some crazy things because of that."

Grandma talks slowly, evenly. Her speech is thoughtful, and as I sip wine, I'm looking forward to hearing how she spins this story.

"Your father briefly ran around with her."

"Mom—" Dad protests.

"Shut up, Ben. She needs to know," she snaps in his direction, then turns her gaze to me and takes a slow sip of wine.

I mimic her. I thought this would be an angry talk. Instead, I'm much calmer than I expected. The wine hits my system, and I feel languid and dreamy.

"Yes, your father was not exactly an exemplary boyfriend," Grandma says with deliberate bitterness. "And yes, he ran around with that crazy woman who almost ruined his and your mother's life. For quite some time. Didn't you, son?"

"Bullshit," I call her out, and her gaze on me hardens.

That's a nice spin to the story. I'm surprised Grandma knows that many details. I want to laugh in her face, but I'm feeling dizzy and thirsty. More wine would help, but my glass is already empty.

"It's not," she says. "That woman dressed like your mother, acted like her. She went around Old Bow pretending to be her. Some people actually called her Elizabeth and thought she was indeed Ben's girlfriend."

Can't be...

Suddenly, I start questioning what's real and whether I made this whole false identity up. There are too many wild stories lately, but no proof of any of them.

"Your mother was a recluse. She hardly ever went out. That woman, Tonya Shaffer? She went as far as following Ben's friends to bars and introducing herself as Elizabeth. Oh, yes. A year later, half of Old Bow knew Elizabeth. Just not the Elizabeth that Ben was with."

My head starts spinning as I set the empty wine glass on the coffee table. My hand fumbles and I almost drop the glass.

I hardly ever drink. And this drink hit me fast. *Too fast.*

"Wait a second," I say, hearing myself slur. My heartbeat is suddenly in my head. "You're saying that—"

"I'm saying, dear, that Tonya Shaffer was a sick woman and did a lot of damage. It took a while to untangle her lies. But she got into an accident, and she was gone. Thank God."

"Wait-wait-wait. This doesn't make..."

I'm trying to say something else, something to contradict her, but the air seems to swallow my words. That could be a legit story if Dianne Jacobson, who knew both girls, hadn't recognized Tonya in the picture. Grandma doesn't know that, sneaky witch that she is. She thinks her botched story will fly.

Another thing bothers me—not a single time did Grandma call Mom Lizzy, though back in the day, she only went by her short name.

I want to laugh in her face, but my laughter comes out as a

whimper. I try to prop myself up off the couch, since I'm sinking into the pillows, but my hands are too weak. My head spins so fast that suddenly everything blurs before my eyes.

"Kiddo?" Dad asks. His face in front of me fades in and out of focus.

"Ben, leave her. Mackenzie, dear? Are you listening?" Grandma's voice is muffled, like a distant echo from a far-far away.

My eyelids are so heavy that I have a hard time keeping my eyes open. I need water. I need to stand up. I need to get out of here. I need to run away from this house.

But I can't even think, let alone move.

In seconds, I slip into darkness.

FIFTY

My head feels like it's splitting into tiny pieces when I try to move. Blood pounds inside my skull. I peel my eyes open and shield them from the bright sun streaming through the window.

It's morning. I'm in my underwear and T-shirt, in my bed, but I don't remember getting here.

Last night's events flash in my mind through a hangover-like fog.

Hangover, right.

I'm not sure what went down yesterday, but I don't have a freaking hangover. I was drugged. I know. I was spiked at a freshman party once. If it weren't for EJ, I would've probably gotten assaulted there and wouldn't even know about it.

Hence the reason I don't drink. I know exactly what it feels like the next morning after being spiked.

How much did I drink last night? One glass. Right, the wine Grandma served me.

The fragments of her story start popping in my mind. Tonya Shaffer. Stalking. Pretending to be Lizzy. Something else, some bizarre stories Grandma cooked up to trick me.

It would be all fine, but she doesn't know about Mom's letters. Or my trip to Nebraska to see Dianne.

Dammit, the letters...

For a moment, panic grips me until I remember that I left them at my apartment in town. *Phew*. Plus, I took pictures of all of them. Just in case. And I made copies at the University library and left them at EJ's. Again, just in case.

I look around my room and register the barely noticeable signs of disarray. Not a mess, per se, but I know when someone moves things around in my room.

My skin crawls—someone searched my room.

I grit my teeth in anger that quickly turns into gloat—I took Mom's original manuscripts to my place in town, too.

Another thought jolts me to sit up.

What if they get to my apartment? They have a spare key, I know Dad does, because he helped me move a new couch there several months ago.

I scramble out of bed and grab my bag, which is sitting on the desk—I never put my bag on the desk. I pull out my phone, swipe the screen, and stare at the message, *Incorrect password*.

Assholes. They tried to get into my phone.

I unlock the screen and dial EJ right away, and he picks up after one ring.

"Mackenzie, what the hell?" he says instead of a greeting. "I called you last night a dozen times, sent messages, thought about driving to your parents'. Are you okay?"

"Not sure. But listen, I need a favor. Are you busy?"

"Seriously? I just about lost my mind waiting for you to call back—"

"I'm fine, I'm fine, EJ! I need you to do something. Take your copy of my apartment key, go there, and take the manuscripts and letters and bring them to your place."

"Kenz?" There's worry in his voice.

"*Now,* EJ. Please."

"Are you all right though?"

"Yeah. I'm fine."

"Sure?"

"EJ, please! Just do it for me. Now! I have to go. Wait! Also, if I don't call you within two hours, call me yourself."

"You are freaking me out."

"Don't freak out. But if I don't answer today at all, get the cops. I gotta go. If everything is fine, I'll call you in two hours or so."

I hang up, quickly pull my jeans on, and walk out of the room. *Creep out* of it, to be exact, because I don't know what's on Grandma's agenda for me after she spiked my drink.

As I tiptoe down the stairs, I hear voices. Grandma is on the phone. Dad is on his cell phone, too—that's unusual, he never gets up before me.

I can smell food. *Good.* Maybe that means Minna is in the house. If she's here, Grandma won't try anything funny.

I tiptoe back into my room and think, think, think.

Yesterday's events replay in my head. Am I crazy? No, I know the letters I got were written by Mom and not the woman who raised me. Now that I think about it, they didn't sound like any of the words that I've heard growing up.

Okay, okay. Now. The only proof that I was raised by Tonya Shaffer is Dianne Jacobson. Unless I do a DNA test. For that, I need something that belongs to the woman who raised me.

Cremation was a smart move. If Elizabeth Casper wasn't Elizabeth, that was definitely a good way to prevent any exhumation for DNA testing.

My nerves on edge, I sneak down the hall to my mother's room.

She and Dad had separate bedrooms. I used to think it was weird. Again, now that I think about it, it makes sense. Her room is the size of four of mine, plus an adjoining room which was turned into a closet. Unlike her office, the room is all pearly colors with burgundy accents, a gold chandelier, and giant posters of Mom from her fashion photoshoots.

Her room has been left untouched since the day she died. I'm not a detective, but if what I know is right, I need her hair.

First, I go to the massive bureau. There's a collection of perfume bottles, makeup jars, and hair products. There are framed pictures of her for magazine photoshoots. This woman sure loved herself.

I spy a hairbrush. There are some hairs stuck in it. In one of the bureau drawers, I find a plastic bag with sponges, dump them out, and put the hairs from the brush into the baggie. Then I look into the little trash bin under the bureau. Bingo. More hairs go into the bag.

If that's not enough, I'll be screwed. So, I walk to the bathroom.

I've never done anything this cringy, but dire circumstances require dire actions. I crouch over the shower floor, inspecting it, and pull out a hairball stuck in the drain. Gagging, I put the clump in the same baggie. Then I inspect the bathtub, but that seems to have been wiped clean.

This is just in case, I tell myself.

Suddenly, another idea strikes me, making my heart race with adrenalin.

How did I not think of it before?

FIFTY-ONE

Back in my room, I lock the door and start digging in my desk drawers, pulling out my old school notebooks and everything I can find.

Where is it? Where is it?

I know I have it somewhere. I used to throw away that kind of stuff, but there are always random things accumulating in drawers for years.

I pull out a folder of my old high school paperwork and start feverishly flipping pages, going through papers, tossing them aside, rummaging through the old school composition books, exercise books, notes, letters, until I stumble on one. And that's all I need.

I close my eyes and thank the universe.

It's an absence note for when my mom yanked me to Key West for a week during high school. She set me up in a hotel, letting me watch cable and order room service while she disappeared for several days.

The absence note is handwritten. She wrote it in front of me, in a hurry, because for whatever reason, that trip was a last-minute deal. I never gave it to the teacher, though.

Now, I pull my phone out and open one of the letter snapshots then put it right next to the handwritten note to compare the handwriting.

My mom never wrote anything by hand—I've never realized that until now. I've never seen her write manuscripts. She never wrote letters. She never *wrote*, period. It always "happened" in her office, behind the closed door. Everything, I mean, *everything* was always done on the computer. Even her notes to me when I was in school were typed and printed. I thought she was a neat freak. Now I know she's been careful for decades.

And she screwed up, just this one time.

This school absence note might be one of the very few things that tell me she's not the one who wrote the manuscripts. She tried, oh yes, she tried to make her handwriting perfect, like it was in the manuscript. But I don't need to be a handwriting specialist to see that the capital letters don't have the same swirls, the small letters are more rounded, and her overall style is more slanted.

There's no mistake—this note was written by a different person than the manuscript.

I put the note into my backpack, next to the clear bag with her hair.

Now I just need to get out of this house.

A loud knock makes me jump.

"Mackenzie, dear, are you awake?"

Grandma's voice behind the door is syrupy sweet, but I know what she's capable of.

I grind my teeth to push aside the slight panic rising in my chest. "Yes, Grandma!"

She tries the door without waiting for the answer, but it's locked. "Can I come in?"

I march to the door and take a deep breath to calm myself. I can't show my anger or I won't get my way. And I *need* to leave this place.

Grandma is already fully dressed in a knee-length tailored

designer dress, makeup on, her red lipstick glaring at me like a stop sign. There's something about this family and red lipstick.

"How are you feeling, dear?" She smiles, studying me, but her voice is steel-cold.

"What happened last night?" I blurt, then curse to myself for being too straight-forward.

"Oh." Grandma scrunches up her pencil-line brows in pity. "I had to help you to your room, dear. I didn't realize that you were such a lightweight." A trill of her fake laughter cuts through my headache. "You were saying some nonsense, then you started slurring. Then we got you to the room, and you shut the door on us. Are you feeling all right?"

Her concern is so genuine that I almost forget the fact that I am by no means a lightweight. Whatever was in the wine she gave me last night knocked me out in less than ten minutes.

Grandma's fake smile is still aimed at me, her gaze unblinking as if she's trying to read my thoughts.

Dread spreads through my body, making my knees weak, but I manage a smile.

"I'm... No, not really," I say, theatrically rubbing my forehead. "God, I can't believe I got drunk." I look at her with as much naiveté as I can muster. "I still feel like I'm drunk. What was that nonsense I was saying last night?"

That trill of laughter from Grandma makes my blood go cold again. "Don't worry dear. A lot of people lately are spreading nasty rumors. We just have to stick together."

"Right. We have to," I echo. "I think... I think I need—"

"You need to get dressed and come downstairs. There's an important legal matter we need to sort out."

"Legal?"

"Yes!" She smiles broadly. "Your mother willed everything to your father, you know. We had a little talk, and we decided it was quite thoughtless on her part to leave you out of it. Your father and I decided it would only be fair to set up a trust fund for you."

My jaw drops. "A trust fund?"

"Yes."

"You mean money?"

"Yes, dear. That's what a trust fund means."

"And I can access it—"

"When you turn twenty-five."

I hold my breath. I hold it as long as I can so that I don't show how much I despise her right now and so I don't spit in her face.

It's a bribe. She knows that. So do I. She wants my silence for the next four years. And who knows what happens to that trust before that. More importantly, she doesn't even know what I know, but she's already cooked up this whole thing with Dad overnight.

That's fast.

I exhale, closing my eyes. "I think I'm unwell, Grandma," I say weakly to switch the topic and give her a pleading gaze. "And I have to go to class today. I really have to leave."

"Today?" Her eyes flash disappointment. "But, dear, today is the Tribute Ceremony at your university."

I completely forgot about it. "Right."

Grandma studies my outfit, jeans that I threw on and the T-shirt I slept in.

"Please, wear something appropriate to the ceremony," she says. "But before you leave, I need you to sign the documents."

"Does my trust fund require an NDA?"

Grandma smiles. "Of course. It's the money that comes from literary profits."

She doesn't say Mom's, because we all know by now that "Mom" means many things in this house.

"And please, join us for breakfast," she adds already turning on her heel and walking away.

Mom's words in the diary come to mind: *Your grandma is a bitch, petal.*

I grit my teeth.

Mom, you were wrong. Grandma is a monster.

FIFTY-TWO

"They are bribing me, EJ," I say, disheartened, as I pace back and forth in EJ's living room.

I finally made it out of my parents' house, but only after signing some paperwork Grandma and the family lawyer made me sign, of course.

EJ doesn't move, sprawled in his computer chair, his hands locked behind his head. Only his eyes follow me back and forth. On his coffee table is a stack of boxes—the manuscripts he brought from my apartment. *Good.*

"First, they tried to make it seem like I'm crazy," I explain. "Then Grandma decides to set up a trust fund for me. You know why? They are afraid that I will start talking to other people and ask questions. With that tribute, Dad is going to do a speech, accept the posthumous award for Mom. Grandma is going to be there, but of course, she doesn't want any unnecessary drama. Or me saying something that will be picked up by the press. To be exact, me saying *anything* suspicious about E. V. Renge for the next several years."

"Maybe they are trying to protect you?"

I stop in front of him, glaring. "Protect me? How about hiding a murder? Or worse."

I start pacing again.

"Snarky," he calls out, but I don't pay attention. "Kenz!"

I keep pacing.

"Dude, you are hyperventilating." He finally gets up and grabs me by my shoulders to stop me. "Relax."

"Relax?" Anger starts boiling inside me. "How about I walk onto that stage and tell everyone that my father conspired to kill my biological mother?"

"Be reasonable," EJ warns, not letting go of my shoulders. "Your grandmother tried to spike you. You need to be smart and keep quiet until you have more proof."

"How about I print posters saying, *Missing: The real E. V. Renge*, and plaster them all over the university campus, huh?"

EJ blurts out a short laughter, but his hands don't let go of my shoulders.

"You are freaking crazy," he says in a half-whisper. "That's why I love you. Come here."

He pulls me into a hug so quickly that I don't have a moment to object. And once he holds me tight against him, I don't want him to let go of me. He's my rock. Who would've thought that by the age of twenty-one, my rock wouldn't be my family but my best friend?

Though, the way his body feels against mine is not the way a best friend should feel. A best friend shouldn't feel like you want to get skin to skin with him, and then some.

"I was up all night," he says. "I was calling you on repeat like a maniac. It sucked. That feeling? That something happened to you? It was awful. Don't ghost me like that again."

"I won't," I say, my forehead against his shoulder as I breathe in his scent. "I didn't mean to."

"I know. Don't go to that tribute," he says softly, not letting me go, his cheek pressed against the side of my head. "Please, don't. I know it's your mom's tribute, or whatever, and your family is there. But they make you crazy. It's not worth it. I don't like seeing you like this. It reminds me of what your mom felt when she wrote those letters."

I shut my eyes tightly and hold my breath so I don't cry. I can't cry. I won't cry anymore because of *them*.

I tell EJ that I'll think about it, but when I leave his place, I already know that I'm going.

It's another event. Remember, everything that has to do with E. V. Renge is an event, right? Publicity, hence, money and ratings.

The Pearl Lecture Hall is packed. By the time the tenth speaker finishes the speech, the audience is restless. Most came because they are part of the college system. Many came because they expected some excitement. Without the actual E. V. Renge, the event is as dry as an overcooked TV dinner. Mom was a legend. Well, *that* woman was, anyway.

Dad's speech was the worst in my opinion. Maybe because the sound of his voice makes me cringe. Even his charming smile with deep dimples looks so fake these days. The smile ruined my mom, my *real* mom.

When the ceremony is over, it's the usual mingling party.

The hall—soon to be E. V. Renge Hall—is full of snakes. Look at them, flicking their tongues, veering among each other, talking, talking, talking, but essentially, waiting to snatch the profit from this event. Literary agents, PR people, the who-is-who of the university's upper echelon.

I stand at the back of the hall, hoping no one would spot me. I'm here to mess things up. Though the more I look at the indifferent crowd, the more I think it could backfire. My life is already hell. So is Dad's. I know it.

I catch sight of Professor Salma. She waves at me as she stands in a group of people. I wave back but turn away, not wanting to talk.

"Fancy seeing you standing at the very back," someone says from behind me.

I turn to see Professor Robertson. "Hi," I say weakly.

"Miss Casper, I was looking forward to hearing you speak." He smiles in that way of his that can calm storms or a lecture hall full of students.

"No, thank you. Not my cup of tea."

He stands next to me, facing the hall full of people, a suit jacket over a cashmere sweater and jeans, hands in his pockets.

"You might not realize it," he says, "but many people have great respect for your mother's works. It's not all fans and hyped-up publicity. Talent is talent. Sometimes it gets lost in the sea of everyday hustle."

Or criminal activities, I want to add.

I could tell him a thing or two about the talent being lost to the ruthless people, who turn out to be your family, but I bite my tongue.

"Your father seems proud," he says.

"My father is a liar," I snarl.

I don't care about explaining myself and don't look at him to see the effect my words had.

"Mackenzie, dear!" The familiar patronizing voice makes me tighten my fists in my hoodie's pockets.

Grandma sashays toward me in a lavish long-sleeved dress that cascades down to the floor and the jewelry that could blind the blind.

And she looks like she is on a mission.

FIFTY-THREE

"How come you weren't in the front row?" Grandma briefly scans my non-glamorous outfit. I know she's pissed at me for not dressing according to the dress code, but she hides it well. "We had a seat reserved for you."

Her observant gaze slowly glides from me to my professor.

"Professor Robertson," he introduces himself.

"Evelyn Casper, Mackenzie's grandmother," she says charmingly, shaking his hand.

For once, she is not introducing herself as the mother-in-law of the celebrated author, like she usually does.

"Is that Professor Robertson of social studies?" she asks hesitantly.

Ugh, not now, Grandma.

"Indeed," he says with a chuckle.

"Oh, then you are definitely her favorite professor."

"Is that so?"

I don't have to look at him to know he's smiling at me while I'm blushing.

There are different types of smiles. I notice my father in the crowd, shaking hands, and smiling, too. But his smile can kill—I know that.

Grandma notices me looking at him. Her eyes latch onto the professor. She knows how to network and make peace. She can be a perfect crisis manager.

"Professor, I would like you to meet my son. He is in charge of the E. V. Renge Trust. If you ever want to work with us, do any social studies, or whatnot, we would be delighted."

I look up at the professor to see him stiffen.

Oh, Grandma is trying to bribe him. Smart. I hate her for that, too.

She smiles at me, that fake smile that actually fools many people. I don't smile back but hold her gaze. And there's something of my mom's gaze in hers—cruelty. Not my biological mom, not the one who wrote the letters, but the woman who raised me, Tonya Shaffer.

She sets her palm on Professor Robertson's shoulder, oh, so, elegantly. "Please, give me a moment, I'll bring him here."

"I'm leaving," I hiss through my teeth, embarrassed. If Professor Robertson wants to kiss ass, that's his thing.

"Is something wrong?" he asks, studying me with concern.

I know that gaze—the lack of interest in me as soon as they get to talk to the actual celebrities. Not that my father has anything to do with the books, but he is the husband and—surprise-surprise—in charge of E. V. Renge's Trust. That's huge.

Suddenly, a thought comes to mind. I want to win this, for once. I want to show people how many lies and poison go into fame.

You just wait, Dad, I say to myself, watching Grandma apologize to the group Dad is talking to and leading him our way.

She beams like a Hollywood star. "Ben, dear, meet Mackenzie's favorite professor," she says as they stop in front of us.

"My pleasure," Professor Robertson responds, stretching his hand toward my father.

I watch Dad closely, waiting for some half-baked line, something to give me a reason to put him to shame. Just because. For what he did. I will never forgive him. I can't.

"Nice to meet you," Dad says with his well-practiced smile, but then something strange happens.

As he shakes hands with Professor Robertson, his smile starts falling, fast-fast-fast, until panic fills his face. It's so obvious that it's uncomfortable.

Grandma notices, too. "It's good to know Mackenzie has someone to look up to in school," she says and keeps pouring praises.

But I can't look away from my dad.

His smile is gone. His face turns ashen-white. Jerking his hand, he tries to pull it out of the handshake with Professor Robertson, but he can't.

I turn to look at the professor, but his gaze is calm, like nothing is wrong.

But there is.

I turn to Dad again. He's never been good at hiding his emotions. Mom, on the other hand? She was a pro. Their coverup, I'm sure, relied solely on her.

Dad finally gets his hand free with a rude jerk. "Excuse me, I-I... I have to talk to someone," he murmurs and walks away hurriedly.

Grandma stares him down, then turns to the professor. "My apologies. This is a busy evening." She gives me her signature snake smile then turns to him again. "I hope you have a great rest of the semester."

With barely noticeable stiffness, she walks away.

"What was that about?" I ask Professor Robertson.

"I'm afraid I have to go," he says and, without looking at me, walks out.

I stand dumbfounded. Puzzled, yes. Feeling angry—absolutely.

Knowing I didn't say what I wanted—no surprise here. Failing to confront the monsters—epic fail.

There is all sorts of wrong with my family's story, and I saw it all over my dad's face. Again.

What do you do when something is off? You chase it, in your mind, replaying it step by step.

Except this time, I start chasing Professor Robertson.

I see him veer among the people in the crowded lecture hall toward the exit door. I follow him through the main hallway and into the side entrance of the main campus. He marches through the parking lot, and there's nothing left of the calm man he was inside.

The wind jerks at his open suit jacket as he approaches his car. He pulls off his jacket, though it's cold outside, and tosses it inside the car. Angrily, he pushes the sleeves of his cashmere sweater up, then takes a cigarette out of his pocket, and lights it.

He looks stressed out, angrily flicking the cigarette ash onto the ground, then pushes his hair back.

I didn't know he smoked. I didn't know he could be like this—I flinch when he angrily bangs his hand on the roof of his car, then takes another nervous drag off his cigarette.

My heart is racing as I walk up to him. "Professor Robertson?"

He whips around, his irritated expression immediately softening as he recognizes me. "Miss Casper." He looks at his cigarette and drops it on the ground, putting it out with his shoe, then he smiles at me, though it's the first time his smile seems forced. "It was a nice tribute to your mother."

I've heard that already.

For several seconds, our eyes lock. I don't answer, don't look away, but try to figure out what this all means.

"How do you know my father?" I ask, probing.

"Pardon me?"

"My father. Have you met my father before?"

"A lot of people know your parents, Mackenzie."

269

Now, it's Mackenzie, so informal. But that's not the answer I was hoping for.

"Your mother had a lecture here." He sticks his hands in his jeans pockets and casts his eyes down.

Liar. He never went to that lecture, he told us so during the time when we were discussing my mother's books.

I need to walk away, but I can't. Something is off. I'm not an expert in people, but I might be one in secrets by now.

He exhales loudly but doesn't walk away either. It's an awkward moment, but I don't care. Stranger things have happened in my life.

"I should go. You should go inside," he says, finally meeting my eyes. "There are a lot of important people there. You should probably network."

He pulls one hand out of his pocket and rakes his hair.

That's when I see it, something that was always hidden by the long sleeves. Now that I think about it, Professor Robertson never wore short sleeves.

As I stare at his arm, my heart starts pounding so loudly that I feel like passing out.

This might be a coincidence, but I've never heard of anyone who has a scar on their forearm in the shape of a star.

Except one person.

FIFTY-FOUR

"Professor John Robertson," EJ reads the info off his computer screen.

"I know that, EJ. We need more!" Impatiently, I pace around the room while EJ tries to find more info online.

"Age, forty-six. Master's and PhD from Rutgers. Bachelor's in social studies from Manford College, Old Bow, Nebraska."

He looks at me over his shoulder, his eyes widening.

"Dammit!" I stop in the middle of the room and rub my face with both hands. "How? How is that even possible?"

EJ spins in his computer chair to face me. "This might be pure coincidence."

I glare at him. "Yeah? Really? You are going to be all logical *now*, Emerson?"

"Oh, big words." He wiggles his eyebrows at me for using his full name.

I roll my eyes. "I need his address."

"Kenz, what you're thinking of doing is—"

"What, illegal? Now you are going to preach about illegal stuff?"

"It's stalking at the minimum."

"I won't stalk him. I just need to talk to him. And I mean, *talk* to him. A crime was committed. Even if he doesn't know about what happened to Tonya, or Lizzy, he knows who is who. If he is *the* John, I'll find out. At this point, I don't even care if I sound ridiculous in front of a stranger."

EJ gets the address in seconds. Apparently, it's the easiest thing to do on the internet—get someone's deets, even if they are buried by the now-popular data removal companies.

Half an hour later, I park my car on the outskirts of town, by a small house in a nice neighborhood.

I recognize the professor's car from the parking lot earlier.

Good, he's home. Let's just hope I don't make a fool out of myself.

Determined, I walk up the steps to the porch and press the doorbell.

When he opens the door, there is no surprise on his face. Maybe guilt, maybe sadness. I don't know what that expression on his face is, but it's not shock. I think he expected me.

His head starts nodding just slightly. His mouth tilts to the side in some sort of contemplation.

He knows that I know. It's in his eyes that calmly keep mine hostage.

"Mackenzie," he says quietly.

"Professor." I nod. "I want you to tell me how you know my mother."

FIFTY-FIVE

If I told anyone at school that I was at Professor Robertson's house, by myself, having a chat, there would be a whirlwind of rumors and suggestive questions.

I sit on a leather couch in his living room and study him as he apologizes for the mess and picks up books and paperwork off the table and armchair. He doesn't know what a mess is. Besides the papers and books everywhere, his living room, with a bookshelf and a fireplace, is pristine.

He goes to the kitchen, brings a glass of water for me, and takes a seat on the armchair across the glass coffee table from me. He leans on his knees with his forearms and studies me with curiosity.

I can't take my eyes off him, studying his gestures and facial expressions. This is the man who was my mom's best friend. I can't even picture him being in his twenties.

He doesn't say a word, just looks at me inquisitively.

"You were my mom's close friend back in Old Bow," I say, starting from afar.

He nods. "How did you find out?"

I could lie and say that she told me this while she was alive. But then, I don't know if he knows anything about the creepy switch-up.

"I read her diaries."

He cocks a brow.

"And then I saw your scar." I motion with my eyes to his forearm, covered by a thin long-sleeve sweater.

"Right, the scar." His lips twitch in a smile, and instinctively, he rubs his right forearm with his left hand. "How do you know about that?"

"The diaries. Like I said."

"What else did the diaries say?" His gaze on me is unblinking.

"Some interesting stuff. You were close, you and her. Before my father showed up in the picture."

"Right."

"Why didn't you ever tell me?"

"Tell you what?"

"That you knew her. At that lecture, the raffle, when E. V. Renge's name came up, you acted all surprised."

"I did." He blinks in confirmation. "I didn't know back then that Lizzy was E. V. Renge."

"No?"

"No." He shakes his head. "I only found out when I read her book."

"You read it?"

"Yes. All of them, right after that lecture. I checked the last name, Casper. I knew *his* name was Casper. I saw her picture."

He stops, contemplating. I wonder if he's deciding how much to tell me. There are only bits and pieces in her diary letters. This man in front of me knew more about her than my dad probably did.

"Did you ever talk to her when you found out?"

"No, but I wanted to. I didn't... I didn't summon my courage until it was too late."

"You didn't go to the funeral?"

"No."

"Why didn't you keep in touch?"

He exhales heavily and rakes his hands through his hair, then leans back in his seat. "One day, they were in town, Ben and her, and the next, they just left. Poof. Just like that. Moved to the East Coast, someone said. She got an agent, you know, was about to sign a publishing deal. And she was about to give birth. I mean, that's a lot. She always had a lot going on for her. I don't know what she saw in Ben. He was handsome and from a good family. But he..."

John goes quiet.

"You didn't like him," I finish his thought.

"I didn't care for him, no. He didn't treat her right. He didn't treat her like a girlfriend." I don't take my eyes off the professor, and he is agitated. His speech gets impatient. "She was just there when he needed a place to sleep or company when there were no other options. Sorry,"—he glances up at me— "it's the truth. She was there for him every time, like a discounted motel room."

I gasp and open my mouth to say something but I don't. He is right. And I don't want to interrupt, because Professor Robertson is losing his cool, perhaps, for the first time since I've known him.

"He didn't deserve her," the professor continues. "She was talented. And beautiful. And sure, her head was filled with all sorts of crazy stuff, because that's part of talent. She had her moods. But God, she was a beautiful person who was just..." He looks away, closing his eyes for a long second like the words pain him. "Used by him," he finishes in a whisper and rubs his forehead. "Sorry," he murmurs. "It's just... Just makes me angry."

I nod. "Were you in love with her?"

He chuckles. "I had a crush, sure."

"Why didn't you try to reconnect with her, find out how she was?"

"Why?"

"Because you had feelings for her?"

He cocks his head as if in a slight reproach. "Mackenzie, I hope you don't mind me calling you by your first name?"

I shake my head.

"You are twenty-one. If you meet the guy who is your soulmate, or at least someone you can envision a future with, you'll forget about what you did two months ago. Let alone last year. Once you graduate, your circles will change. So will your friends. And if you are not in the same city, trust me, you'll never think twice about some person you had a crush on in college."

"You didn't think it was strange? That they just left?"

He shrugs. "His parents never wanted to get to know her. But after they found out she was pregnant and about to sign the book deal? I guess they figured out that she was better for Ben than anyone else. She always wanted a family. I assumed, once they accepted her, she was all in. She never talked to anyone in Old Bow again. Not that I know of. Not to me, anyway. She said she hated that town, wanted to get away from it. Funny. She used to love it when she first moved in. Only when she met Ben and caught him cheating did she start saying that she hated that place. She should've left him. But no, she stuck around. She never emailed me, I'll tell you that much. Never tried to talk after she left town."

He gives me a meaningful stare, and I'm wondering if we are thinking the same thing, if he *knows*.

He looks away. "I moved and didn't care, really. I met my wife soon after. No one cares about former crushes."

I want to see if he knows, if he noticed the difference in the author picture. Dianne Jacobson did. Would *he*?

"You knew Tonya Shaffer, right?"

His head snaps toward me with obvious shock in his eyes. "Why are you asking about her?"

I'm trying to choose my words carefully. "Dad was running around with her. But you knew that. My mom told you that. She came crying on your shoulder, probably more than once. And you had a fight with him. Hence—"

I nod at the scar on his forearm.

"Right." The shock in his eyes dissipates. "And you know that because of her diaries?"

I nod. "Do you have time? Right now?"

He smiles. "Yes. I have all the time in the world."

I pull out the letters from my backpack. They are in a folder, pinned together in the right order. So are the envelopes. Not that I'm going to do a forensic analysis, but I have them all.

"What are those?" he asks.

"Diary letters from Mom. Letters that she wrote before she gave birth to me."

He tears his eyes from the pages and looks at me.

"She wrote about you, you know," I say with a smile.

He reaches for the letters, then stops himself and looks at me again. "May I?" he asks almost in a whisper.

FIFTY-SIX

It's getting dark outside, and Professor Robertson gets up quickly to turn on the lights. He does this without taking his eyes off the letters in his hands.

He reads them greedily, quickly, one by one, his eyes flying over the pages. When he finishes the last page, he turns it back and forth, then looks at me with a question.

"That's it. That's the last one," I say and wait while he briefly rereads them all.

I know how he feels. I know how *this* feels—reading someone's private thoughts, their happiness and pain, watching them gradually fall apart.

"Now that you know what this is, tell me." I want him to talk. I need to know what he knows. "What do you think happened?"

He shakes his head and passes me the letters. "I have no idea."

"When was the last time you saw her?"

"Well... That night"—he tips his chin toward the last letter in my hand—"she told me she wanted to leave Ben."

"You didn't tell me that."

"That's a complicated topic. She wanted to confront him, see if he was willing to change his ways. She's done it many times before, and she was sure that was a wasted hope. She truly thought that she would be leaving him."

"Before giving birth?"

He nods.

I drop my eyes to the letter, confused.

"She... She asked me if I would help her move," the professor says. "Of course, I would have. She knew I would. She knew I would help her financially, though I was working several jobs and trying to graduate, too. She knew I would help her with the baby. She knew she could turn up at my door any time, and I would let her in."

"If that was the case..." I stall. I think I've gotten it wrong all this time. "I don't get it. How did you not contact her later? When she was gone for days?"

"Because she hurt my feelings, all right? She was saying one thing that night, and the next thing I know, they moved away. What was I supposed to do? Ben always had a strong hold on her. She always took him back because he promised her the world."

"Did you do research on her? Before she died? When you wanted to talk to her?"

"I did."

"Did you see the pictures of her when she first published?"

Our gazes lock, and he swallows. "I did."

"What was your first thought?"

His chest stills. I can tell he's holding his breath. "Listen, Mackenzie, I think you..." Of course, he doesn't finish and looks away.

"How about this?" I take out my phone and find the video from the memorial services. I rewind it to the picture that I showed to Dianne Jacobson and pass my phone to Professor Robertson.

My eyes are glued to him, trying to catch every tiny reaction as he studies the picture, then rubs his eyes with his fingers.

"That's Mom, Dad, and me," I say. "When they moved to the East Coast."

He doesn't answer, doesn't look at me, doesn't look at the picture anymore, just rubs his eyes as if this would change what he sees.

"Tell me. Tell me *who* that is," I plead barely audibly.

I can't help the tears that well up in my eyes, because I can't take another person lying to me.

"Tell me, please," I whisper. "Because I think I'm going crazy, and I think something terrible happened, but no one tells me anything," I plead, my voice shaky. "Tell me I'm not crazy. Tell me who that is in the picture."

He finally meets my eyes. "Tonya Shaffer."

FIFTY-SEVEN

I should feel awful at this confirmation, but relief washes over me knowing that one more person knows the truth. That means Dianne is not crazy, and neither am I.

My fast-beating heart is ready to jump out of my chest.

"Right." I brush my cheek with the back of my hand, wiping away a falling tear. "That's the mother I knew. That's the woman who pretended to be Elizabeth Casper for twenty-plus years."

The silence between us is tangible, like a monster that grows teeth. It grows claws, scratching at my heart, making it bleed.

One more person knows that something horrible happened. It's a relief, but the fact spins my head with even more questions.

"When did you know it wasn't the actual Elizabeth Dunn?" I ask.

"I followed her."

I stare at him in shock. "Who?"

"After that lecture, when they said you were her daughter, I read the thriller. Lizzy used to read to me, back then, before.... Before Ben. I knew the book, I knew what it was about. When I read it and put your last name with your father's name, I knew it was Lizzy, E. V. Renge."

His sad smile quickly vanishes.

"I didn't want to just show up at her house, you know. It had been over twenty years. True, I wanted to talk, see how she was. Ask why she never, not even once, got in touch. Why she left town with Ben without saying goodbye."

He takes a deep inhale, then exhales heavily, goes quiet for a moment, staring down at his hands.

"She was important, back then, Lizzy. I got divorced recently. And I kept thinking for several days about how things went down back then. How it could've been different. Thinking and thinking and thinking. That's how you make irrational decisions. And I did. I got obsessed, I suppose." He smiles, glancing at me. "Obsession is the primary target of marketing, you know."

I know. We had a lecture about it.

"So, I did drive to her house. Didn't quite make it, sat in my car on the side of the road at that turn into the property. I sat there for an hour, maybe two. Sketchy, I know. But I was trying to muster up the courage to actually drive to the house and ring the doorbell."

"And?"

"And then a car pulled out of that driveway and into the road. It was her. Or so I thought. Sunglasses, raven hair, red lipstick. I followed."

He rubs the scar on his forearm again, and I stare him down, willing him to go on.

"I followed her into the plaza with the coffee shop. She used the drive-through, then went into the nail shop. I watched her walk in, catching every detail. She was confident, lovely. I thought, twenty years did her good, you know? Fame would. But something was off. There was this air about her... I don't know. Lizzy was always humble. She was shy. I don't think fame would change that. This woman was glowing. When she went inside, I got out of the car and walked into the nail salon."

"Sketchy."

"Right." He chuckles, slightly embarrassed. "It was a small

place. I walked in, and she was right there, right in front of my face, taking her sunglasses off..."

He sucks in his cheeks, and his expression darkens.

"I knew both of them, but Lizzy... Well, I knew Lizzy up close, very close. I knew her for three years back in Old Bow. And I knew that no years, no plastic surgeries, no makeup or hair color would change a person *that* much. From a distance, or if you didn't know her well, sure, the woman was strikingly similar. But I was close this time, only several feet away. She gave me an amused once-over. So did the other ladies there. 'I'm looking for my wife,' I said apologetically. 'A man with a lost wife is a lost man,' she joked, studying me. And here's the thing. Lizzy would've recognized me. She would've. After twenty years, forty, it doesn't matter, I didn't change that much. This woman didn't. But I recognized *her*."

"Tonya Shaffer."

"Yes. Except the receptionist turned to her and said, 'Hi, Elizabeth. Good to see you. How is the book business going?'"

I bite my lip, anger and helplessness mixing inside me.

"How?" I ask him.

"How what?"

"How could she make someone, my dad, do something to another person?"

"Tonya? Tonya knew how to say the right things at the right time to get what she wanted. She had that gift to suck you in. I don't know. Mysterious words, jokes, clinging to you then pulling back. Push and pull like a tide." The professor rubs his forehead. "She made you feel great about yourself. She felt like your best buddy. You drank? She drank. You read? She read. You played video games? So did she. You were into football? She had a collection of trading cards. You worked at a cafe and gave her a free coffee? She'd stop by late one night and help you clean up the tables."

I roll my eyes. "Oh, please."

The professor shrugs. "For her benefit, of course. She was

everywhere, you know. Later, only later did you realize there was something about her, a sort of stickiness. You didn't want to be the one she picked. That meant trouble. You couldn't just get rid of her. You'd be stuck with her until she was the one who lost interest." He raises his worried eyes to me. "I'm afraid she never lost interest in your mom. Your real mom."

The silence between us grows heavy again.

"What are we going to do about it?" I finally say.

"What *can* we do about it?"

"Isn't that identity theft?"

"Sure. But we don't know what happened, what they did. Whatever they did, Ben Casper is in on it." He winces when he says that.

"But... She disappeared. My biological mother. Something must've happened to her. They disposed of her?" Jesus, I'm talking like a cop. "That's a crime. Worse than identity theft."

"We can't prove it, Mackenzie. Are you willing to go to the police and pose horrible accusations against your father only for them to be dismissed and for him to hold it over your head for the rest of your life? You'll ruin your life and his and many other people's."

They all sound the same—Dianne, EJ, Professor Robertson—and I want to cry at how helpless we all are.

"Do you..." I stall because I'm grasping at straws here. "Do you think it's worth flying to Old Bow?"

His face breaks into amusement. "For what?"

I shrug.

"What exactly are you trying to find there?"

I shrug again, helplessly staring at him.

"What do you think you can find twenty years later?"

I shrug, ready to cry. "Talk to people? Professors? The landlord? Someone? I don't know."

A soft smile tugs at his lips, but his gaze is disappointed as he looks away. "I don't think there's anything we can do. Unless the police are involved."

"Right. You said that."

We sit for a minute in silence, then I try one more thing.

"Would you—" I hesitate, wondering if he'll think that I'm obsessed. "Would you like to go to Old Bow sometime?"

His eyebrows shoot up. "Old Bow?"

"Yes. For… I don't know. I'd like to see where she lived, where she went to school, where you worked. It's… I think it's closure."

He stares at me like I'm going cuckoo.

"I know it's a strange request. I'm your student and all."

Jesus, I might have just embarrassed myself and made things weird between us. He stares at me like I just proposed something explicit.

My face catches on fire, and I get up from the couch, ready to leave.

"I'm sorry," I say quickly, wanting to fall through the floor. "It's just—"

"Yes," he says, and I flinch in disbelief. "I'd like that."

I feel like hugging this man who is yet another thread to my mom's past, because now, I have a tiny bit of hope to learn more about her.

FIFTY-EIGHT

Two days later, Grandma calls me and asks me to come to the house to sign more papers.

"Sure. I'll stop by with EJ," I say obediently, cringing at how fake I sound. In reality, I want to scratch her eyes out.

"Come alone, dear. We need to talk. Your father needs moral support."

"I have to get ready for a test. I'm coming with EJ and leaving right away. Maybe next week, Grandma?"

The number of times I say "Grandma" with an overly loving voice makes me want to throw up in my mouth. But I need to play nice. For now. I've seen enough horror movies to know that the stupidest thing is to rebel against dangerous people who have power over you.

That just so happens to be my grandma right now, and she's been in town for days, which is unusual.

EJ texts me every hour when I'm in classes or at my studio. I think he's making sure I'm not kidnapped or going crazy. When I ask him to drive with me to my parents', he agrees right away.

"Should we tell someone else?" he asks.

I frown. "What do you mean?"

"In case something happens to us?"

I widen my eyes at him. "EJ, what the hell? Are you serious? Is that... You think that's a possibility?"

He shrugs.

"I'm about to sign another NDA. It's a bribe," I say. "They know that. They think it'll work. I'm making sure I act like it'll work. So be nice. Be extra nice, EJ. Like... Like nothing happened... Like my mom never passed. Especially with Grandma. Kiss ass. You know how."

"Snarky?" He stares at me in reproach. "I got your point."

He comes to pick me up at my studio at five.

It's getting dark outside already. I hurry out of the building and am about to jump in the passenger seat when a male voice at a distance stops me.

"Excuse me. Miss Mackenzie Casper?"

I squint at the tall shadow of a man approaching me. His mustache looks vaguely familiar.

"Detective Jimenez," he introduces himself and shows his badge.

Right. "I remember you," I say. "At the memorial services. And back at the house, before that."

"Indeed."

I'm not sure what he wants, but now that I know how many secrets my family has, I'm not surprised he's still snooping around, more than a month after Mom's death.

"Is it true?" I ask.

"About?"

"That you had suspicions that my mother's death wasn't an accident?"

"Unfortunately, yes. Well, that was a brief theory and wasn't confirmed."

"Based on what?"

"We found fresh tire tracks not far from where your mother

was found. Could be nothing, but we were checking all possible scenarios."

"Still checking?" I coax. There must be a reason why he is here.

"I am, yes."

"You found the car those tracks belong to?"

He chuckles, his inquiring eyes studying me up and down and returning to my face.

"No."

I stare at him. He at me. Then slowly, he pulls several pictures from his pocket and hands them to me.

"I was wondering if you recognize this man."

The pictures are screenshots from CCTVs. One from the memorial service. Another is from our house patio. I check the date on the last one—four months ago.

I can't see the man's face on the pictures, but I recognize the baseball hat.

"Have you seen that man before?"

I nod. "At the memorial service, yes."

"You talked to him?"

I shoot him a surprised look. "No. I saw Dad talk to him. I think they were arguing."

"About what?"

"Not sure."

If I don't get a chance to uncover Mom's identity fraud, then I will feed the police little bits and pieces so they dig into other stuff.

"So, you don't know who he is," the detective states.

"No. Did you ask my family?"

"We did. They think it was a stalker."

Interesting.

The detective can't miss my bitter smirk. "You don't agree?"

"Oh." I feign naiveté. "I don't know. He could be, I guess. Did you check the footage at our house? To prove your theory? A year ago, there was a man—"

288

"I know about the incident a year ago," he cuts me off. "This man doesn't act like a stalker. Yes, we requested the footage from your property and didn't find anything."

"But...?"

He stares at me. I stare at him. I can't trust him yet, but if he is this diligent, maybe I can tell him something to raise suspicion.

"I still don't think your mother's death was an accident," he explains. "But somehow, your family is not very cooperative. I think this gentleman had something to do with it."

I want to tell him that Elizabeth Casper is not Elizabeth Casper. I gaze at him for some time, wondering what he'll say if I tell him the crazy story and show him the letters. He's in his fifties, I think. No wedding ring. Maybe he's the type who gets obsessive with cases and likes to bring justice and not just clock in work hours.

I bait him. "If I tell you something, can you promise me that you won't tell my family I'm the one who told you that?"

His poker face is great. It doesn't change a bit. Except his eyes, that bore into me with even more intensity.

"Sure, Miss Casper."

"You might want to check the CCTVs again, from two days ago. I am pretty sure that the man was at our house."

The detective cocks his brow. "Was he?"

"In a white pickup. Having a meeting with my dad and my grandmother."

The detective nods. "Anything else?"

"That's the last time I saw him.

"Did you ask your family about it?"

"They said it was blackmail."

"Did they?"

I smile coldly. "I'm pretty sure blackmailers are not invited for family meetings where an agent is present."

"An agent?"

"Right. Laima Roth, my mother's literary agent, was there, too." I gloat when I say that. *Fuck you, Laima.*

The detective takes out a card from his pocket and hands it to me. "Please, don't hesitate to call if you... if you want to talk about your family or anything."

"Anything?"

He nods and steps back without turning around. When he finally does, I call to him. "Detective!"

He whips around right away, his expectant eyes on me.

"Have you ever worked identity theft cases?" I ask.

I shouldn't do that, but I want to make someone see that there are messed up things going on. Maybe, if I give him a clue, he'll start digging in a different direction.

The detective takes a few steps in my direction, suspicion on his face. "Why would you ask me that?"

"Oh, just wondering." I shrug. "I'm doing a report for one of my classes. Maybe I could get some advice from you."

His face relaxes. "I have."

"You have." I nod. "If I have questions, may I call you?"

I know he's not my friend. And no student calls a detective about their assignment. He knows that. I hope he doesn't think I'm stupid.

But I don't smile when I say that, don't look away. Our gazes stay locked, and I keep his stare. If he is a good detective and can read body language, he will go home and ask questions. Hopefully, those questions lead to the real Elizabeth Dunn. Maybe, this tangle of lies will come loose, and I won't be the one who ruins people's lives in the process.

That's wishful thinking, of course.

"Yes." He smiles. "You do that. May I call you if I have any questions?"

"Yes. I'll give you my phone number—"

"No need. I have it."

We both smile, and I finally get in the car.

"I see what you are doing," EJ says as he turns on the engine.

"What am I doing?"

"You are giving him clues to dig deeper without actually coming off like you know anything."

"Do you blame me?"

He looks at me for the longest time, then says, "No. I would've done the same thing."

He fastens his seat belt, and we are off toward the lion's den.

FIFTY-NINE

An hour later, we pull down the familiar private road that leads to my parents' house.

For once, I wish we had neighbors, so that there would be witnesses. To what, I'm not sure, but I'm paranoid.

My parents' house greets us with lights in every room of the ground floor, the smell of roasted chicken and pie and candles lit up, and Grandma's Hollywood smile as she greets us in the hallway.

EJ kisses her hand—a perfect gentleman.

Dad greets us with a whiskey glass in his hand. I grit my teeth as I hug him, then go to the kitchen and exhale in relief when I see Minna. I almost cry when I wrap my arms around her from behind. She pauses stirring glazed carrots on the stove and laughs when I say, "I missed you."

Sadly, our housekeeper is the only person I actually love seeing at the house right now.

Our family's lawyer is here, too, an older guy who talks like he's the king of Wall Street.

Grandma takes me and Dad to Mom's office where the lawyer

has me sign more papers. I briefly scan what they are about, but again, it's NDAs and a bank transfer.

Look at us, a happy family, I think with bitterness as we all finally sit down at the dining table.

Grandma orders Minna to pour wine.

"Not me," I say. "I don't think I can handle liquor well."

I smile down at my plate as Grandma laughs.

"Me neither," says EJ.

"Emerson? Dear? You won't have a glass with us?" Grandma asks while our lawyer is already chugging his.

"No, Mrs. Casper. Thank you so much."

"Well, I hope you are hungry."

"Actually, I am not eating either." I shoot him a surprised glance. "I had bad food poisoning the other day. Still recovering. Grits, bread, soups—that's about all I can handle in the last couple of days. Thank you. Mackenzie didn't tell me we would be having dinner."

He grins at me, then looks at Grandma and raises his palms in apology. "Sorry."

I think he's being cautious. Seriously, he should've been an actor. He's definitely a charmer, though, because while we are having dinner, and I pick at the food on my plate as if it's been poisoned, he constantly asks questions. Grandma—about her house, and Mr. Casper, and her rose garden. Dad—about golfing, though I'm pretty sure EJ hasn't golfed a day in his life.

When we finish dinner, EJ keeps Grandma and Dad busy with conversations while I excuse myself and run upstairs.

I don't go into my room. Instead, I go to Mom's, flip the light switch, and stand in the doorway, startled.

The only things left of Mom in her room are the bed frame with the mattress and the bureaus, but there's nothing in them. I bolt to the walk-in closet the size of a bedroom itself and pull the doors open—nothing, no clothes. Everything is cleared from the bathroom as well. Mom's room is clean as a whistle.

Anger rises in me like a wave. It's a no-brainer that Grandma and Dad are making sure that there's no trace of the woman who pretended to be Elizabeth in this house.

I don't say a word when I go downstairs. Instead, I talk to Minna and manage my fakest smile at my family when EJ and I leave the house.

"They cleaned Mom's room," I say when EJ and I get in the car.

"Vacuumed and bleached?"

"No, EJ. I mean, there are no personal belongings of hers in that room. It's empty. Completely. Closets, drawers, walls —everything."

We both look at each other in grim realization.

My family is cleaning up their messy trail.

And there is nothing I can do.

SIXTY

A week goes by with nothing much happening. I go to classes. I reread Mom's books.

I call Dianne. She actually answers. I tell her about John and that I want to go to Old Bow. I tell her about the man at our house, what Grandma told me about Tonya.

"Horse shit," Dianne replies, and I laugh loudly, though it's not a laughing matter.

I go to the social studies lecture and sit in the front row, something I've never done before. Professor Robertson is not as composed as he usually is. His glances at me are inquiring. He can feel me staring him down, and when the lecture is over and everyone files out of the hall, me among the last students, I don't cringe when he asks, "Miss Casper, may I have a word, please?"

We both wait until the last students leave the hall. Then he finally says, "I thought about what you said."

"Which part?"

"Old Bow."

I don't say a word but wait for him to continue.

"I think it might be a good idea."

"What?"

"To go there. For you. It would be some sort of closure, I suppose."

"And you?"

"I will go with you, yes."

That very evening, EJ stops by my place for a minute before one of his Zoom meetings with some software developers he's working with.

I sit cross-legged on the couch, a book I've been reading set aside, while he takes a seat on the bar stool by the kitchen island and studies me as I tell him that the professor and I are flying to Old Bow this weekend.

"Isn't that kind of inappropriate?" he asks. "Considering he is your professor."

"I mean, we are just traveling together. One day. In and out."

"Hmm."

"You don't think it's good idea?"

"No, I think it's good for you."

"I think so, too. I want him to show me where Mom lived, where she studied, the cafe, all the places, you know."

EJ nods. "Want me to come?"

I give him a little smile. "No. Probably not. I think I'm going to cry a lot. And you don't like that sort of stuff."

"I'm okay with you crying," he says, chuckling. "On my shoulder."

"Whatever." I snort out a laugh.

"Who else will let you soak his favorite hoodie with your bitter tears?"

I roll my eyes, grinning. "True. By the way, I called Dianne again last night."

"Yeah? She actually picked up again?"

"Yeah. I called like three times until she did. But then, she said I can call her if I had any questions."

"What did you ask her?"

"Told her about the trip. She said she'd pick us up at the airport and drive us to Old Bow."

"Dianne?" EJ's eyebrows shoot up.

"Yeah. I told her John knows about the group home. About Tonya. About... You know, the switched identities. She lives about four hours away. But she said she has nothing else to do."

EJ rises from his seat, ready to leave, but hesitates for a moment, giving me awkward glances.

"Heya, when you get back..." he finally says. "When you get back, want to go for dinner?"

I give him a surprised stare. We've done plenty of dinners, at home. But even when we went out for food, he never phrased it this way.

I look away, trying to hide the awkwardness. "We can do the usual takeout and chill, sure."

"I meant like a dinner date."

I don't answer. I can't look at him. This should be normal, *is* normal for anyone but me. I've gone on dates before but have never done dinner dates. And something about EJ makes me super nervous.

I throw my usual quip at him. "Your cyber queen buffet ran dry?"

And I know it's a weak jab, so weak. It's an overused joke, we both know this.

I lift my eyes to meet his, which are unusually intense.

His lips curve in a disappointed smile. "Is it not obvious enough lately that I'm not interested in those? Or are you the only one who doesn't see that I have a thing for you?"

A nervous chuckle escapes me, and I fumble with the sleeve of my hoodie I'm picking at, avoiding looking at him.

"Look, just tell me how it is, Kenz. If you are not interested, I'll understand."

My heart screams in protest right away.

"I'd love that, yeah," I say and purse my lips. I think I might pass out from nervousness.

"Good," EJ says. I hear him picking up his backpack. "Cause I would've asked again until you said yes."

I'm pursing my lips really tightly so as not to smile, but there's no way to hide my blush. I'm pretty sure my entire body is blushing.

I hear him approach from behind.

He leans over the couch back, and his arm gently wraps around my shoulders, his lips in my ear. "Don't freak out, Snarky."

"I'm not freaking out."

"You are freaking out. Internally."

"Right, 'cause you can see it."

"I always see you."

Then his arm is gone, and I force myself to breathe evenly, though my heart is pounding like a drum.

I can hear a smile in his voice that comes from the door as he opens it. "Kenzie?"

I turn around and meet his boyish grin that I freaking adore.

"Relax. It'll be great." He winks and leaves.

Somehow, despite the trip to Old Bow being at the top of my list, this dinner with EJ is already becoming something I'm looking forward to. Even if everything else in my life fails, I still have EJ.

SIXTY-ONE

We fly into the airport that's located over an hour away from Old Bow.

Nebraska is cheerful under the November sun, despite the air being crisp and biting with low temperatures.

Dianne looks just like the first time I met her—bib overalls, flannel shirt, boots, duck jacket, her gray hair tied in the back into a bun.

She and John are in the front seats of her pickup truck. They talk about Nebraska, John being from somewhere she used to fish.

I stare at the window, my mood even more melancholic with this sunny weather. Some dark things often happen right in broad daylight. And then there are decades of horrendous consequences that tarnish so many lives.

There's nothing but forests and fields, with occasional small towns that look like they were left behind a century ago. Windmills. Hunting signs. Tourist attraction billboards, though I have a hard time figuring out what tourists can potentially entertain themselves with here.

We ride through the forest when a giant sign with a fish on it catches my attention.

I laugh quietly. "That's some weird-looking fish," I say from the back seat.

John turns to smile at me.

"There's a lake out there. Private properties, I think, a camp with cabins. The fish is called garfish, and it's not very common in the States, but it exists in that lake."

"It looks like a fish with long duck mouth."

John chuckles. "It has sharp teeth."

"The fish?"

"The locals call the fish Sharp Teeth."

My stomach turns at the words. "Mom's latest book was supposed to be called *Sharp Teeth*."

I see John and Dianne exchange glances. I know they think I have some sort of PTSD from the letters and the things I found out.

I don't. It's just that everything makes me think of my mom. My real mom.

Old Bow is a small college town. All kinds of businesses dot both sides of Main Street that stretches for about two miles. The college campus is at the very far end of it, taking up over a hundred acres with its campuses, sports fields, and dorms.

We first stop at the main campus.

An old man in a fancy suit and tie greets us in the hallway. It turns out, it's Professor Robertson's former teacher.

John—Professor Robertson insisted that I call him that during this trip—introduces me as E. V. Renge's daughter.

"Yes. We are very proud of Elizabeth Casper," the man says. "Despite her refusal to do a commencement speech here. Well, the five times we invited her."

The man laughs cheerfully, while John and I exchange understanding glances.

They laugh and talk about the old days while Dianne and I walk around the hall and read the accolades for other students and professors. Not that either of us care. We stumble upon a board with notable alumni. Sure enough, there's Mom's poster and the accolades for her books there. Her picture is one of the most recent, the same that's on every book and press release.

"I can't look at her," I say, turning away.

Dianne doesn't reply.

Next, we drop by the apartment building above a convenience store.

Five floors. Old facade. Students walking to and from on Main Street in front of it.

"That's where Lizzy lived for four years," John says with hard-to-miss nostalgia.

The three of us walk through a side street to the back of it and the ugly green door with a buzzer next to it.

A man is sweeping the backyard. It turns out, he is a super.

John shakes hands but doesn't introduce the rest of us, and I'm grateful.

"Does this place have the same owner?" John asks.

"Yeah," the short skinny super with a goatee says. "Same one for, I wanna say, forty or so years."

"I used to come here often," John says with a smile that's charming and friendly. "Used to study at the college. I'm just visiting."

"Oh, yeah? That woman, the famous author, used to live here, you know. E. V. Renge. For three years. You knew her?"

John nods. "I did."

"Oh, man. She's a millionaire. A best-selling author."

"Right."

"Her fans come here occasionally. Ask questions. Some creepy ones, too. They hold gatherings with candles. Had to call the police a month ago. I guess that author died or something."

"She did."

"Once in a while, journalists come here, too."

"You knew her?" John asks carefully.

"Nah." The guy looks disappointed. "I came here several years after she'd moved out."

"I see. Did you by chance know the previous super?"

That's Grunger—I know the name from Mom's letters, though John said he'd only met the guy once or twice.

"Nah. Never did. He was the nephew of the owner, I know that much."

"Was?"

"Yeah. He went to prison before I got here."

"Prison?"

"Yeah, for a long time. He used to deal drugs."

My heart sinks into my stomach. I was hoping to find someone who knew Mom, even someone insignificant. But maybe Dad was right. She was a loner and didn't get out much.

We drive around town for some time. John shows us the places they used to hang out at, the bars he used to frequent. He doesn't know where Tonya used to live, so there's that. And though the day is cheerful and he and Dianne laugh and crack jokes, my mood is less than fine.

We end up back on Main Street and stop at a cafe to grab lunch. When I finish my sandwich, John and Dianne order coffee and I excuse myself and tell them I need to go for a walk.

They nod in understanding. I need some time by myself. I want to see this town with *her* eyes. Feel how she felt when she walked to college.

I also know that John and Dianne want to talk about Mom as well as Tonya. But mostly, about me. They think I'm too young to be involved in a secret like my family's. Sure, they want to discuss what happened and what might happen in the future.

I aimlessly roam the town for over an hour until my hands are cold, my nose is an icicle, and my phone finally rings with a phone call from John.

"We should probably head back to the airport," he says.

"Yeah. I'll meet you on Main Street, by the cafe."

When we get in Dianne's truck, my chest tightens in disappointment.

I feel sad and angry. I don't know what I was hoping to find here in Old Bow—something, at least a hint at what happened to Mom.

But there's nothing.

We leave Old Bow, and I stare out the window at the forests lining the road. They are dark and shady, the sky suddenly gray, weighing down on them. By now, I feel like crying.

And there it is again, that weird fish sign.

We pass it too quickly, and I turn and repeat on reflex, "Sharp teeth."

John looks at me over his shoulder, then looks at Dianne and back at the road. "Maybe one day, we can come here and I'll show you the lakes. We camped out by the lake when we were teenagers."

"You're from here, right?" I ask.

"Not quite, but the lake was a hidden gem."

"Maybe. One day," I echo.

And just like that, with the reference to a far-away future, my only hope to find anything about Mom is completely gone.

SIXTY-TWO

Dianne turns at the sign to a small town off the highway. She needs gas.

I walk inside the gas station and get coffee, then take small sips of the steaming liquid as I watch through the window while John talks to Dianne as she pumps gas into her truck. They are not smiling anymore. Their conversations are hushed. I wonder if they came up with some way to find out the truth about my mom. I will never stop being hopeful.

I don't have a mother—the thought strikes me. It feels so heartbreaking all of a sudden that I have to clench my jaw to stop the tears from coming.

I was so close to finding out the truth. Just not close enough to get to the bottom of it. It hurts. No, no, that's the wrong word. The realization is devastating. I might never find out what happened to my mom.

A sudden screech of tires from across the road makes my eyes snap to a pickup truck that swerves so dramatically out of a shop parking lot that it leaves a cloud of burned tire smoke in the air.

"Dipshits," the guy at the cash register curses.

Then I see it.

Huckleberry Supplies, the shop sign says.

I chuckle at the name. Like Huckleberry Finn.

Suddenly, a memory zips through my mind—*Huckleberry Supplies.*

I stare at the sign and feel the floor drop from under my feet.

It can't be.

I run outside. "John, John, I know that name."

"What name?"

"The shop." I nod across the street. "They called several weeks ago saying we didn't pay the bill. I didn't know what bill, didn't care. But why would my parents have a bill here?"

"Maybe just a similar name?" He exchanges worried glances with Dianne like I'm going crazy.

"Maybe. But what if not?" I give him a pleading stare.

I see reluctance on his face, but he obliges. "Come on." He nods. "We'll be right back," he tells Dianne.

"Hurry up," Dianne grunts. "Or you'll miss your flight!"

John and I walk into the small shop that looks like the owners piled the products on the shelves without bothering to make it look like a store.

"Can I help you?" an older lady behind the counter asks as she turns away from a desktop computer.

"Yeah," I say hesitantly. "My parents have an account with you. Maybe," I add, wondering if I'm indeed going crazy. "You have such a thing? Accounts with other people? For supplies and services?"

"Sure. Hundreds. We deliver all over the county."

"Can you look it up?"

"I can't just give away information, sweetie."

"Right. Except I think they owe you money. The account is overdue."

Her expression loses some of its haughtiness. "What's the last name?"

"Casper."

"Casper, Casper, Casper..." Her eyes bore into the computer screen as she clicks the mouse. "No, not in the system."

I almost whimper in disappointment. "Maybe they used a different name?"

"You have that name?"

My heart falls. "No."

John next to me stirs. "What phone number did they call? The supply store?" he asks me.

"The house phone." The realization hits me. "Could you check by the phone number?"

The lady shrugs. "Shoot."

I tell her the phone number, and she goes back staring at the computer screen. Then her frown smoothens. "Yep. Sure thing. Seven weeks overdue," she says. "The phone number is Etched Properties LLC. That theirs?"

She gives me an inquiring look.

I look at John. "I've never heard of that company. But if the phone number is my parents', that means it's theirs, right? Wait." Another realization hits me.

I pull out my phone out and dial EJ, but the phone call drops. There's no connection. My hands are trembling as I try again.

The doorbell dings as Dianne walks in. "You'll miss the flight. Or I'll have to drive like madman," she says, but John gives her a meaningful stare, and Dianne turns to look to me in question.

"Listen," I say, and at this point, my heart is beating so fast that I start panting.

"Mackenzie, calm down. Breathe," John says to me. "Did you take your medication recently?"

I shake my head. "It's not that. It's... My friend and I did some research weeks back. And Tonya inherited a property outside Old Bow about the time Mom and Dad were in college. She sold it years after to an LLC. I don't remember the name but I think... I think it might be the same one?"

John exchanges glances with Dianne.

I'm not crazy. I was right. My parents have something to do with this supply store. "If that same LLC belongs to my parents and has a bill here—"

"Are you paying the bill or what's going on?" the lady behind the counter interrupts rudely, watching us, not a tiny bit amused.

I turn to her. "Do you know how long they have had an account with you?"

The woman hesitates before she peels her irritated gaze from me and looks at the computer. Her brows tick up. "Over twenty years by the looks of it."

I feel my knees buckle.

John rakes his fingers through his hair.

Dianne steps to the counter. "Ma'am." She nods in greeting. "Where do the ordered supplies go?"

"To an address."

"Do you have the address on file?"

"Sure, they do," I say.

The lady gives me a dirty stare. "I can't just give away personal information."

Dianne leans on the counter. "We understand. But we might have a criminal case here."

"Ex-*cuse* me?" The lady glares at her.

"What I mean is that we either check out the address you have on file, or we have to go to the police and give them information, and they will come with a warrant to get the address."

"Oh, yeah? You threatening me? Let 'em come." The lady at the desk puffs out her chest.

Dianne stays cool as a cucumber. "I understand. The problem is that they will probably confiscate your computer. And lock down the shop to do a search. We don't want that, do we?"

The woman's glare doesn't subside, but she shifts her gaze to the computer screen and spits out the words.

"22 Gar Lane," she says. "About twenty minutes from here."

SIXTY-THREE

I can't calm my trembling as we drive back toward Old Bow.

"You will miss the flight," Dianne warns.

"It's all right. Maybe not," John answers. "But we need to check this out. If anything, I'll book us a flight for tomorrow morning. We'll just stay at a hotel."

He glances over his shoulder at me. "You all right?"

I nod, but my heart is racing. I'm not all right. Not by a mile.

And neither is John. He keeps rubbing his jeans with his palms, and the next twenty minutes pass in complete silence.

I keep glancing at the offline GPS on my phone and the final destination, a dot by a lake without any seemingly visible road leading to it.

I exhale loudly at some point.

"Mackenzie, it'll be all right," John says, trying to calm me without looking. "There are probably renters there."

"And my parents have been paying for supply deliveries for twenty years?"

"We should've asked about those supplies. Maybe it's firewood. Coal for the furnace. These things—"

"John," Dianne interrupts him then turns her head to me. "Hang in there, sweetie."

I don't look at the road, I only stare at the dot and the turn that's approaching with excruciating slowness.

"Right here," I say finally, glancing between my GPS and the road turning at the ugly fish sign.

"At the sign?" Dianne asks.

"Yeah." My heart gives a thud so powerful that I feel like it's going to break my ribcage. "Sharp teeth," I murmur again.

A mile after the turn, our truck pulls up to a clearing in front of a small log cabin.

There's an old blue Toyota parked out front. The lake flickers between the trees.

"Can we go in?" I ask.

Dianne sighs with resignation. "While in Rome. Come on."

We all get out.

I come up to John and stop. All three of us stand by the car, looking at the house but not moving.

I take a shaky breath. John shifts, and I feel his hand on my shoulder. "Mackenzie?" I look up at him. "It's not her. Relax. Just breathe, okay? It's probably not what you expect."

I take a deep breath and exhale loudly. "Right."

But I'm terrified. Terrified that we are wrong. That we are too late. That we'll find something more sinister here than what we thought.

All three of us start taking slow steps toward the house when the door suddenly opens, and we halt.

So does my heart.

I think I'm about to throw up in nervousness.

The woman who comes out is in her forties, wearing sports sneakers, nurse's scrubs, and a parka. Her dark hair is tied in a messy bun on top of her head.

I look at John in question.

"It's not her," he reassures me. "It's not her, Mackenzie. Breathe, okay?"

"Uh." I exhale, swallowing the bile in my throat. A chill pill would've been really handy right now.

"Can I help you?" the woman asks loudly as she walks down the steps and toward us.

I look at John again. I don't think I can talk. I'm not even sure what to say.

"Hi! Yes. We are looking for someone," he says. "Not sure if we have the right address."

He chuckles as the woman stops several feet from us, her hands in her parka pockets as she stares at me unblinkingly for several seconds, then looks at Dianne and John.

"Is this your property?" he asks.

"No. I just work here." She stares at me again.

"Work? What sort of work, if I may ask?"

She peels her eyes off me. "I'm a caretaker."

"A caretaker?"

"Yes. I work for private nursing services. I take care of people."

"You work for someone here?"

"Yes. For a family. What is this about?"

I study the house behind her, the smoke coming out of the chimney, the clean porch, and the flowerbeds that are empty but clean, as if they had flowers in the summer.

"What's the person's name?" John asks.

The nurse takes a step back. "Listen, I don't want any trouble. And I'm not authorized to give out personal information. I get paid for my services, that's it."

"I understand. We are looking for someone... Well, actually we are not sure who we are looking for."

The nurse snorts and takes another small step back, retreating.

My eyes shift to the house windows, and I see a face in one of them. I can't make out who it is, but the curtain moves, and the face disappears.

"There's someone inside the house," I murmur.

John looks at me, then at the nurse. "Do you know who lives here?"

The nurse looks at me again, up and down, then at John, and cocks her head, her eyes narrowing in what looks like suspicion.

"You are some type of relatives or something?"

"Maybe?"

She nods, giving John a suspicious once-over. "Never seen you here before." Right away, her eyes are trained on me again.

"We... We actually just learned she might live here," I say vaguely and with hesitation.

The nurse's face softens. Her eyes slightly narrow on me. "No visitors are allowed here," she says. "I have strict orders. No personal info is disclosed." Her eyes shift to John. "Sorry, folks. I wish I could help."

"Why is that?" John insists.

"My client is in a fragile state."

"Wh-what does that mean?" I ask, my heart in my throat. I'll take any clue. I might just come later and sneak into the house to find out who lives there.

"Today is one of her better days." The nurse nods at the house. "The weather affects her. She doesn't speak much. She says words. She writes. Writes a lot of beautiful stuff that doesn't make much sense. She doesn't connect well with most people. That's the issue. I have strict rules to keep her from anyone who might trigger another episode."

But with everything she just said, I latch onto one word —*writes*.

"She is writing?" I whisper and look pleadingly at John, then Dianne. "She writes. The person inside writes."

"She doesn't go outside much," the nurse says. "Not in this weather. And I can't let you in, either. Sorry, I get paid quite well to keep my client safe."

We all exchange glances.

I'm sad. And anxious. And nervous. But most of all, I'm desperate to know who is inside.

During this trip, I was hoping to find pieces of myself in this place, this state, anything, something that I could never find in the woman who raised me or in the man I called my father.

I can tell John is probably even more nervous than me.

"So." The nurse puffs out her chest and picks up the phone. "I have to ask you to leave. Otherwise, I'll have to call security."

My heart thuds violently in my chest in despair.

That's when the door squeaks open.

The nurse turns at the sound. "Oh, that is unusual," she murmurs, her hands dropping in shock, as we see a woman walk out. "She rarely goes outside. You have visitors, Tonya!"

The name makes the hairs on the back of my neck stand on end.

"Jesus Christ," Dianne whispers.

The woman who walks out looks like she's in her forties. Her thick hair is loose, falling down onto her chest. She's wearing a thick knitted sweater, sleeping pants, and house shoes.

She stands still on the edge of the porch, her face turned toward us.

There's a loud exhale and a murmur—Dianne again, who covers her mouth with her hand, staring at the woman on the porch.

"Oh, God," John gasps next to me. He rakes his fingers through his hair, his eyes wide at the woman.

"Is it... Is it her?" I ask in a whisper as if afraid of my own words.

But when I study her, I don't need a confirmation. I see it now, too, the resemblance. If I used one of those apps that can age your photo by twenty years, this would be me—the woman with dark graying hair and soft features, who starts taking slow steps down the porch and toward us.

The nurse raises her hands just slightly toward the woman, palms out, as if the woman is about to fall.

We don't know yet what exactly is wrong with her, whether she is a functioning person or not. But as I study her, my eyes well up with tears.

"Oh, Jesus," John exhales again, and I briefly glance at him to see his face frozen in shock.

But my eyes are back on the woman, my heart beating so fast that it's ready to jump out of my chest.

They weren't lying—I'm a carbon copy of her.

There's no mistake—though the woman who raised me looks similar, you would've known the difference if you knew them.

My chest shakes with a tiny sob. I've never met this woman, my biological mother, but that's not what makes me want to break down in tears.

You know what's cruel? Stripping an innocent person of their talents, achievements, loved ones, and locking them up for twenty-one years.

You know what's worse than murder? Burying someone alive.

The approaching woman's gaze only briefly pauses on Dianne. Then, it's on John, lingering for a little.

She walks slowly, her gait a little unsteady, her steps uneven, like her legs don't quite work properly.

Then her gaze shifts to me and latches on, whipping me back to the diaries and the story of the beautiful mind who was cut off by an unspeakable act of cruelty.

The woman slows down, her eyes roaming my face, and when she finally walks up to us, she stops in front of me.

The same height as me. Same build. Same face. Her arms hang loosely by her sides. She smells like fireplace smoke and flowers. The wind ruffles her long strands, grayish, though I can tell that, a long time ago, they were raven black. Her lips are chapped, her skin pale. Wrinkles etch the corners of her eyes. There's beauty in her, weathered by years of solitude and some type of sickness that nevertheless hasn't marred her face.

There's no mistake as to who she is—looking at her is like looking into my future.

I feel like I'm about to fold. The world suddenly stills around us.

Her eyes are calm but somewhat vacant, her gaze roaming my face as she slightly cocks her head.

"Hi," I say. The word comes out like a whisper.

My chest feels so tight that it's hard to breathe. The only thing that makes me smile is the fact that this woman's eyes are not etched with sadness or trauma or any sort of madness. They are calm like the ocean.

She raises her hand slowly, as if with great effort. I flinch a little when her fingertips, inch by inch, trace the contours of my face.

Her touch is warm, feather-like. Motherly. Though I don't know for how long in the distant past she got to be a mother.

For a moment, I feel like my heart breaks. It aches at the fact that this woman will never truly know who I am. These are the slowest seconds of my life, the feeling of my heart cracking just a little more as her eyes wander over my face. I stand frozen in time, afraid to move and scare her away.

She lowers her hand, and the corner of her lips lifts a tiny bit in what looks like a smile. Her eyes begin to glass over.

Is she retreating into herself? No. Please. No-no-no.

But she's not. Her eyes are glistening, I realize. I think it's tears. Can it be?

My own heart is too big for my chest, about to explode. My eyes, too, well up with tears that are about to spill.

"I'm Mackenzie," I say in a shaky voice and smile at her.

That's when her soft gaze locks with mine, her eyes glowing with kindness, and her lips part with the first word.

The word I've repeated so many times, reading it from her diaries.

The word I've never heard out loud.

It's a soft whisper that feels heartbreakingly loud when she says, "Petal."

SIXTY-FOUR

A YEAR LATER

"Hurry up!" EJ shouts from the living room.

"I need a little help here!" I shout back from the kitchen, struggling to pull the tray of baked Brussels sprouts out of the oven.

I hear John and Dianne's laughter in the living room, and though I burn myself a little with the hot tray, I can't help but smile in excitement.

We've had these gatherings at John's house almost weekly since, you know, we found Mom a year ago. But this is our first Thanksgiving together: me, EJ, John, Dianne, and Mom. Dianne calls it the "justice crew."

Technically, EJ is the one who dug out all the info about my mom's past, including Dianne's address. Thanks to him, the crazy chain of events in the last year unraveled the storm. But it was thanks to Dianne and John who took me to Old Bow that we finally got to the bottom of it. We are, indeed, a crew.

I set the tray on top of the stove and lean in to smell it.

Quick footsteps approach. "Need help?"

EJ's arms wrap around my waist, and he nuzzles my neck. "Hurry up, turtle."

"I'm trying. Stop distracting me," I quip, giggling as he kisses my neck.

"I wouldn't distract you if you weren't so distracting," he murmurs into my ear.

"Hey, watch your grabby hands."

"You keep being rude, I'll have to take you somewhere secluded and teach you a lesson." His one hand snakes under my blouse.

I burst out laughing and swat his hand away.

"Everyone's waiting," I whisper.

He leans from behind to give me a peck on the cheek and goes for the stack of clean bowls. "The sprouts go here?" He picks one of them.

"Yeah."

I watch him helping like a good boyfriend and can't stop smiling.

I'm lucky. I tell him that every day, and he gets cocky and proud. But seriously, I'm the luckiest girl in the world.

"Go-go-go. Everyone is waiting." He nudges me as he's carrying a bowl of sprouts and a bottle of soda.

This Thanksgiving, I have a whole table of people to be grateful for.

John—he is *John* and not Professor Robertson anymore—is checking something on his phone.

Mom is next to him. She's going through extensive therapy, and the doctors said that she won't ever be back to her full capacity, not even half. She barely speaks, but I know she understands a lot, feels it. I love the way she looks at me, like I'm her entire world.

Mom smiles softly at us when EJ and I step into the living room.

Dianne has been staying in town in a rental for the last year while the trials and the media circus were going on. She testified numerous times against Ben Casper and Evelyn Casper, as well as Tonya Shaffer, who was living under the Elizabeth Dunn identity all this time.

"Look at this," John says, reading from his phone. "The latest from the New York Post:

FRAUD, ABDUCTION, SLAVERY.
WHAT HAPPENED TO THE REAL E. V. RENGE?

They call it the literary fraud of a century.

Of course, it is.

When we found Mom, my *real* Mom, the FBI got involved. We stayed in Old Bow for a week, John, Dianne, and I. EJ flew in. So did Detective Jimenez.

And then our lives exploded, to put it mildly.

Dianne was the first witness in the identity theft case. Then there were several people from the group home who recognized Tonya from her earlier pictures with Dad and identified her as Tonya Shaffer. Several of Dad's friends from college came forward about Tonya and Lizzy. College professors from Old Bow. Someone dug out the old commencement photos. It turned out John had the negatives from back in the days he never developed. Sure enough, there were several pictures of Lizzy.

There was a DNA test, which confirmed that the woman living in the lake cabin was indeed my biological mother. A number of nurses who had been hired in the last twenty years gave the insight into what medication was given to her, mostly sedatives, which the nurses cut back on after a while. None had met the real Tonya Shaffer who posed as Elizabeth Dunn in person.

The paper trail of the LLC that bought the property and paid all the expenses in supporting Mom at the cabin was traced to my parents.

My parents should've gotten rid of the diaries and original

manuscripts—those had fingerprints of the woman from the lake cabin.

Here's the thing. If Grandma hadn't snapped that one picture of Tonya and Dad back in the day, it would have been much harder to identify Tonya at a young age. In fact, this whole investigation might never have started.

They never located the man who was blackmailing my family and who was paid for years. Dad blamed his wife, accused her of cheating and paying off. He went to prison for a lifetime.

Grandma, too, on conspiracy to identity theft and conspiracy to assist in fraud charges. She would've been spared if the nurses who took care of Mom hadn't confirmed that Evelyn Casper visited multiple times in the last twenty years. In fact, as soon as Tonya and Dad moved to the East Coast, Grandma flew to Old Bow to "take care" of legal things. She's been in on the whole thing from the very beginning. On top of that, she's been taking a large cut of E. V. Renge's royalties. We are talking a quarter of those. Now she's stripped of the funds and in prison.

See, Mom? I told you Grandma was a monster.

I don't feel bad for her. Not when I saw where my biological mother lived for years. They found the papers with her writings at the cabin, hundreds of them. God bless the forensics that proved it was the same writing as in the original manuscripts for the already published works.

The identity theft unraveled a monstrous beast.

Copyright lawyers were involved. My trust fund was the only thing that was left untouched. Everything else was confiscated from my dad and grandparents—properties, funds, savings, future royalties.

The entertainment and copyright lawyers had a field day with that trial. Mom got the best one in the country to represent her. She won. And though she got her funds and royalties back, at least some of them, she couldn't use them legally because of her mental state. So, I was appointed a caretaker of the E. V. Renge's trust. And hers.

Most importantly, Mom got herself back, her name, Elizabeth Dunn, and the rights for her books. She doesn't understand much of it, nor does she care. But I can see it in her eyes when she looks at me and John—she is happy she is around us, and that's all that matters.

That bitch Laima Roth? Well, she was questioned and charged with conspiracy. But of course, her publishing house and PR team got a good lawyer.

"I was unaware of the false identity," she said in a statement. "I'd never met Elizabeth Dunn in person until the signing of the contract. I am the biggest victim in this case."

Laima might've gotten away with it legally, but the journalists buried her. NDAs were NDAs until feds were involved. She couldn't explain why the so-called Elizabeth Dunn-Casper had to hire ghost-writers to write the missing pieces of her own manuscripts.

John has already found new literary agents for Mom. The previous publishing house lost their rights to the published E. V. Renge's books. What a circus it was. We signed a deal with a new publisher. And while the old copies are sold and traded for extraordinary money, the new copies' pre-orders are raking up unheard-of numbers.

I talked to Detective Jimenez the other day. He is a local celebrity. He still teases me about the so-called identity theft class report.

So, here we are, celebrating our victory. Mine of finding Mom. Hers of finally getting justice.

She smiles softly when I glance at her. They say she probably had a stroke while giving birth. It caused brain damage and memory loss. And she was heavily sedated for quite a while until the nurses who took care of her decided something wasn't right and started cutting down on her medication. But Mom's lack of speech is apparently her own choice. Maybe, one day, she'll talk more to me. She loves hearing me read her my stories, though.

She's been staying at a physical rehab facility for a year now. But we are looking for a house for her. Once we get it, we will set it up with the appropriate nursing care.

"What did the new agent tell you?" John asks me as all of us finally sit at the dinner table.

"He asked me if I'm interested in writing a book about Mom."

"Do it," EJ says, shoving sweet potatoes in his mouth. "You are talented. Who else will write that crazy story better? You can call it *Sharp Teeth*."

I give him an alarmed stare then glance at Mom again, feeling bad for mentioning the words.

But she smiles, looking down at her plate. I think she understands most of what we say.

"We'll see about that," I murmur.

"Can I be in it?" EJ asks.

"Brat," I whisper, grinning as I roll my eyes.

John and Dianne laugh.

Right now, Mom is a celebrity, her picture—no lipstick, graying black hair—is viral. She is a new legend and sort of a martyr.

Our Thanksgiving is a cheerful one. John is attentive to Mom and pours her water and brings cake. I think he did love her once. I think he still does, in a different way.

The doorbell rings.

Eyebrows raised, John gets up from the table. "It'd better not be paparazzi," he murmurs.

He comes back a minute later, confusion on his face as he holds an envelope.

"No one at the door," he says, but his gaze is worried as he passes me the envelope.

To Mackenzie Dunn. From #1 fan. XOXO

SIXTY-FIVE

I swallow, scanning the people at the table, who look at me expectantly.

"What is it?" EJ asks impatiently, his eyes glued to the envelope.

With shaking hands, I open it.

It's one page, just like the pages I got a year ago. The same journal. The same handwriting. The page starts with a cut-off sentence.

maybe, just maybe, and please, forgive me for this, my beautiful girl,
but maybe Ben has nothing to do with you at all.
Love, Mom.

I stare at the words in a stupor, trying to remember what came before that, in the last letter that I haven't reread in months.

"Kenzie, spill. What does it say?" EJ prompts.

My mind sifts through the memory—of the last letter, where Mom was at John's house, while she was still pregnant and wanted to leave my father. The letter ended abruptly.

If Ben lies to me again, I'll snap.
It's either she's gone or he is.
Ben will have to make that choice himself. But

I look at the page in my shaking hands.

maybe Ben has nothing to do with you at all.

"May I?"

I look up at John and on reflex, hand him the page, unable to look away from him.

John was always there for Mom at Old Bow. John was the one who she came to for help. John was the one who promised to help her get away.

"Excuse me," I say and get up so abruptly that my chair tips over.

"Mackenzie..." John's voice echoes behind me as I dart to the bathroom, lock the door, turn on the water, and close my eyes.

It's hard to breathe, but even harder to contemplate the truth that slaps me in the face.

"Can't be..." I murmur, looking in the mirror, and try to find the traces of my dad in my reflection.

Tears start streaming down my face. I try to take a deep breath, but my chest feels like it's gripped by iron claws, blood pounding in my ears.

I need to calm down, but my hands are shaking, and the icy cold water that I put them under doesn't help a bit.

Still shaking, I open the bathroom cabinet. I need a painkiller, or a sleeping pill—anything to calm down. There are a number of bottles on the middle shelf, including prescriptions, and I stare, stare, stare like a zombie at just one of them—the familiar drug name on it.

I wouldn't have known what it was if I hadn't been prescribed the same one—for my hereditary condition, passed on usually from a parent.

My mouth opens in a silent gasp. Memories reel like a pack of flies in my head—Mom's letter where she talked about the night she came to John with a bottle of booze. Then her words in the last letter:

Right now, while I'm writing this, John is making us dinner.
He's throwing awkward glances at me.
I know he has questions, but I'm not ready to answer them.

I remember the way John stared at me after the lecture when he asked about my health and I told him about my condition. No, it wasn't pity in his eyes. It was shock at the realization that we had the same condition. He already knew then I was Elizabeth's daughter.

Tears spill down my cheeks as I close my eyes and remember how it felt over the last year going through the trials, the hate I felt for my father, for what he had done to Mom. The hate was so bitter that I told him just that when I visited him in prison, "I wish you weren't my dad."

I smile through tears and sob, unable to process how I feel right now.

"Mackenzie? Kenzie?" John's soft voice comes from behind the door, followed by gentle knocking.

I can't help but sob as I take in that voice, more caring than any other voice I've ever heard.

"Please open the door," he says softly. "It's all right. Let's talk."

I unlock the door and open it slowly, revealing the part of my life that I never knew existed.

John stands with the letter in his hand, his eyes searching mine, pain reflecting in them as he registers my tears.

I lift the prescription bottle in my hand and summon my strongest voice. "You knew," I whisper.

He glances at the page in his hand, at the medication again, then at me. "Yes," he says barely audibly.

"When?"

"After your episode at the lecture." He smiles weakly. "When you told me about your condition."

"Wh—" A sob escapes me. "You knew all this time? Why didn't you tell me?"

He swallows hard. "I wanted to get to know you better. And you had a lot on your plate. You needed time, Mackenzie."

A shadow appears behind him, a hand softly touching his shoulder.

It's Mom.

She looks at him, then at me, at the bottle. There is a question in her eyes. Or maybe she's trying to understand what's happening. I wish she could've told us the full story.

But then she smiles and leans her cheek against his shoulder.

And he nods. "It'll be all right," he says, smiling weakly but with that powerful gaze that can calm storms, or a lecture hall full of students. Or erase years of lies. "Let's talk, Kenzie. Please. It's time."

I nod, smiling. Him, her, me—finally, the puzzle is complete. "Yes, let's talk."

SIXTY-SIX

DIANNE

They say, when you are old, you want to have lived a life full of stories to tell. I wish I didn't have so many. And I sure wish mine weren't so dark.

I haven't celebrated Thanksgiving in years, but this feels special, seeing this family come together. Especially Lizzy. That poor girl's been through hell.

And now there's another letter, on a day like this. The news that just broke—John might be Mackenzie's father. They are in the other room, talking it over. John, Mackenzie, Lizzy.

Mackenzie got her mama's kindness but also her determination. I don't know John all that well, but with parents like those two? That girl's gonna conquer the world, no doubt about it.

This kid Emerson and I, we are the strangers here but we have ears. Emerson digs into the turkey, gives a little shrug when I chuckle at him, then slides the sweet potatoes my way.

"They'll be a while," he says. "Might as well eat."

"You go ahead, kiddo," I tell him with a smile. He's a good kid.

What can we do? Lord knows, this family's been through

enough already. I just hope they don't go digging up more secrets from their past.

I have no children of my own, you see. But in all my years working at Keller's, I've seen plenty of them, each with their own stories and troubles and hopes.

I tried to keep tabs on both Lizzy and Tonya once they left for the world.

Tonya? She got herself pregnant while she was still in the group home. Some agency paid her a good sum to have it under their watch, and she gave it up for adoption. The likes of Tonya would figure out how to profit from that sort of thing. She never had a notion of caring for someone else.

Lizzy went off to college. She'd call now and then, on my birthday and Christmas, then she disappeared. No hard feelings. Lots of kids don't need a reminder of where they came from.

Then, about three months ago, I walked into the gas station where I usually shop. Mary was behind the counter, with a book in her hands.

Lies, Lies, and Revenge, it said.

"Any good?" I asked.

"I'll be darned. Let me tell ya. Can't pull my eyes off them pages," she said, shaking her head. "Get this. This young gal grows up in one o' them group homes, and three boys go and do her wrong, y'know? Ain't nobody liftin' a finger to help, neither. 'Cept for the housekeeper, bless her heart, she's the only one that cares a lick. So, this girl grows up, gives those boys one heckuva run for their money. Then she goes and does somethin' downright wicked to 'em. Not exactly my cup o' coffee, but heck, they sure had it comin'.'"

I took a look at the back cover and froze, staring at the author photo.

I do believe in coincidences. And I don't go to bookstores. But I did that day, drove ten miles to one, bought the book, and read it in one sitting.

Now, I don't have a computer, just my old flip phone. So, I went to Mary's place. Her nephew's good with all that tech stuff.

"Elizabeth Casper," he told me. "That's the author's real name." He pulled up pictures, everything he could find online. But no matter how hard I looked, I didn't see a trace of Lizzy in that author's face.

It was Tonya, clear as day.

He got me her home address, said he had to work to dig it up, so I slipped him a twenty for his trouble.

And then I decided I needed to see for myself.

An old bird like me? I've got plenty of time on my hands. I drove all the way to the East Coast. Took me three days. I brought my shotgun along, just in case.

E. V. Renge. Fancy name. Fancy house. Fancy car. No right to any of it. The moment I laid eyes on her, in the shopping plaza parking lot near her house, I knew she wasn't Lizzy.

I got out of the car. "Tonya!"

You should've seen how she froze, like a deer in headlights. But she didn't turn around, just fumbled with something in her purse and kept on walking. She'd always been good at acting.

I followed her into the store, trailed her down the aisle.

Fancy hair. Fancy makeup. Fancy clothes. But none of it could hide who she was.

She saw me following, tensed up when I stood in line behind her, nearly broke into a trot when I followed her to her car.

She whipped around. "What do you want? Why are you following me?"

She didn't recognize me, you see? Lizzy would've known me in a heartbeat.

"How does it feel to play Lizzy?" I asked, and then added, "Tonya."

Her eyes froze on me, filled with the same hate I'd seen in her back at the group home.

"Stay the hell away from me," she hissed.

"What did you do to her, Tonya?" I pressed, stepping closer.

She gunned the engine and nearly ran over my feet pulling out of the spot.

I didn't come for revenge, or money, or blackmail. I just wanted one thing—the truth. I wanted to know what happened to Lizzy.

I kept watch on Tonya, that fraud. Don't ask me how an old bird like me can pull it off. I hunt. I've worked with tougher prey than her.

There was a lake by their property, a small state park with trails. She walked there every day, chatting away on her phone most of the time.

One morning that same week, there she was again, walking one of those trails, heading into the woods. I parked my truck on the side of the road, took my shotgun, and followed her.

Sometimes, all it takes to get the truth is a little scare.

She saw me coming. I wasn't hiding, just walking about forty or so feet behind her, my shotgun at my side. I didn't care if anyone saw me. I wasn't there to hurt her, just wanted to talk.

But that morning, there wasn't a soul in the woods.

"What do you want, old hag?" she shouted, then stopped, turning toward me, with those hands on her hips like she was posing for a photo. That chin ticked up at me like she had the upper hand. Her sunglasses the size of half of her face hid her shameful eyes.

I told her who I was, told her what I knew.

"What did you do to Lizzy, Tonya?"

She laughed. "Go away, you old witch. What, you thought you'd come here and get me to tell you some crazy story?"

"No. Just the truth, Tonya."

Her mouth curled in an ugly smirk. "You want money? You won't get any. That"—she nodded at my shotgun—"won't help you. As soon as you fire, this place will swarm with joggers, and you'll go to jail. So, get your fat ass out of my sight."

I wanted her to admit what she'd done to Lizzy, whatever that was.

But she laughed in my face, and then I raised my shotgun.

"You'll tell me, Tonya." I pointed it at her as I walked up to her. No shame in a little scare. She could use some intimidation.

She still laughed, the evil thing that she was. She never took off those damn sunglasses either.

"Oh, I'm so-so-so scared," she taunted with a giggle, wiggling her fingers in the air.

A sociopath? Don't think so. There are sociopaths, and there's Tonya. She was something else—evil and vile.

She still chuckled as she walked backward, my shotgun barrel pointing at her. She spat insults and poison at me when I nudged her with my gun.

You see, I only wanted to scare her. Tonya brought it all on herself.

She slipped and fell backward.

Funny how fate works in mysterious ways.

Lizzy wrote in her book that punishment is white, revenge is red.

Mine had the sound of Tonya's skull cracking against a rock. She never got up.

And you know what? I don't feel bad. That's how justice works.

Lies, lies, then revenge, right?

EPILOGUE

WALLACE KING

"I'll be damned."

I snort at the open newspaper in my hands, then pull a joint out of my mouth and take a swig of Budweiser.

My fishing yacht bobs softly on the waves. The azure waters of Key West around me reflect the bright morning sun. It's paradise.

I crush the empty beer can, toss it aside, and reach into the cooler for another.

This is the life, man. Later, I'll dock, hit the local bar, grab some oysters, down a few drinks. If luck is on my side, I'll pick up a tourist chick and bring her to my crib. They always get more enthusiastic when they see my house.

I deserve this. Fifteen years locked up for it.

Damn shame about Tonya. That woman, man, she was a riot. Knew how to give good head, too.

I take another gulp of beer, the headline still rattling in my head. Halfway through the can, I read it again.

CRIMINAL MASTERMINDS:
BEN CASPER AND EVELYN CASPER.
CONSPIRACY IN CRIMINAL IMPERSONATION,

ABDUCTION, FRAUD, UNJUST ENRICHMENT AMONG MANY CHARGES IN THE TRIAL OF THE CENTURY

There're too many damn fancy words in there, but Benny-boy's locked up for life. That dumbass had it coming.

I spit overboard and down the rest of the beer.

I never could figure out what Tonya saw in him. When she first rolled into Old Bow, she picked me up at the bar.

I was first, for the record.

Fine smile, great rack, even better ass. Sassy, too. That girl had some spark, I tell you. You don't meet girls like her every day. Not in Old Bow.

Tonya fucking Shaffer.

Half an hour after she walked in, she had her sweet ass parked on my lap. Couple hours later, she was at my place, doing lines and downing beers like a pro. I didn't mind sharing my stash with a fine girl like her.

She came back the next day, all fired up like a cat in heat. I told her my uncle owned the building, free rent 'cause I was the supervisor. But when she started asking about Lizzy next-door, that's when I knew Tonya was there for a reason.

'S all right by me. She wanted a copy of Lizzy's apartment key. Illegal? Sure, but who was gonna find out, right? Telling you, she was a fine lay. Worth it.

Then I found out what she had cooking with that dumbass Ben. It pissed me off. But Tonya explained that he owed her money. Said she had to keep it friendly. So, she'd sneak over to see me, making sure that Lizzy and Ben didn't know Tonya kept an eye on them.

Smart girl, Tonya.

I didn't get a whiff of what's going on 'til a year later, right before I got busted for selling blow and a bunch of other stuff.

Last time I saw Tonya, she was sneaking into Lizzy's

apartment. We had a "goodbye fuck." That's what I called it. Two days later, I was locked up. But that day, when she told me to lay low and disappeared into the bathroom, I swiped a fancy leather notebook off the counter. Turns out, it was Lizzy's.

Not like I cared at the time. Figured, I could always slip it back when no one was around. Hadn't seen Lizzy in days anyway, and she was about to pop a kid.

But that notebook? It changed my life.

It was Lizzy's diary. Turns out, our quiet little mouse was about to score a publishing deal. Plus, it looked like she was starting to lose her marbles.

And Tonya? She was messin' with Benny-boy way more than I figured.

Well, damn.

I was pissed at first, but then it hit me—Tonya wasn't just after small-time money. She was playing the long game.

Like I said, smart girl.

Two days later, cops came bustin' in. Some rat tipped 'em off. Fifteen years behind bars 'cause of it. I wish I knew who snitched. I'd break their bones, one by one.

The prison library is no Library of Senate, or whatever that big place is. But they get some donations. I stuck to magazines, mostly for the pictures.

Lies, Lies, and Revenge. The second I spotted that book on the shelf, something clicked in my head. I'm a smart man. It hit me right then—Lizzy's diary, that's where I saw that name.

And who's staring back at me from the back cover? My fucking Tonya, all dolled up, trying to pass off as that mouse. Tonya was no mouse, but I laughed like a lunatic at the picture on that dust jacket. I cut it out, too, hung it above my bed. It came in handy, if you know what I mean.

I started digging into every article about her, every newspaper I could get my hands on. Another book came out later. Hell, when you're stuck in prison, you got nothing but time, so I read it. Took me a while, but I went through all her books. The third book got weird, but still a bestseller. Tonya was raking in cash. All while I was rotting in a cell.

After fifteen years in prison, I am out, flat broke, with all my stuff packed up in my uncle's storage. God bless that man.

What did I do? I grabbed Lizzy's diary and headed straight for the East Coast.

Now, let me tell you about the East Coast. Fancy looks, but no guts. Tonya? (Pardon me, Elizabeth Casper) Now, she was finer than fine wine. Mid-thirties, she had the body of a freshman. And her so-called daughter? She ain't hers. I knew exactly where that scrawny thing came from.

Tonya tried to play it smart, acted like she didn't recognize me the first time I showed up. But I had to jog her memory, remind her we went waaaay back, and that I knew Lizzy well—she sure as hell was no Lizzy.

"What do you want, Grunger?"

See? She suddenly got her memory back.

I didn't like that name. In prison, they called me Kingman, after my last name.

I told her that. She laughed. I knew she'd get a kick out of it.

I wanted her to run away with me like she'd promised once. But I had nothing, and she had it all—that fine house, the maids, the cars. So, I told her my loyalty wasn't cheap. I brought up the diary.

"Liar," she snapped.

That hurt, but then again, I am a smart man. I laid it out like it was.

"Two books she wrote while she was knocked up. I know what the books are about, the barn fire, your old flame at the group home, your dealings with Benny-boy."

"You are lying. How'd you get the diary?"

"Remember the last fuck we had, in Lizzy's apartment? I

swiped it off the counter, just for kicks. You wouldn't believe what I found inside."

"What's inside?"

I smirked. "Wouldn't you like to know? It's in a safe place, in case you try something funny."

"Give me time. Two days."

In two days, we met at her place—a mansion, of course. There was this old woman there.

"Who the hell is that?" I asked.

That Cruella de Vil looked at me like I just walked out of prison. I mean, I did.

"I'm Ben's mother," she said, all proper-like.

Turns out the old witch was the sharpest one in the whole room. Was in on the secret the entire time, too.

Crazy, right?

I didn't find out 'til later, when Tonya was screwing me on my boat down in Key West—the first one I got with her cash. She told me that the first night she and Ben and the baby moved to the Coast, the old witch sat her down and told her straight up, "I'm not a fool. And you are not that smart. I want to know who you are and where the actual Elizabeth Dunn is."

"Where is Lizzy?" I asked Tonya then.

She never told me.

At the time, I figured she and Benny-boy pulled off a nasty on that girl and dusted her. I told Tonya my theory, and she just laughed, didn't care for my questions. She knew I was solid on my end. Sure, I can keep secrets. I'm a simple man. All I wanted was a house in the Keys, a nice boat, and to be set for life. Is that too much to ask?

Tonya tried to break it off with me several times, but that wasn't happening. She was my golden goose. Benny-boy? He was a lousy lay, she told me so. Me, I made her happy. She always came back.

So, that was the deal with her and that old bitch. Easiest money

I ever made. I got my cut for keeping quiet. Every six months, like clockwork.

But then she was gone.

First thing I thought was Benny pulled a nasty one. Of course, he knew about me and Tonya. But he wasn't the type to kill. Too weak. His mama though? Different story.

I went to talk to Benny-boy. You know what he said?

"That's it. The free ride is over."

"Nuh-uh. You've been riding this gravy train for years. I'm late to the party, sure, but how 'bout you stick to the plan?"

He laughed, the prick. Shouldn't have done that. The minute he said I was worthless scum, I knew I was gonna mess his whole world up.

"You stay away from me and my daughter, you hear me?" he demanded. Demanded! Can you believe that?

What's the best way to ruin someone? You bring their secrets right out in the open.

I ain't rich, but I got all I wanted from Tonya. Now Benny-boy, he was getting on my nerves.

So, back to Lizzy's diary.

I sent a couple pages to his daughter. Figured, I'd rattle his cage and stop. But Benny-boy threatened to cut me off for good, so I went all in.

See, back in Old Bow, I dealt drugs. When you're in that game, you learn to keep an eye on what's going on.

One morning, just after dawn, I was coming back from a deal. Town was dead quiet. But who do I see standing by my building entrance? Sweet Lizzy, looking all ruffled and guilty, with some guy next to her. I know a sidepiece when I see one. He leaned in to kiss her, and she jumped back and looked around like she'd just robbed a bank.

"It was a mistake," she mumbled. "Please, don't tell Ben."

I minded my own business. But the day I swiped her diary and read through the sad mess, I knew what the last page meant. Sweet

Lizzy played Benny-boy dirty, and the fool didn't even suspect he might not be the baby's real daddy.

Whatever. That's some Lifetime channel stuff. But revenge is revenge, right? That's what Lizzy wrote in her books.

So, when Benny-boy told me to piss off, and Tonya was now gone, there was nothing stopping me from making his life hell. I just had to be careful, so no fingers pointed at me.

You ever play blackjack? Best thing about it? You watch the pattern, figure out how you win. That's what I wanted that girl, Mackenzie, to do. I sent her the first pages of her mom's diary. Lizzy's, that is. Then a few more...

You see, if that girl read between the lines, she'd catch on and start digging. She did. Got more smarts than I gave her credit for. Ain't from Lizzy, though, that's for sure.

Now that I think about it, not sure what this has to do with blackjack.

Anyway.

When it all came down, I don't know how she found her mom, Lizzy. The whole mess blew up as I sat on my boat in Key West and watched the news, cheering to Tonya in heaven (your #1 fan, baby!), Lizzy in a loony bin or wherever (bless her heart), and laughing at Benny-boy (may he rot in prison). If I knew they kept Lizzy locked away, I woulda' asked for more money. But that's not how things worked out.

In case they were too slow to catch on—the goth girl and that John guy who'd gotten all cozy with Lizzy back in Old Bow—I sent 'em another diary page on Thanksgiving. A little holiday surprise, you know?

So, now Benny-boy is truly screwed.

Oh, and Benny's mama? Hope the bitch enjoys rocking prison blues.

Cheers!

AFTERWORD

For news and updates, please, join my mailing list:
https://www.ilianaxander.com/
For questions and comments, email:
ilianaxander@gmail.com

Thank you for reading **_LOVE, MOM_**.
Please, leave a review:
GOODREADS
AMAZON

Made in United States
North Haven, CT
10 December 2024

62152757R00207